THE DREAM MAKER

BOOK 2
TRILOGY

Arnaldo Ricciulli

authorHOUSE®

AuthorHouse™
1663 Liberty Drive
Bloomington, IN 47403
www.authorhouse.com
Phone: 1-800-839-8640

Published by AuthorHouse 12/19/2013

ISBN: 978-1-4918-4065-8 (sc)
ISBN: 978-1-4918-4066-5 (hc)
ISBN: 978-1-4918-4067-2 (e)

Library of Congress Control Number: 2013922194

TABLE OF CONTENTS

PREAMBLE

On the way home from visiting their eldest son at university, Dan and Malou Politano had stopped in Pahokee and had both decided to take up an offer from an old Seminole Indian to re-visit their past. During their journey, they went through an incredible adventure which drove them to relive many of Dan's childhood memories and some fantastic ancestral events while completing twelve tasks. These tasks were all designed to reinforce or ignite desires for Dan to redress his family life after a horrible skiing accident, which had occurred thirteen years earlier, had left him questioning his destiny and ignoring his future – or the future that was staring him in the face.

While returning to the present, Dan and Malou were separated. Malou was the only one who made it back to 2013. As for Dan, he had unfortunately returned further in time and had lost all memory of his travels into the past with Malou. He had been found in a forest clearing – unconscious – and had been transported to the nearest hospital in Key West, Florida. When he woke up and regained his senses, he soon realized that he didn't even know his name. Suffering from post-traumatic amnesia, the only name he remembered was the one of an old shepherd – *Damianos*. Not having anywhere to stay – he couldn't remember where he lived either – Dan was sent to a shelter where he was to share a room with another man named Gustavo.

CHAPTER ONE

It was all Malou could do to keep her eyes on the road. The Sunday afternoon traffic didn't help either. She was drifting in and out, thinking of how she would be able to locate her husband, Dan, and bring him back to her.

When she arrived home – their beautiful property in Davie, Florida – Malou grabbed Dan's and her traveling cases out of the trunk, fumbled to find her house keys in her purse and finally opened the front door with a sigh of relief. At least, she had made it home in one piece.

"Hi, Mom," Gaby, their seventeen-year-old, yelled from the kitchen, after she had heard the front door close on her mother, "how was your trip?" She stopped and stared when she saw Malou's devastated face. "Mom? What's happened? Where is Dad?"

Malou rushed to her daughter and took her in her arms. "I don't know...!"

"What do you mean you don't know?" Gaby queried, pushing herself out of her mother's embrace. "Did he stay with Stefano...?" She peered into her eyes. "Come on, Mom, what's going on?"

"Where is Daniel?" Malou asked, switching her gaze to the living room.

"He'll be back by six, I'd imagine. I told him I was preparing Dad's favorite eggplant parmigiana..."

But Malou wasn't listening. She went to sit on the sofa and began crying – bawling her eyes out to be precise.

At a loss to know what was happening, Gaby rounded the sofa and sat down beside her mother. Wrapping an arm around her shoulders, she whispered, "It will be okay, Mom. I'm sure everything will be fine," trying to soothe her mother's obvious anguish. "Dad will find his way home..."

1

In a jerk, Malou straightened up and shouted, "NO!" to her daughter's face. "That's just it, Gaby, your dad is lost in time," she added between hiccupping sobs. "He won't be able to find us…"

"I think you better explain that one, Mom. How could Dad be lost in time?" She pulled a few more tissues from the box on the coffee table and handed it to her mom. "What about Stefano – did you see him?"

Malou nodded.

"Does he know that dad is…, I mean does he know what's happened?"

"No, of course not. How could he know…?"

"Okay, Mom," Gaby said, getting up and going back to the kitchen. "I'll get Daniel to come back right now." She picked up her cell phone from the counter and scrolled down to find her brother's number. As soon as he was on the line, she said, "Hey, you; you better get your butt home on the double… I don't care what you're doing…" She paused, lifting her gaze to the ceiling in visible exasperation. "I don't care, Daniel!" she shouted. "Something's happened to Dad, and you need to get home. Is that clear enough for you?"

With an arm stretched over the back of the sofa, Malou was watching her daughter. *Like her dad; she won't take no for an answer*, she thought.

"He can be such an idiot at times," Gaby remarked, regaining her seat beside her mom. "He was saying that he was in the middle of some video game or other and he couldn't just leave his friend before winning the war – or some such thing!"

Malou had to smile.

"When he'll get here, I think we should call Stefano on Skype and then you can explain to us what's really going on, okay?"

"Yes, I guess that's best," Malou agreed, wiping the tears that were still streaming down her cheeks.

A half-an-hour later, Malou, Daniel and Gaby were looking at the laptop screen from which Stefano was participating in their conversation.

"What are you saying, Mom," Stefano questioned, "that Dad has gone with you to Pahokee and there you found this old Seminole Indian who sold you a trip to your past for five bucks? Of all the crazy things to do…! And Dad went along with that? I can't believe this."

"Yes, Stefano, and your dad was actually keen to go back…"

"What on Earth for?" Daniel interjected.

Malou raised her face to him. "Because he wanted to see if he could change anything about his skiing accident..."

"But, Mom," Stefano cut-in, "that's insane. No one can change the past, even if you tried."

"That's probably why your dad went down that slope anyway and relived the accident."

"You mean you guys went through that whole thing again?" Gaby asked. "But why?"

"In a way, I think your dad thought God would change things for him."

"Okay. And what happened next?" Stefano asked, having calmed down a little.

"Well, while your dad was in the hospital, we got the visit of a man by the name of Damianos."

"Like the Greek Damianos — the tamer?" Daniel interposed.

"Exactly. And as in the Greek mythology, this man led us first to find a book that contained the guidelines to our redemption."

"Wow! Are you sure you didn't get a sun stroke or something, Mom," Gaby said, staring at her mother.

"No, Gaby, this was all real, as real as your imagination can be." Malou fingered the little amulet hanging from a leather strap around her neck, and brought it closer to the screen for Stefano to see. "You see this? This is a dream catcher. It actually catches bad dreams and let good dreams go through. And that's what your dad and I bought from the old Indian. It's some sort of protection against evil. And during our journey, it did in fact protect us from being killed..."

"But, Mom, what I don't understand," Stefano said, "is if everything you went through was in your imagination, how come Dad is not back with you. Didn't you guys wake up from that dream?"

"That's just it, Stefano. We did "wake up" as you said, but we were still in the past — thirteen years ago — and the only thing we forgot to do was to hold hands when we came back to the present. And..., well, I was the only one who made it back to today's date."

"And what did the old Indian have to say about Dad being lost?" Stefano asked.

"He didn't say anything except that Dad must have gone through another portal and found another life somewhere. More than that, I couldn't tell you."

3

"What about that Damianos guy; what happened to him," Gaby asked.

"Before I tell you more about him, I have to tell you that, in reality, he is the cat who was sitting on the window sill beside the old Seminole. He has powers to transform himself in anything that would guide or "tame" the spirits in his charge apparently."

"Okay, and did you see that cat again when you came back?" Daniel queried, quite interested now. Even at twenty years of age, the supernatural always captured his imagination it seemed.

"Oh yes. He was there – sitting on the window sill – when I came back. And I told him that I would be seeing him again. I'm sure he understood me, too."

"Okay, Mom, I'll drive down with the Caddy and…"

"No, Stefano…, I don't want you to interrupt your…"

"Mom! I love you, but you don't tell me what to do anymore, remember? And I'm sorry, but finding Dad is much more important for all of us than keeping my head in the books right now. I can always go back and re-take some of the courses I would have missed, so don't worry about that, okay?"

During his first night at the shelter, Dan awoke from a nightmare, screaming the name *Damianos* until his roommate woke up, startled.

"Hey, mate, what's the matter with you?" Gustavo demanded, after going to Dan's bed and looking down at him. He was drenched in sweat and his eyes seemed unfocused or still lost in his dream.

"I'm okay…," Dan replied a few seconds later, sitting up. "Sorry if I woke you," he added, getting out of bed.

"Did you have a bad dream or something?" Gustavo inquired, returning to sit at the edge of his own bunk.

"Something like that, yeah." Dan was now rummaging through his locker box at the foot of his bed.

"What did you dream about?"

"I can't really remember…," Dan answered evasively, while digging every piece of clothing out of his duffle bag. "Ah-ah, there you are," he shouted, brandishing an amulet and passing the leather strap around his neck.

"What's that?" Gustavo asked, squinting at the little piece of carved wood when he stepped closer to Dan to examine it under the dim light of the room.

"That, my friend, is a dream-catcher. It protects me from having bad dreams."

"Neat!" Gustavo said. "Where did you get it?"

"I can't remember yet, but at least I know what it is and what it's for," Dan replied, replacing his duffle bag into his locker and locking it.

"How come you remember that little thing but you can't remember your name?"

"I don't know, Gustavo, but when I do, you'll probably be the first to know," Dan said, smiling now and returning to slide under the covers.

After eating their dinner practically in silence, Daniel asked his mom, "Do you remember anything of that trip into your past?"

"Yes, actually I'm surprised that I remember so many of the places we visited," Malou replied, somewhat vaguely. But then she recalled what she had been told: *You will remember all of the places you have seen — the pictures will be locked in your memory.* "Solange was right…"

"Who's Solange?" Gaby asked, stopping her hand from grabbing the empty plate in front of her brother, and staring at Malou.

"She is like a guardian angel," Malou replied, switching her gaze from her son to her daughter. "She and her husband, Damian, were watching over us all the time we were performing the twelve tasks."

"Do you have any way to contact them now?" Daniel asked, fingering his napkin to occupy his hands absentmindedly.

"Don't be silly, Daniel," Gaby put in, taking the dishes away from the table, "guardian angels don't show themselves, they're just watching over us, like your instincts or your "little voice". That's all."

"Yeah, but if mom saw these two, maybe they know that Dad has been lost…"

"Well, you might have something there, Daniel," Malou said, "Because, they said that they would be watching us even after we returned home." She paused. "But I don't know if there is any way to contact them." She looked up at her daughter. "As you said, it's up to them to contact us or make us see what we tend to ignore or do not want to recognize."

"Like premonition you mean?" Daniel suggested.

"Yes, something like that, so that we don't get into trouble."

"What about that dream-catcher, Mom," Gaby asked, "returning to the table with a coffee pot and some cups and saucers, "wouldn't that be a way to contact them?"

"I don't think so, Gaby. These amulets"—Malou touched her pendant and looked down at it—"are only supposed to catch bad dreams before they get into your mind..."

"But didn't you say they protected you while you were in danger?" Daniel argued.

"I'm sure they did, but Damianos was really the one who was always there to organize each of the dreams – or tasks – making sure we came to no harm."

"Sounds like this Damianos guy played an important part of this whole adventure, didn't he?"

"And you know, the funny thing was," Malou went on, "your dad thought he was really evil at first. But in the end he began to trust him – we both did."

"But if he's that cat in Pahokee, and he can actually talk, couldn't we go and see him when Stefano gets here tomorrow?"

"Yes, Daniel, I think that would be the first thing we should do. But let's see what your brother has to say about all this before we start anything, okay?"

CHAPTER TWO

When the morning sunrays awoke Dan out of his restless night, he sat up and shook his head. Noticing that Gustavo was not in the room, he decided to wander down the hallway and take a shower. Beforehand, and when he opened his locker box, he found a piece of paper at the bottom of the duffle bag that must have fallen out of his pants pocket when Mrs. Stevens, the social worker, packed his clothes. It read: *Meet F. at the hangar on the 10th.*

Dan sat on the floor and stared at the note for a while, bewildered. There was something about the writing — it must have been his own, he concluded. But who was "F"? And what "hangar" was he referring to? He couldn't think of it at the moment. He folded the note and put it in his jeans' pocket.

After taking a shower and getting into some fresh clothes, he went to join Gustavo for breakfast. The so-called dining room could have easily hosted a hundred patrons, but this morning there were only a few tired-looking men eating some porridge, slurping the warm concoction noisily. Somehow, the sight of these poor souls disturbed Dan. He knew he didn't belong in this place, and he knew that he would have to find out his name sooner than later.

"I thought you said that thing around your neck protects you from having bad dreams," Gustavo said, after drinking some of his coffee, "so why do you wear it during the day? Do you expect to have bad daydreams, too?" He chuckled.

Dan shook his head, while munching on a piece of toast. "No, not daydreams, Gustavo, but I know this dream catcher will protect me from bad encounters or pull me out of tricky situations, somehow."

"How do you know that? Has it protected you before?"

"I can't remember; but something tells me that I have to trust my instincts."

"Okay, good enough for me," Gustavo replied, finishing the last of his porridge. "What are you planning to do today then?"

"I'm going to find out who I am," Dan stated matter-of-factly.

"And how do you plan to do that? Didn't your doc say that you'll regain your memory bit by bit?"

"Yeah, that's what he said alright, but I need to trigger something in my brain to remember the bits and pieces."

"And where do you expect to find this trigger of yours? It's not like you can go to the library…" The look on Dan's face stopped Gustavo in mid-sentence. "Did I say something funny?"

"No-no, you didn't. But you gave me an idea."

"Glad I did, but what idea was that?"

"The library, Gustavo, that's the idea. I'll go to the library."

"What do you hope to find among thousands of books…? It's not like your name is gonna be written in gold letters on some book or other…"

"Inspiration, that's what I'm going to find at the library." Dan fixed his gaze on his new friend. "Are you coming with me?" He had a slim hope that Gustavo would agree to accompany him. It seemed the more he talked to him, the more thoughts or images would come to mind.

Gustavo drank the last of his coffee and got up. "Sure, I'll go with you. I haven't been there in ages, and it'll be good for me to put some more bricks on the pile of my practically non-existent knowledge."

One thing about Gustavo that amazed Dan was the fact that the man sounded much more knowledgeable than he led on. He wasn't a drunken vagrant. On the contrary, this guy sounded as someone who had fallen on hard times.

Stefano arrived at his parents' home late in the afternoon of Monday. He parked his Caddy on the street and went around the house to find his mother sitting in one of the lounge chairs that surrounded the shallow pool and oasis that his father had constructed soon after they had bought the house. It was such a peaceful place that Stefano remembered the many evenings he spent studying or reading, sitting in the very same chair where he found his mother.

"Oh God, you can't imagine what a relief it is to see you, Stefano," Malou said, getting up and giving her son a big hug.

"Well, you knew I was on my way, so here I am, and nothing happened, as you can see."

"Yes, yes, but I don't know why I was afraid you would have an accident..."

"Come on, Mom," Stefano said soothingly, "it will be okay. We will find Dad. That's all there is to it."

"But what if he's gone too far into the future, what then? We can't go in the future..."

"Exactly, Mom. That's precisely what I thought. After I heard your story, and mulled over all of the events that happened during your journey, I came to the conclusion that Dad is gone back either to 2000 or some time earlier than that."

"But how are we going to pin point the date or even his location? We have nothing to guide us." Malou looked up at her son, pleading for answers.

"Come in the house, Mom, and I'll explain, but first, I need to take a shower, change and eat something. Where are Gaby and Daniel? Didn't they stay with you today?"

As the two of them made their way indoors, Gaby looked up from her laptop. "Oh there you are; and it's about time," she teased. "I thought maybe you got lost, too..."

"That's not funny, Gaby," Stefano replied admonishingly. "And where is that brother of ours?"

"At the library. He's got some test coming up and he needed to get some back-dated newspaper clippings or something."

"And he'll be back for dinner I suppose?" Stefano asked.

"Oh trust me, he'll be back. His stomach is still like a bottomless pit."

While Malou and Gaby were preparing dinner, Daniel and Stefano sat at the table.

"So, did you get all you needed at the library?" Stefano asked Daniel.

"Yeah, and then some. I could have found most of the stuff I needed for my test on the internet, but I wanted to look if they had some old books on Damianos or on Hercules."

"And what did you find out?" Malou asked from the kitchen.

"Well most of it was "Greek to me"," Daniel quipped, smiling furtively at his mother, "but I found out that the tamer – Damianos – only put the animals he couldn't control in cages. He was like the animal whisperers of today."

"That's exactly what I saw the first time I was with him. He had brought me to this sort of zoo where he had imprisoned several beasts. I guess – and he told us later – that they didn't want to be guided."

"Yeah, that sounds like what I've read," Daniel agreed.

"What about Hercules, what did you find out about him?" Stefano asked.

"There are probably hundreds of volumes about him and his twelve Herculean tasks, but the interesting thing was that all of his tasks were related to human virtues."

"Like what?" Gaby asked, putting a dish of vegetables on the table.

"Like vanquishing demons or demonic beasts that would prevent people from being free, or having choices in life."

"Something like having good moral ethics?" Stefano asked.

"Yeah, but all of his tasks were demonstration of strength of character," Daniel went on.

When Gaby and Malou had brought the rest of the food to the table and were sitting down, Malou remarked, "Again, what you're describing, Daniel, sounds very much like what your dad and I went through."

"Did Dad have to fight ugly beasts, too?" Daniel asked, a smirk drawing on his lips.

"No, he didn't, but he had to fight his own instincts like being frustrated or being impatient."

Stefano had to chuckle. "Yeah, that's Dad alright," he said. "Always wants things done yesterday."

"Yes, and I think the hardest one for him was to fight stubbornness. He had the habit of confusing determination and stubbornness. Anyway, we – I mean he made it. . ." Malou's voice trailed off. "And now he's lost. . .," she added, tears pearling at the rim of her eyes again.

"As I said, we will find him, Mom," Stefano said, trying to return his mother's mind to the positive prospect of locating his dad.

As they were walking toward the library, Dan remarked, "You know, Gustavo, this city is very familiar to me. I must have been here, but to tell you when, I can't say."

"But you're still a young guy, so maybe you lived here with your parents."

"No, I don't think so," Dan replied. "Somehow, I was here, probably stayed here, but I know my parents live somewhere else."

"And what would you be doing here? Were you on holidays?"

"I don't think so. I think it's got something to do with the naval base. For some reason I went there yesterday. I had to see the ships and was looking for an aircraft carrier. Don't ask me why, because I have no answer for that one."

"Maybe you were a naval officer..."

His eyebrows raised, Dan said, "How could I be an officer when I am only in my early twenties?"

"Simple. If you studied engineering for example and had a degree, you could have enlisted as an officer; maybe they've got some records of you at the recruiting office."

"Do you think they would recognize me if I walked in?" Dan asked, visibly more than hopeful. Although he couldn't remember ever taking a college course of any sort, Gustavo's suggestion made sense.

"How about we go there now, instead of you searching for "inspiration" at the library, as you said?"

"I don't know if I've got enough money for even a bus fare," Dan replied.

"Don't worry about that, I got my check yesterday, so I'm loaded, as you might say."

"Thanks, buddy, I'll reimburse you as soon as Mrs. Stevens gets her act together and sends me a check, too."

Coffee mug in hand, Malou and her three children went to the lounge room to continue their conversation.

"Okay, Stefano," his mom began, "you said something about knowing exactly what I meant when I said we wouldn't be able to travel into the future to find Dad. What did you think then?"

"Well, like you described, Mom, first you and Dad returned to 2000 and once you woke up from your imaginary trip, you came back to 2013, to your time of departure. And, while you were on your journey, you always went further into the past, like going back to World War II, when Grandma escaped to Venezuela. You never went into the future, right?"

"Yes, that's right. And that's why I think if your dad is gone further into the past, he wouldn't be able to travel into the future."

"Sorry, Mom, but that's where you might be wrong."

"How?" Malou questioned, wide-eyed.

"I think I know what Stefano is getting at, Mom," Daniel interposed. "You see, when you and Dad traveled into your past, you were able to come back to the present. If it had not been for you two not holding hands, you would be both back into your future."

"Precisely, Daniel," Stefano rejoined.

"So, you're saying that a person traveling in his past could always come back to the present, right?" Gaby asked, sipping on her coffee.

"Yes. Although you couldn't travel to 2014 for example, you can return to the time you left, as long as it is not beyond the date at which you left. Does that make sense?"

"Yes, Stefano, it does," Malou agreed. "But the question remains: how do we find Dad? It's all well and good to know that we could bring him back, but we've got to find him first."

"Yes, and to do that, Mom, I think the four of us should have a chat with the Seminole Indian and see what he can suggest."

"Why?" Gaby asked. "It's not like he knows what could happen during our search. He's only offering an open-door into the past, that's all, as I understand it." She looked at her mother.

"Yes, Gaby, but I think it's a start," Stefano agreed, "However, he probably would know something about saving us from growing younger..."

"Oh, I see what you mean," Daniel cut-in, "if we go into our past even thirteen years in time we'd only be kids then. And if Dad is gone further back in time we wouldn't have been born then, is that it?"

"Yes," Stefano said. "But this is where I thought of what you described as your visit to Sumperk, during World War II, neither you nor Dad was born then, yet you relived all of the events as they occurred in reality."

"So, you mean we could go back in time for only a few days maybe, and then take a trip further back in time until we find the date at which Dad landed?"

"Yes, Mom. That's exactly what I'd like to do. We would not lose any of our maturity, but we would have the opportunity to visit the past, such as you and Dad did during your journey."

"Okay then, if you think it will help, then we should drive to Pahokee tomorrow..."

"Hold on, Mom," Stefano cut in, "As I said to Gaby a minute ago, it's a start, but we can't go navigating in the past searching for Dad without guidance. So, we would need to "talk" to Damianos, the cat, before we start – don't you think?"

"I don't think he would be able to "talk" to us in his present state, but I am absolutely convinced, he can hear and understand everything he's told. Besides, we are souls in his charge and one of the last things he told us was that he would be "there" – where ever "there" is – if we needed him."

CHAPTER THREE

Dan stopped dead in his tracks when both he and Gustavo arrived in front of the recruiting office of the naval base.

"What's the matter now?" Gustavo asked, turning to face Dan.

"I don't know if I can do this, Gustavo. I'm not sure.... What if they say they've never seen me before?"

"And what if they say you're Officer So-and-so and ask if you had a good weekend?"

Dan looked up at Gustavo. "I guess there's only one way to find out, isn't there?"

"Then, let's get in there, okay?"

Before leaving on the Tuesday morning, while Malou and her children were sitting having breakfast, Stefano said, "Okay, I've done some research on the internet, and I found out that the woods beside our old house in Pennsylvania still exist. So, if that's where we want to land, say before the last weekend, we should be okay. But the house belongs to some other family now and..."

"That doesn't matter, Stefano," Malou interposed. "You see, when we landed in 2000, yes, we went to our house, but once we met with Damianos, he led us to the house at a time it belonged to Solange and Damian. So, he should be able to do the same now."

"But didn't you say that the old Indian told you that you could never go back to the same place...?" Gaby asked.

"Yes, but what I think he meant was that we couldn't go back to the house in 2000 – and that's not what we're intending to do today, is it?"

"Alright then," Stefano said, getting up. "Are we ready?" He looked at Daniel.

"Don't look at me like that! I'm ready as I'll ever be," Daniel retorted, scraping his chair back from the table.

"Alright, you two," Malou said, "I don't want any arguing from any of you, understood? We've got a couple of hours driving before we get to Pahokee, so be mindful of what's ahead of us, okay?"

Although no longer teenagers, the three children nodded. Mother had spoken!

Still apprehensive, Dan let Gustavo enter the office first. The words on the piece of paper he had found at the bottom of his duffle bag rang through his mind and he couldn't help but feel uncertain. Finding out his name, who he was and everything he could was of course very important, but somehow knowing was more frightening than being left in the dark about it all. Nevertheless, he stepped toward the desk and riveted his gaze on the uniformed officer behind the counter. He didn't think he had ever met him before today, but that didn't mean a thing under the circumstances.

Unexpectedly, the young man stood up and saluted. Dan was floored. He couldn't believe it. The man obviously recognized him, even out of uniform. "At ease, Sergeant," he said, putting his elbows on the counter, suddenly relaxed, as if he had been there every day of late. "I'm just going to show my friend here"—he nodded to Gustavo at his side—"around the place. But before I do that, would you have my file handy? I wanted to check something. . . ."

"Yes, sir, of course, sir," the sergeant said, turning toward a filing cabinet to his left.

"Thank you, Sergeant," Dan said, when he had the file in front of him. As soon as he opened it, the flashbacks of his life seemed to pass in front of his mind's eye as if he were in a movie theater. His name was Dan Politano. His place of residence was Boca Raton, and he had attended Lynn College in that city, obtaining a Bachelor Degree in Engineering. This allowed him to be automatically engaged as an officer. He was due to commence his pilot training in the next two weeks.

Closing the file, he said again, "Thank you, Sergeant. I will be back on the tenth then."

"Yes, sir, certainly, sir," the officer replied, taking the file from Dan's hands and replacing it in the filing cabinet.

"Well?" Gustavo asked as soon as they were outside. "I didn't want to intrude in there, but did you find out who you are then?"

Dan nodded all smiles. "Yes, yes! I am Dan Politano, Gustavo. My name is Dan Politano! I do remember my college and my friend Fabio. He is Professor Hugo's son. And apparently, according to the file, he enlisted with me."

"Wow, but hold on a little minute. So, I was right; you did go to college, didn't you?"

"Yes, Gustavo. I must have come here with Fabio for some reason, which still eludes me, and then something happened. I don't recall everything yet, but at least I know who I am and where I live. And the other thing I found out was that I am due to start training in two weeks' time. Which means I'll have time to go home and find out what happened. I don't know, maybe my family is searching for me."

The note in his jeans' pocket made sense now. He was to meet Fabio on the tenth in the hangar. Which hangar, he still didn't know, but that was a detail.

"I am still broke, but would you mind if we went for a pizza somewhere to celebrate?"

"A pizza? What on Earth would you want to eat a pizza for?"

"I don't know, Gustavo, but I feel like it — how about it?"

"Okay, a pizza it is then."

When they reached Pahokee, Malou slowed down and pointed to St. Mary's church. "That's the church where your dad and I went through our first task."

"What was that task about?" Daniel asked.

"Tolerance. The priest showed us images of despots and tyrants who were cruel and intolerant toward their own people."

"It was like showing you the reverse of the coin?" Gaby remarked.

"Exactly. By showing us how intolerant human beings could be, we understood the importance of tolerance toward our fellow man."

"So, you came back here during your journey?" Stefano queried.

Malou shook her head. "No, not exactly. Damianos managed to transport the church from here to Pennsylvania…"

"Neat!" Daniel exclaimed. "Can hardly wait to meet the man — sounds like my kind of people…"

"Cat..., Daniel," Gaby corrected. "He's a cat, remember?"

Looking in the rearview mirror at her son, Malou smiled and said, "Anyway, whatever he is, if he's here, you'll see him as soon as we get to the hotel."

A few minutes later, Malou parked the car by the curb near the Seminole Indian. The old man hardly raised his gaze to her as she climbed out from behind the wheel, but smiled. Stefano, Daniel and Gaby gathered around their mother while shooting furtive glances at the black cat with a patch of white on the top of its head. The animal was lying on the window sill, impassible, but watching the four visitors carefully it seemed.

"Do you remember me?" Malou asked, bending down to the old Indian.

"Oh yes, Mrs. Politano, I do," he replied, putting the amulet he had been carving on the table beside him. "And you have come with your children to take another trip into the past, have you not?"

"Yes, we have. But before we do, could we talk to your cat?"

"If you like to do that, I'm sure he would listen to you, but he will not respond. Of course you realize that, I'm sure."

"Okay then, and thank you," Malou replied, turning her gaze to Damianos. "I am sure you are aware that Dan is lost in his past; our children and I need to find him, Damianos, and since you told us that you would be "there" if we needed your help; we are here to ask you to come with us in our search."

An almost inaudible purr and a paw passing over his eyes and nose was the only answer Malou got to her request. Yet, for her, it had been all she wanted to reassure her that Damianos would be there, on the other side of the painting.

As if mesmerized by Damianos's green, vibrant eyes, Gaby had a hard time looking away from him when her mother grabbed her arm and led her to the paintings leaning against the wall beside the old Indian's chair.

"I was expecting you to return," the latter said, standing beside Malou now. "I believe this is where you wish to return." He pointed to a painting depicting a forest clearing and a small log cabin in the background."

"Yes, absolutely," Malou blurted, "but how did you know?"

The old Seminole chuckled, although his sad eyes didn't show the hilarity he expressed. "*A little bird told me*, as you people say."

"This looks like a beautiful place," Gaby remarked from over her mother's shoulder.

"Yes, it was, Gaby," Malou replied.

"Are we going to find Damianos in that cabin?" Daniel asked, determined as ever it seemed to meet the man, and not the cat.

"We'll just have to wait and see, won't we?" Stefano said, looking at his brother, a frown crossing his brow.

"Okay then," the old man said, "come with me first; you need to buy your dream catchers and listen to my instructions before you leave."

"You mean we've got to wear that silly thing around our neck..."

Stefano was about to grab his brother by the shoulders to throw him in the gutter when Malou intervened. "You are both behaving like kids, and I won't have it! Is that understood? And as for you, Daniel; everything you will see or hear during this journey may be the strangest or silliest things you've ever experienced in your life, but I warn you, God will be watching and I or Stefano won't be the ones correcting your errors."

Stefano pulled his wallet out of his jeans' pocket and paid the old man fifteen dollars for the three dream catchers that he, Daniel and Gaby would need to wear during their journey.

"Don't I need a new one?" Malou asked, looking down at her own amulet.

"No, Mrs. Politano, you don't. You need only one dream catcher for your entire life. Keep it around your neck — all of you — and it will protect you." He looked at the three children, each in turn, as they passed the leather strap around their heads. "Now, as I told your parents before they took their first trip; you will need to hold hands to enter the painting and do the same when you return. You have seven days to spend in your past. On the seventh day, you need to return to the exact spot where you landed, hold hands and return here to the time you left. If you stay longer than seven days, you will not be able to come back. If you should lose your dream catcher, not only will you expose yourselves to grave danger, but you will not be able to come back."

"What if we get separated while we search for our dad, what happens then?" Stefano asked.

"Nothing will happen, unless you are not at the spot where you landed before the seventh day has elapsed."

"And if we don't hold hands on the way in or on the way back, you know what could happen, don't you, Daniel?" Gaby was glaring at her brother.

"Alright, alright, I'm not a child anymore, okay?" Daniel blurted.

"Then stop acting like one," Stefano rejoined.

"Are we all set then?" the old Indian asked.

"As we will ever be," Malou replied, going to stand in front of the painting – Gaby and Daniel to her right, and Stefano to her left – the four of them holding hands.

Such as Malou felt on their first trip into their past with Dan, they began to feel lighter and lighter, and lights began to flash back and forth, along with fog and winds blowing from different directions. Then, all of a sudden, everything stopped.

CHAPTER FOUR

There was a sense of awe pervading Malou and her three children's minds when they found themselves standing in the middle of the forest clearing near their old house. They looked around them and remained silent for a few moments before Malou said, "Well, here we are then. Are you okay?"

Stefano and Gaby nodded, their eyes still traveling to the canopy of trees surrounding them. As for Daniel, he seemed indifferent to the beauty and tranquility permeating the woods, yet searching for something.

"And where is the cabin?" he asked. "Isn't there supposed to be a cabin somewhere around here?" He took a few steps in the direction of the edge of the meadow.

"Are you looking for me, Daniel?" Damianos asked, coming toward him. His attitude and attire was obviously disconcerting.

His long beard, his cloak and the walking cane he held in his right hand only served to baffle Daniel a little further than he already was. "Are..., are you Damianos?" Daniel stammered, backing away from the old man.

"Yes, Daniel, he is," Malou replied, stepping beside her son. "He is our shepherd." She threw a pleading glance at Damianos. "Will you help us?"

"Indeed, Mrs. Politano. I will help you, since it is my help that you sought. I had offered my assistance in time of need; therefore, I am committed to respond to your call presently."

"Thank you, Damianos," Malou said as Stefano and Gaby came to stand beside her. "These are my three children – Stefano, Daniel and Gaby – but you know that already, don't you?"

"Oh yes, I know that already, as you say, my dear lady. And I should add that Daniel here is the most inquisitive soul among you, and perhaps the one for whom taming will be recommended."

"Oh no, you don't, you old wizard – you're not putting me in a cage like you did all these other people…"

Damianos guffawed. "As I guessed it, rebellion is in your blood, son, such as it was in your father when he was young."

"Yeah, well…, I guess he's done pretty well for himself, hasn't he?"

"Not without a little guidance, he didn't, son." Damianos chuckled again. "And I believe I should re-assure you that I have no plans – thus far – to encage you. You need a little taming, no doubt, but nothing that could drive me to incarcerate you."

"Are you going to be able to help us in locating our dad?" Stefano interposed, feeling that someone needed to re-focus the conversation onto the subject at hand.

"Yes, Stefano, I will assist the four of you in locating your father and your husband, Mrs. Politano. However, my assistance will be far from enough in this task. As you probably guessed, the burden of this task will rest mainly on your work and your acumen. The four of you will need to return to your house once again and find a book that will guide you to achieving your goal."

"But, Damianos, Dan and I already…," Malou began objecting.

He shook his head and pointed to the cabin that was now visible at the edge of the clearing. "I believe we will be more comfortable talking about this in my lodgings." He began walking toward the little house. "Yes, you did accomplish twelve tasks after finding the book that concerned your previous dilemma, Mrs. Politano; however, this is quite a different problem, isn't it?" He turned his face to her.

"Yes, it is, Damianos, and if we need to find another book in the old house, we will do so."

As they approached the cabin, Gaby finally opened her mouth. "Didn't you say we needed to go to our old house to find the book, Mr. Damianos?"

The shepherd threw her a gentle smile. "You have acquired the trait of impatience from your father, Gaby, and impatience will only lead to frustration. So, I propose you abide by my suggestions and follow my lead with patience." He stopped on the front stoop. "And by the way, just call me Damianos." He smiled again.

Munching on the last piece of their pizza, Dan frowned. "You know, Gustavo, it's very strange; I can see things I've never considered before…"

"Like what?" Gustavo asked, wiping his mouth with his napkin – another thing that somehow attested to the man's good upbringing.

"This," Dan replied, pointing to the empty dish between them. "I mean our pizza. I see it in another place at another time."

"You probably went to a pizza place with your mom and dad not too long ago…"

"No, Gustavo, it's not like that…"

"Like what then? Like in a daydream you mean?"

"Yeah, I see my brother…" Dan's face lit up suddenly. "Yeah, I've got a brother too, and I see him, Rafael, taking a pizza out of an oven…, and…" He stopped talking, and shook his head. "It's gone – sorry."

Gustavo had let his friend talk. It was important not to interrupt him when he seemed to recall things, people or events. "Well, not bad for a first recall. You just discovered that you have a brother named Rafael. That's good, isn't it?"

Dan appeared to be lost in thought. He looked up and across the table. "Yes, I suppose it is, but he's baking a pizza. That's totally bizarre!"

"Why should it be strange, Dan, he's probably a cook in a pizza restaurant somewhere…"

"No, Gustavo. He's much older and I've never seen this place before." Dan shook his head again. "Anyway, I'll piece all this together some day, I suppose…"

"What about your friend Fabio, any more memory of him?"

"No, nothing. I remember us going to college together, and his father, Professor Hugo, but apart from that, I can't recall anything else."

"Well, your doctor did say that your long term memory was okay, but the short term one was going to be a bit harder to come back to you."

"Do you have a quarter?" Dan asked suddenly, looking at the couple of coins he had pulled out of his pocket.

"Sure…, here…," Gustavo replied, handing Dan what he asked.

"I'm going to call Mrs. Stevens, so she can find out if I have any other residence than Boca Raton, and get her to call my parents…"

Dan got up and was on his way to the payphone near the restaurant's counter, when Gustavo stopped him. "Hold on! Maybe it would be better for you to wait until you know if you live here before she calls your folks…"

"Yeah…, perhaps you're right. If I call my parents and tell them my story when there's no need, it wouldn't serve any purpose. Anyway, I'll call the old dear and see what she's got to say."

Gustavo leaned against the back of his chair and watched Dan go to the phone.

As the four of them followed Damianos inside the cabin, Stefano gasped.

"This is exactly like our living room in our house in Pennsylvania." He looked around him in disbelief. "How did you do that?" he asked Damianos.

"Why don't we sit down first," Malou told Stefano, leading him by the arm toward the couch.

"But, Mom, this is extraordinary!" Stefano argued mildly, plopping down beside his mother, while Gaby and Daniel sat in the two chairs opposite them.

"Didn't you hear what Mom said before we left? She said that what ever we saw or heard might look or sound strange," Daniel remarked, visibly happy to be the one recalling his brother to attention for once.

"Yeah, I heard what Mom said, but this is still beyond belief."

Walking up between the two chairs and now only clad of his flannel pants and shirt, Damianos said, "This is one of the reasons for which I brought you here. I feel that you three children need a little explanation before you start on your journey." He pulled one of the wooden chairs that had been standing by the door and sat down. "You see, Stefano, everything all of you will experience during the next days will be the product of your combined imagination. In this instance, your mother remembered the inside of my cabin the way she saw it the first time she and your father paid me a visit, or were led here I should say. So, it was imperative to respond to that recollection and for you to see what she saw." He looked around him at the faces staring at him. "Ha-ha, I see that you don't quite believe your eyes or ears yet, do you?"

"Oh no," Gaby was quick to say, "It's not that, Damianos, it's just hard for us to grasp the idea of us traveling in our imagination as if everything was real."

"Oh but, my dear girl, everything you will hear, feel, touch and experience from the moment you landed in the clearing is and will be very real. You're not sitting on the cloud of your dreams right now, you are physically living that dream."

"A bit like an insomniac would do," Stefano remarked.

"Exactly like it, yes." Damianos nodded. "Perhaps with one exception though, no one will wake you up or no one will be allowed to do you harm. And things will not hurt you either, as long as you keep your dream catcher close to your chest."

"But Mom said that you can't touch it either, does that mean you're evil?"

"Daniel!" Malou shouted in surprise.

Daniel had to be the one voicing his father's initial reaction to Damianos's presence in the hospital when he first appeared in their lives.

"No, I am not evil, son, far from it, but my task requires me to stay outside and ward off malignant spirits that could try and hurt you. Moreover, I have to make sure that you perform what ever is required of you, whether the task is difficult or not."

"Are you going to tame us into submission then?"

"No, Daniel, I will not beat anyone of you into submission. Yet, I am a hard master when it comes to abiding by the precepts of God."

When Dan hung up the phone and turned around to look at Gustavo, his face expressed his obvious annoyance.

He must have learned something unpleasant, Gustavo thought, but smiled. "Okay, what did the lady have to say for herself?"

Dan sat down. "She must have been a school teacher or even a principal," he replied. "She said that I'll have to go to her office and explain how I discovered my identity." He chuckled. "How can I do that?" He fixed his gaze on Gustavo. "I can't very well go back to the recruiting office and ask to borrow my file, now can I?" He grabbed his napkin and threw it on his empty plate. "This is absurd. She wouldn't even give me an answer to my question about where I lived. Can you believe that?" He sniggered.

"Maybe, we should go back to the recruiting office and ask the good sergeant for copies of your application and a duplicate of your photo..."

"Oh yeah, that was the other thing she wanted – a photo identifying me as Dan Politano. How can I go back, Gustavo? What reason would I have for asking to copy my file?"

"I don't know, Dan, but maybe simply asking would be the answer. You never know what the answer would be. See, by my way of thinking, you're an officer, and anything you ask should be provided without explanation."

"But that's ridiculous…"

Gustavo shook his head, visibly disagreeing. "No, it's not ridiculous; it's simply a matter of believing in who you are and what you can do."

A couple of hours later, Gustavo and Dan were coming out of the recruiting office, Dan holding a large envelope in his hand.

"What did I tell you," Gustavo said. "All you had to do is ask and the sergeant obeyed you without batting an eyelid. Didn't he?"

"I thought he would ask me why, at least question the purpose…"

"No, Dan, the army or the navy doesn't function that way. When an officer asks you to do something, you just say "Yes, sir, right away, sir," and obey the order."

"It sounds like you've been there before — have you?"

"Yeah, in another life I was obeying orders too," Gustavo replied pensively.

"Why are you living in a shelter, if I may ask?"

Gustavo stopped walking abruptly and turned to face his friend. "I've done one too many tours to the Middle East, Dan, and I couldn't cope with my old life when I got home — that's all." He looked down at his feet for a moment. "And if you were ever sent overseas, when you've completed your training, just remember one thing — you won't be the same person when you get back."

CHAPTER FIVE

When Dan and Gustavo returned to the shelter, they went up to their room for a while. Dan was curious about Gustavo's past, but didn't want to press the man into divulging anything of his personal life until he was ready to do so. Nevertheless, Gustavo opened up a little and Dan learned that he had been married to a lovely lady, but when he came home from his last tour of duty, he couldn't keep it together. He couldn't hold a job for very long and was always late at work for the sole reason that he "wanted to be left alone to clear his head." A few months later, things went from bad to worse. His wife kicked him out when she discovered that he was roaming the streets aimlessly instead of going to work, when he had a job, or searching for one when he was laid off.

Fortunately, they didn't have children — they had wanted to wait until he was demobilized to have a family — and the divorce had been swift and final in a matter of months.

"And you know what the weirdest thing about that is?" Gustavo said, looking up at Dan from his bed, "It's that she still loves me, or so she said the last time we met."

"Why would you find that weird?" Dan asked by way of a reply.

"I don't know. I guess I was expecting her to be mad at me for not assuming my responsibilities."

"I've never been married, but what I know is that true love is not fickle. When I remember my folks..." Dan stopped and stared into space. "Yeah..., I can see them now, Gustavo; that's great!" He laughed. "My mom..., her name is Daniela..." His voice dwindled down to a mere whisper then. "And my

33

father..." He shook his head. "Darn it, I can't hold these images; it's like you shut off the TV." He looked at Gustavo for a long moment before he added, "Anyway, I was seeing them arguing just now and that's why I was thinking that even when they get mad at each other, that love of theirs is still very much overseeing everything they say or do."

"Sounds wonderful, but I don't think that's the kind of love we had. I mean I was a bastard for not caring about what happened to her while I went to "clear my head", and I don't think I would forgive myself either if I had been in her shoes."

"You don't know that," Dan objected. "Maybe now that you've got a clear head and that you're back, you could find work, couldn't you?"

"I don't know, Dan. It's been a couple of years since I came back and I'm losing everything I've learned..."

"And what were you doing before you left?"

"I was a crane operator..."

"You mean you hung around and maneuvered these tall building cranes...? Wow! That must have been fascinating."

Gustavo chuckled and sat up. "I don't know about fascinating, but it was a solitary job, which is what I always wanted. But the fact is, to do that job, you've got to have your head on your shoulders, otherwise you could kill someone just because you touched the wrong lever. And when I came back, I was far from being able to concentrate on a job like that. I was often back in the middle of a war that brought too much misery to all of us and I couldn't escape from reliving the killings, the bombings and from hearing these screams..." Gustavo's voice trailed off. He remained silent for a moment and then added, "Anyhow, enough of my story; why don't we go down and watch a bit of TV. What do you say?"

"Yeah, sounds good to me, let's go," Dan agreed, getting up. "What about Mrs. Stevens?" he asked; his hand on the doorknob.

"There's no rush to satisfy the lady, is there?"

"No, Gustavo, there isn't."

Throughout the little exchange between Daniel and Damianos, Malou had been observing their cat. *The man is definitely comfortable in his own skin* — a remark she recalled making when she had first come to the cabin with him. However, this time Dan wasn't expected to burst through the door and question Damianos about his beating him with a cane to teach him how it would feel when he would be at the end of his tether. Her face clouded over at the recollection.

Noticing the dreamy look in her eyes, Damianos said, "I think it is time for us to hit the road, don't you think so, Mrs. Politano?"

The children's faces turned to her. "Hum…., yes, yes, of course. I'm sorry; I was just remembering when Dan and I were here."

"I know," Damianos rejoined. "But unfortunately, it's no time for recollection, my dear lady." He got up from his chair, grabbed it and dragged it back to where he had found it. "We should go to the house now. Solange is waiting for you."

"That's our guardian angel, isn't it?" Gaby said, rising to her feet.

"Yes, Gaby, but for the moment, she will only try guiding you to finding a book."

"Why wouldn't she get the book for us?" Daniel asked. "Wouldn't that be simpler than us searching for it?"

"Seek and you shall find; isn't that what the Lord said?" Damianos countered.

"Yes, Daniel," Malou interposed, "And I wish you would stop questioning everything we'll have to do during this trip. Otherwise, we'll be here for ever, remember?"

"Okay, okay, Mom, I'm sorry, but this is so weird."

"Right. And this is only the beginning," Stefano said, following his mother and sister to the door. "I think things are going to get much weirder before we're done."

As they opened the door of the cabin, a cold breath of wind swept over them.

"Would you look at that? It's been snowing," Gaby said, surprised to see the snow-covered clearing. "We should have packed something…."

"No need," Malou said, pointing to the anorak and boots Gaby was now wearing.

"Wow! Talk about practical," Daniel said, patting his own jacket. "I guess we don't need to pack a bag when we're traveling with you, eh?"

Having donned his cloak once again, their shepherd no longer appeared in a mood for any bantering. He closed the door and began marching through the snow in front of them until they reached the edge of the meadow. He then turned to Malou. "It is now time for you and your children to find your way back to the old house, Mrs. Politano. Your children need to realize how difficult the forthcoming journey will be. They need to build an inner force that will guide all of you to the house. I will be waiting for you at the end of the trail." And with these words, Damianos snapped his fingers and disappeared, and so did the cabin at their backs.

"That's all we need!" Gustavo said to Dan, taking a seat in one of the chairs in the lounge room, facing the TV. "Another war story…"

"Yeah, and it's a good one too," an older fellow countered, looking at Gustavo pointedly.

His pronounced accent didn't leave any doubt in Gustavo's mind that this Australian guy had landed in Florida by mistake. He grinned at the thought but remained quiet.

"What is it about?" Dan asked, plopping down in another chair beside Gustavo.

"That's about the landing on the beaches of Gallipoli…"

"Say what?" Dan shouted unexpectedly. "Did you say Gallipoli?"

"Yep, that's what I said; why? You got anything against our Aussie vets, hey?"

"Sorry, man, I have no idea what you're talking about, but I just remembered…," Dan replied, turning to Gustavo who had been taken aback by Dan's sudden shouting. "That's Fabio's last name, Gustavo. Gallipoli is Fabio's last name. Do you realize what that means?"

"You got it wrong, mate, Gallipoli is not a bloke's name, it's the place where…"

"I don't care…," Dan blurted, shooting a dirty glance at the old Australian guy. He got up and grabbed Gustavo by the arm. "Come on, we've got to phone him."

"Okay, okay, I'm coming," Gustavo said to Dan. Then he turned to the Aussie man. "I'll come and watch it with you later…, alright?"

"Sure, sure, but don't be too long, you're gonna miss all the good parts."

As soon as they reached the reception desk, Dan looked over the counter. Harrison was there, doing another crossword. He looked up. "What can I do for you?"

"You could give me a phone book for a start," Dan replied, still excited at the thought of being able to meet with his friend shortly.

Without a word, Harrison took the hefty volume from under his table and plunked it in front of Dan with a thud. "Anything else?"

"A smile would be nice?" Gustavo said to Harrison's scowl.

All he got was a shrug instead.

"Okay, here it is…, Gallipoli, F. That must be him. Look." Dan turned the opened phone book toward Gustavo.

"Okay, that's the name alright, but his address is nowhere near here. That street sounds like way out by the airport or something."

"Well, at least we could try phoning him, if you've got another quarter to lend me?" Dan said, extending his begging hand to Gustavo.

"I'm going to have to run a tab on you, you know that?"

Dan Guffawed, but wrapped his palm around the precious coin. "I'll be right back," he said, practically running to the payphone.

Fighting against the howling wind that whirled relentlessly through the trees, Stefano wrapped an arm around his mother's shoulders while Daniel and Gaby trudged through the snow, tracing a path with each of their steps.

"Are you alright, Mom?" Gaby asked, the words reverberating through the gusts of wind as she turned around.

"Don't worry about us," Stefano replied, still holding Malou tightly against his side. "We'll be fine. Just don't walk too fast so we don't lose sight of you two."

Daniel swung on his heels. "What do you mean lose sight of us? We're only three feet ahead of you guys. How could you lose sight of us?"

"I wish you would stop arguing with your brother, Daniel," Malou blurted. "You never know what Damianos could do to make this little trek through the woods more difficult than it is."

A moment later, as if Malou's words had been heard, Daniel shouted and fell to his knees, screaming, "My eyes! Something got into my eyes!"

Stefano rushed to him and lifted his brother to his feet. "What's the matter with you, idiot, this is no time to joke around." He pulled Daniel's hands away from his face. "Open your eyes! Come on, I can't help you if I can't see what the problem is."

By this time, Malou and Gaby had gathered around the young man. "What happened; did you feel something hitting your eyes?" Malou asked Daniel.

"No, Mom, it's just that I can't open them. It's like if I opened them, they're gonna burn."

"Don't be silly, Daniel, just open your eyes so we can be on our way, okay?"

"Stop it, Stefano; I'm telling you I can't open my eyes. That's all."

"Well, if that's the way you want it, you'll have to hang on to Gaby and let her lead you out of the forest."

"What if this is permanent and I'm blind? What then?"

"Now, Daniel," Malou interposed, "just remember this is all in your imagination and nothing of what you will experience during this journey will be permanent. So you're not blind, you just need to cope without your eyes."

"Come on then," Gaby urged, taking Daniel by the arm and leading him to walk beside her."

"Are you sure I'm gonna be okay?" Daniel asked again, hanging onto his sister's arm as if he was at the edge of a precipice, afraid to fall.

"You'll be just fine," Stefano replied. He turned to his mother. "Does this sort of thing happen often?"

"It might, Stefano. You see everything Damianos does..."

"You mean this is of Damianos's doing?"

"Oh yes. He hears everything and sees everything and always tries to teach the spirits in his charge something they need to redress or control in their lives."

"And what is he trying to teach Daniel right now, how to see in the dark?"

Malou had to smile at her son's remark, but said, "Don't be so dismissive, Stefano. I believe Damianos wants Daniel to understand that he needs to trust in his own abilities and to rely on someone's helping hand. He wants people to do things for him..."

"Like Solange getting the book for him?"

"Exactly. But in order for him to accept his share of the responsibilities during the journey, Daniel will need to ask for assistance when needed and trust in his ability to do anything by himself and for himself."

"You know, Mom, I wish my classmates could experience some of this. It's turning out to be a very interesting trip."

When Dan hung up the phone, he shook his head in dismay. "There's no answer," he said to Gustavo, obviously disappointed.

"Maybe he's out somewhere and won't be back until later tonight," Gustavo suggested. "Let's go watch the movie with that Aussie bloke, and we can call back in a couple of hours. What do you say?"

"I guess so; but what is he doing going out in the middle of the week?"

"Now, come on; you sound like a mother-hen. He's probably not expecting your call..."

"You know, you may be right," Dan replied, his face brightening up a little, "his note said that he would meet me on the tenth..., maybe he's out of town until then."

CHAPTER SIX

I t seemed as if they had been plodding through the snow for hours when Gaby saw the path ahead of them open up and letting more light through the dense forest.

"It looks like we're getting to the end of the trail," she announced, turning her head toward Stefano and Malou behind her.

"Makes no difference to me, I still can't open my eyes."

"You know, Daniel, it's a good thing you can't see anything right now," Stefano said, "Otherwise you'd see my fist just in front of your nose..."

Daniel's reaction was instantaneous and fierce. He swung around and adopted a pugilist's stance, ready to tackle an invisible adversary.

His brother, sister and mother burst into loud laughter.

"You're just a sight for sore eyes," Malou quipped. "But, really, Daniel, you need to control your impulses or you'll find yourself in a heap of trouble some day."

"Very good advice, Mrs. Politano," Damianos interposed, appearing from behind a tree unexpectedly. "Your son, although slightly incapacitated, still needs to be reined in as a wild colt..."

"Stop referring to me as an animal," Daniel shouted in the direction of Damianos's voice. "Why don't you let me open my eyes so we can get to the house, eh?"

"All in good time, Daniel. You still need to rely on your instincts rather than on anyone else guiding you."

"How could I rely on what I don't see?" Daniel argued, turning toward the spot where he thought Damianos had been standing.

"Your sight only confirms what you perceived before your eyes were able to see."

"You mean like I can hear where you are, but would only be able to confirm your location once I opened my eyes?"

"Now you're getting somewhere," Stefano remarked, having observed Damianos's maneuver to guide Daniel toward him.

"Yes, Daniel," Damianos went on, "and now that you've reached the end of the trail, you are the one who is going to guide your family to the house."

"ME?" Daniel shouted, "How do you expect me to guide everybody when I don't see anything and when I don't even know where we are."

"But you know very well where we are, Daniel," Malou said, "You just need to remember where you were playing all the time when you were a kid."

"Yes, Daniel, your mother is right; you were about seven years' old and you came here to play in the snow...," Damianos rejoined, opening his arms wide, a gesture that parted the drapes of foliage barring their passage, so that everyone could see the edge of the woods and the hill leading to their old home. "And now, you're going to follow my voice. It will lead you and your family back to the house."

"But..."

"NO, Daniel, stop arguing," Malou urged. "And do what you're told. We'll be right behind you."

Damianos cracked a smile and then returned his attention to the old mansion ahead of them. He began walking and started whistling quietly.

Gaby, the compassionate one, grabbed her brother by the arm and turned him toward Damianos's back. "You go now and follow the whistle," she whispered, pushing him ahead of her.

Dan was up bright and early the next morning. He had decided the night before to make his meeting with Mrs. Stevens the first item on his agenda. He needed her to tell him where he lived, given that he believed he was staying in Key West for a purpose, that of attending his pilot training right on the base. As for Fabio not answering his phone, he surmised that his friend had probably returned home and would be back on the tenth.

As they were eating breakfast, Gustavo asked, "Are you going to call your parents today?"

Dan shook his head. "No. I mean I will. As you said, it will be better for me to call once I know for sure whether I've got a place here or if I only came to the navy base to enroll. Once I know what I was doing when I fell in that park, I'll call them just to check in."

Gustavo drank the last of his coffee and stared into space for a minute before he said, "You know what you said yesterday got me thinking…"

"About what?"

"About me getting a job again. Since I've met you, my visions or daydreams about the war have not been so prominent. It seems that when my mind is busy with something else, it doesn't have time to wander down memory lane so much."

"But didn't that happen when you had a job?"

"No, not really. See, I didn't have a break when I got back. I should have taken Liz on a holiday or something, but we didn't. I just got off the plane one night and a week later I was working."

"How about working with someone – like going back to operating a crane but only part-time and with another guy – would that be possible?"

Gustavo laughed. "Yeah, anything is possible on a construction site, but I don't know if they even would consider hiring me…"

"Well, you won't know that until you ask. Isn't that what you said to me?"

"I guess so, but you know; the whole thing scares me a little."

"That's another thing you told me; the worst answer you could get is "no", isn't it?"

"Okay, okay, I hear you, man. I'll think about it."

As Gaby, Stefano and their mother were walking up the hill toward their old home; they couldn't help but reminisce about the days they were living in Pennsylvania.

"It was cold, wasn't it, Mom?" Gaby said, lacing one arm into the crook of her mother's elbow.

"Yes, it was. We forgot about the cold, the snow, and only remember the good times we had."

"But we were happy here, weren't we?" Stefano remarked musingly.

Malou looked up at her eldest son. "Yes, we were, actually. Winter or summer, we enjoyed living here."

When Daniel managed to trip and fall flat on his face into the snow, everyone laughed, except for Daniel who was more enraged than ever.

Damianos stopped but didn't turn around. "Are you going to get up, brush yourself off and continue following the whistle or are you ready for your next tantrum?"

"I'm up, I'm up. Just go ahead; I'm listening," Daniel replied, tilting his head to the resuming sound of the whistle.

It took the four of them and Damianos another few minutes to reach the front steps of the house.

"Here we are then," he declared, moving backward and away from the front porch. "I'll leave you in good hands, I'm sure." He looked at Daniel. "You can open your eyes now!"

"You're right, I can!" Daniel shouted, looking around him. "I never thought I could do that. Wow! That was something else." He stared at his mother. "You know, it was strange but I could hear everything so clearly.... I think next time I need to find my way somewhere, I'll close my eyes." Which remark provoked another round of laughter among his siblings and mother.

"Where's Damianos?" Gaby swung on her heels and threw a glance down the hill. "Why is he gone?"

"Never mind, Gaby. He'll be back, don't worry," her mother replied, turning to face the door. "Okay, now, please remember – again – this is all in your imagination, so please don't be surprised, alright?"

"Alright, Mom," Stefano said, "Do we knock or do we go in?"

"Just see if the door is open. If it is, let's go in."

Stefano tried the knob and it turned very easily. "Hello...?" he said quietly, pushing the door open. "Hello...? Anyone home?"

"My goodness me, son; don't just stand there," Solange said, trotting down the hallway, "let your mom and siblings come in. It's still cold out there." She smiled brightly as soon as her gaze rested on Malou. "Time has treated you well, my dear; you look wonderful." She took her visitor in her arms and embraced her. "But come on in and take a seat by the fire. You must be frozen."

"Thank you, Ms. Solange...," Stefano said, taking his boots off. "I'm Stefano and this is my brother, Daniel, and my sister, Gaby."

"Very nice meeting you all in person at long last, I'm sure," Solange replied, making her way to her favorite chair, the one facing the fireplace.

Imitating Stefano, everyone took their boots and anoraks off, and followed Solange to the living room.

"Wow! How many books are there on these shelves?" Daniel asked, looking up to the ceiling.

"There must be thousands, Daniel. But to tell you the truth, I've never counted them."

"But I guess only one of them will interest us," Malou said, taking a seat on the sofa beside Gaby.

"Yes, my dear. However, to find that particular book, you will need to answer a riddle."

"What sort of a riddle?" Stefano asked, plopping down into the other chair beside Solange.

"It is getting late, so why don't we have dinner before we begin our quest, shall we?"

"You mean it has something to do with food?" Daniel asked. He was still standing, his back to the fireplace.

"No, my dear Daniel, but I hate rushing things, as your mother will tell you, and I couldn't possibly remember everything on an empty stomach." With these words, Solange got up and made her way to the kitchen.

"Do you want some help?" Gaby was quick to say, already on her feet.

"Yes, yes, my dear. Why don't you come and help me with a few things."

As soon as the two women were out of earshot, Daniel went to sit beside his mother. "Do you think she'll tell Gaby what we need to know?"

Malou patted her son's knee. "If she took Gaby aside, she has her reasons for doing so. It's best to let things happen rather than trying to second-guess an angel."

"She sure doesn't look like one," Daniel said.

Chuckling quietly, Stefano said, "Did you imagine she'd be floating about the house with wings at her back maybe?"

"No, but I never thought to see an old, crippled woman..."

"You've missed the point, Daniel," Malou countered. "Appearance will deceive you and she needed to return to the person she was when she occupied this house at the time these books were placed here."

"Do you think each of these books have answers to someone's problems or dilemma?"

"Yes, Stefano. I didn't realize it until I went back to 2013, but I now believe each of these represents an experience or are the written answers to someone's questions."

"That's why there are so many of them, I suppose," Daniel said.

"And you haven't seen them all yet. There are book shelves in every room of the house, including the basement."

In the kitchen, Solange was putting the last touches to the spaghettis and meet sauce.

Gaby watched her with interest. "You know, spaghettis are one of my mother's specialties — you might have to give her your recipe. These look and smell great."

"Oh but, dear, this is her recipe. I spied her many times while she was cooking — she is a wonderful cook."

"You could say that again," Gaby rejoined, giggling. "Okay, what can I do?"

"Why don't you take the salad out of the fridge and get it ready to serve?"

Gaby turned and stepped to the fridge, opened it and was surprised to find only the solitary bowl of salad standing on the middle shelf. Although strange at first, she remembered that Solange being here, in the flesh, so to speak, was only temporary and that an angel wouldn't need to eat anything. ...

"Looks like you've raided the grocery store, Ms. Solange," Gaby remarked, bringing the salad bowl to the table and starting to toss it.

"Oh no, my dear, I don't go out anymore. I have everything brought to my door, for the time being anyway."

"Do you have many visitors like us?"

"I shouldn't say 'many', but enough to keep me occupied," Solange answered, stopping whatever she was doing to turn her gaze to Gaby. "But while you and your family are here, *I would like you to go down the cascade of your memories; your mother and brothers will need to come to the surface of the pool with the reeds of your father's life.*"

"What does that mean?" Gaby asked, slightly baffled. She wondered if this description was part of the riddle.

"You'll soon find out, child." Solange grabbed the spaghettis and sauce and headed out of the kitchen to the dining room.

CHAPTER SEVEN

When Dan and Gustavo walked into the department of the social services where Mrs. Stevens worked, they were taken aback by the many people sitting at tiny desks and practically hidden behind heaps of paper and files of all sorts. One or two of these people had word-processors with large monitors occupying half the remaining space on each of their work tables.

"Amazing," Dan whispered into Gustavo's ear, "I never imagined the social services being so busy."

"Ah, there you are," Mrs. Stevens said, appearing at Dan's side unexpectedly. "Let's go to our interview room. We'll be more comfortable there. Shall we?"

"Do you mind if I attend the meeting too," Gustavo asked timidly.

"If Mr. Damianos has no objection..."

That's all Mrs. Stevens had to say for Dan to flare, "I've told you on the phone my name is Mr. Dan Politano, so..., if you don't mind..."

"We'll see about that, sir," Mrs. Stevens snapped back, opening the door of the interview room. "Please come in and have a seat." Her tone was harsh and unyielding.

Once Dan and Gustavo were seated across from Mrs. Stevens, she began: "So you say you are Mr. Dan Politano, is that correct?"

"Yes, that's what I found out yesterday when I went to the naval base and examined my enrolment file," Dan replied, putting the folder he had brought with him on the table.

"Are those copies of your enrolment papers?" Mrs. Stevens pointed to the file.

Dan pushed it toward her. "Yes, it contains copies of my birth certificate and a copy of my photograph, plus all of the forms I had to fill out at the time I filed my application."

She opened it, put her glasses back on the bridge of her nose and began examining every sheet of paper carefully. "May I keep the file?" she asked.

"Yes, I have no objection," Dan said, shrugging. "But now I have a question for you, Mrs. Stevens; would you be able to tell me if I had taken up residence in Key West since my enrolment?"

"I should have thought that since you have now identified yourself conclusively, at least as far as you're concerned, you would have been able to find that out for yourself."

"Okay then," Dan said, getting up, "let's go, Gustavo. Since I will have to find out the rest of my story on my own, I don't think we need to detain Mrs. Stevens any longer, do you?"

"Wait a moment, Mr. Politano…, you can't just leave…"

"And why not? I have just given you all the proof you need to close my case file and let me resume my life. That's all we have to discuss, isn't it?"

"Except for a little matter of reimbursing this office for the hotel expense…"

"You mean "the shelter expenses", don't you, Mrs. Stevens?"

"Well, yes, but what ever you wish to call it, there's still a night unaccounted for…"

"I think you are mistaken, Mrs. Stevens. You see, you did not acknowledge my name or my identity until a few minutes ago. So, I think that last night at the shelter is still on you. Isn't it?"

"Who says I didn't accept your identity until this morning…?"

"I do," Gustavo cut-in. "I've heard you call my friend "Mr. Damianos" a few minutes ago, and I'll testify about it in court if need be!"

"Alright, alright," Mrs. Stevens said, rising to her feet and taking the file with her. "But be sure to vacate your room by tonight, Mr. Politano, or…"

"Or what, Mrs. Stevens? Are you going to kick me out? I'll be sure to pay my bill personally and sue you for wrongful eviction under false pretense if you were to attempt to chase me out of the shelter."

"But how are you going to pay for it? You're not working…"

"Listen, Mrs. Stevens"—Dan had enough—"I appreciate what you've done for me when I came out of the hospital, but now, I suggest you stay well away from me, okay?"

And without another word, Dan marched out of the interview room, Gustavo in tow.

Having deposited the spaghetti, sauce and salad bowls on the dining room table, Solange raised her voice to say, "Dinner is served!" looking at her guests with a broad grin appearing on her lips.

"Smells delicious," Malou said, taking a seat to Solange's right.

"We didn't see anyone setting the table; did you do that magically?" Daniel piped up, sitting down beside his mother.

"Oh no, Daniel — no magic tricks in this house — I simply set it before you came in, that's all."

The plates, glasses and cutlery were all a reflection of another era. Their fine design and the exquisite, almost transparent porcelain of the plates gave one the impression of being dining in one of the finest European houses.

"These are beautiful," Gaby said, taking her salad fork gingerly and admiring the delicate silver engravings.

"I bet they cost a mint."

I'll have to wash his mouth with soap one of these days, Malou thought, but said nothing.

"Actually, Daniel, they were wedding presents when Damian and I were married," Solange said, throwing a quirky smile in the young man's direction. "But we're not here to discuss the price of my china, so just help yourselves."

Malou took the salad bowl and after serving Solange, passed it around to her children.

Stefano took the opportunity to pour a glass of red wine for everyone around the table. Gaby looked at her mother before accepting to have a glass.

Solange had to smile. "If you wish, I have some juice in the fridge," she offered.

"That's fine, Ms. Solange, I think Dad wouldn't mind if I had a glass with dinner."

"I'm sure you're right, dear. Besides, wine is good for you, if you don't drink too much of it, of course." She looked around the table. "Oh my, I forgot the bread," she exclaimed suddenly.

Gaby was up already. "Where is it? I'll get it."

"In the oven, dear. And there's a bread basket on the counter. Thank you."

The conversation during dinner turned rapidly to Solange's life and her travel adventures with Damian.

"And you know, nothing could really stop us," she remarked. "When Damian had some time to spare, he would organize a trip for us. I generally kept a suitcase packed, just in case"—she giggled at the recollection—"but I was usually wrong.... One time we went to Africa and all I had packed were winter outfits."

"Did you have to buy everything while you were there then?" Malou asked, imagining how she would fare if she had to buy any sort of clothes in the markets of an African town.

"Oh yes. At first it wasn't easy, but I got used to these surprise expeditions eventually."

"Which country did you particularly enjoy visiting?" Stefano asked, between mouthfuls of spaghettis.

"I think Australia was the most intriguing to me."

"Why?" Daniel asked. "Did you see any kangaroos?"

Solange laughed outright this time. "We saw kangaroos and wallabies and koalas and all sorts of strange animals, yes, but these were not what remained etched in my memory, it was the age of the continent, which was evident everywhere, that retain my attention."

"Did you meet any aboriginal people?" Gaby queried.

"Oh yes. Most interesting people indeed. You see, according to some scientific studies, they are the oldest humans on Earth. And if I had to differentiate colors between races, Australian aboriginals are, in my opinion, the blackest people on the planet. I couldn't believe it when I saw them for the first time. Even the darkest African person literally "pales" in comparison."

"They apparently live off the land pretty well, don't they?" Malou remarked.

"Yes they do. But when the white man introduced alcohol to their tribes, it was the end of their natural and ancestral mode of living. They became despondent and restless. Being illiterate, they were treated extremely badly by the people who came to Australia over the past two centuries."

As Dan and Gustavo made their way back to the shelter, they passed by a clothing shop. Somehow the shop window retained Dan's attention. He stopped and turned to look at the mannequins outfitted with various apparels.

"Do they remind you of something?" Gustavo asked, looking up at the display.

"Not really, but there's something about that summer dress that triggered an image in my mind; it looks the same as I saw on a woman. . ., I don't know." Dan shook his head and resumed walking. "It's like snap shots appear and disappear in front of my eyes, and I can't place the people or the event. It's very strange."

"Why don't we go back to the park where they found you?" Gustavo suggested. "Maybe you'll remember what happened and it might tell you what you were doing to fall like you did."

"That's a good idea. But I should really phone my parents – just to say "hello". Do you think they'll be annoyed if I call collect?"

"Why should they? You might not have the change in your pocket, or if you were traveling, it would be expected for you to call collect. I don't see the problem."

"I guess you're right," Dan agreed. Yet, he was still in two minds about making the call. He didn't want to have his parents worrying about him.

"Why don't we go to the coffee shop beside the shelter and you place the call from there?"

"Why not from the shelter?" Dan asked, raising a questioning eyebrow.

"I don't know, but I've got a hunch that old Harrison is keeping an eye on you for some reason. And I don't know why he would, but he's a sneaky bastard if you ask me."

"Okay then, let's use the phone at the coffee shop."

As they entered the little café, it was nearly empty. Only two young people were sharing a piece of pie facing each other across a table.

"Love birds," Gustavo remarked, whispering in Dan's ear as they took a seat in a booth close to the payphone.

"Do you think I've got a girlfriend?" Dan asked out of the blue.

Gustavo chortled. "That I don't know, man. But if you had, I'd say that would be one of the first things you'd remember. Girls have a way of leaving a deep impression on your mind."

"I suppose so," Dan replied pensively. "You know, Gustavo, the people I knew before the accident..." He stopped in mid-sentence.

"What accident?" Gustavo was quick to ask, hoping to help Dan retain the snippet of memory that seemed to have passed in front of his eyes just now.

"I fell and hit my head.... I was skiing," Dan said evasively. "Sorry..., it's gone."

"I'm sure that didn't happen out here though – no skiing in these parts."

"It wasn't here; of that I'm sure. And I was older. Maybe it was somebody else, I don't know."

"Well, maybe your parents could tell you...?"

Dan shook his head. "No way I'm going to talk to my mom about anything like an accident, when I don't even know if it happened to me or to someone else."

"Are you gonna have something to eat or just coffee?" the owner asked as he came around the counter and approached the table.

"Just coffee, man, thanks," Gustavo replied quickly, before looking at Dan. "Do you want to eat something?"

"No thanks, not for now. Maybe later," Dan said, throwing a glance at the owner.

The burly man didn't seem too pleased with that answer. "Coffee coming right up," he said, walking away with a shrug.

Once the two coffees were in front of them, Dan got up and went to the phone. He pulled a piece of paper on which he had written his parents' number out of his jeans' pocket and dialed the operator.

After a few interminable seconds, he finally got connected. He recognized his mother's voice instantly. "Hey, Mom, how are you?"

"Goodness gracious, Dan. Where were you? I called your apartment and got no answer for the past two days. Dad and I were getting worried. Why didn't you call on Sunday?"

Dan could only smile. Truly, he didn't know what to say or how to explain his situation, not that he wanted to anyway. "I'm fine, Mom. I just stayed with a friend over the weekend and they don't have a phone at their cabin...," he lied. "But here I am, and I'm fine."

"Well, next time you decide to go traveling, just let us know, will you?"

"Yes, yes, of course." Dan paused. He wondered how he was going to ask for his address in Key West since it appeared that he must have an apartment somewhere in town. "Well anything happening with you guys?"

"Nothing much, dear. Just that your dad has got it in his head to get a pool installed in the backyard."

"A pool? What on Earth for? We're five minutes from the ocean..."

"He says it's getting too hot around here."

"Okay, well if that's what he wants to do..."

"Yes I know, dear, but it's going to take all the space..."

"Don't worry about it, Mom, I'm sure Dad will think of everything."

A few words later, Dan hung up; tears pearling at the rim of his eyes. He couldn't even remember his own home.

CHAPTER EIGHT

When they had finished their meal and the dishes were cleaned and put away, Malou, Solange and the children retreated to the living room. And that's when Gaby finally asked for an explanation from Solange. "What did you mean when you said that you *would like us to go down the cascade of our memories,*" and something about Mom, Stefano, Daniel and I *"needing to come to the surface of the pool with the reeds of our father's life"*?"

Malou turned her face to her daughter; she was surprised. "Was that a clue, Solange?"

"What cascade are you referring to?" Stefano piped-up, curiosity deepening the lines of his face. "Is that a location or a metaphor?"

"What about us coming to the surface of a pool? Are we drowning or something?"

"No, Daniel. Not in reality, you're not. Yet these two sentences are the first of the riddle that will help you find your book."

"So, we should think of a cascade and a pool," Malou suggested musingly.

"Yes, but I should think the book in question relates to you plunging into the past and coming up to the surface with the reeds of your father's life."

"What does "reed" mean then?" Gaby asked.

"Well, reeds are very well anchored at the bottom of any pool or lake — they're hard to pull up. They're resistant…"

"You mean like Dad not wanting to let go of his past, is that it?"

"Something like that, yes, Stefano."

"What about the rest of the riddle?" Daniel asked.

"I think you will need to remember your geography…"

Daniel mumbled under his breath. "Of course, geography. Why not math or even chemistry? I hate geography!"

Solange laughed with Malou while Stefano frowned. That brother of his was going to be more than he'll be able to take, he reflected somberly.

"The third line of the riddle," Solange went on, "as I remember it, goes like this: *Victoria falls into a lake of joy when memory trespasses time.*"

"What does geography have to do with that?" Daniel queried.

"*Victoria Falls*, you idiot, that's what it refers to," Stefano retorted, visibly irritated.

"Yes, Stefano, you're correct," Solange said. "But you must remember the riddle only refers to the title of a book. Once you've figured out the title, it'll be simple to find the book, will it not?" She looked at Malou.

"I hope it's not in the basement this time," Malou replied, tittering. "But if it is, be it then."

"Do you have a piece of paper and pencil, Ms. Solange?" Gaby asked. She wanted to have the whole riddle written out. It would help them decipher the title.

"Sure, dear. You'll find a note pad and a pen in the bureau beside the window." Solange pointed to the antique desk in question. "Oh, but let me give you the key," she added, rummaging through her apron's pocket. "Here, here. Damian always kept that bureau locked for some reason." She giggled, handing the small key to Gaby. "He must have had love letters stashed somewhere in there…."

Once Gaby had found what she had been looking for and came back to sit beside her mom, she wrote down:

Go down the cascade of your memories;
Come to the surface of the pool with the reeds of your father's life.
Victoria falls into a lake of joy when memory trespasses time.

She raised her gaze to Solange. "If I read this correctly, we will need to find a book entitled with the words: Victoria Falls, Pool, Memory, Father and Time, right?"

"Yes, I believe that would be a good starting point," Solange agreed. "However, I also believe that you should concentrate on the more salient words, such as Victoria Falls, Memory, and Father."

"Do you recall the title of the book then?" Malou queried, knowing that Solange in her present state would be subject to memory lapses.

"Not exactly, dear, but I seem to recall Damian mentioning something to the effect that people could easily drown in the memories of their past and have no vision of their future."

"But that would be depressing," Malou went on, "If say someone has no ambition or goals, that would leave them living in the present, wouldn't it?"

"That's what I thought, too." Solange paused for a moment, her hands in her lap. "I know this must be very confusing for all of you, but I think if you started searching for a book with the words *Victoria Falls*, it would be a step in the right direction."

"Where do you suggest we start?" Stefano asked, looking at the enormous bookshelf to his left. "It's not like they're sorted alphabetically, are they?"

"Well, no time to waste," Malou declared, standing up. She turned her gaze to Solange. "Is the step ladder still in the basement?"

"Oh yes, yes, dear. Yet, I would suggest you start at the top. The attic perhaps?"

"The attic?" Daniel blurted. "Are there more books up there too?"

"Oh yes, Daniel. But my point is that you're looking for a book, which deals with the tallest fall on Earth, and "falling..." Do you understand what I mean?"

"Not really, but if you suggest we look in the attic first, we'll do that, won't we, Daniel?"

He shrugged. "I guess. But, Mom, how do we get there?"

"Simple," Stefano said, "we find the attic access door and climb up."

"Why didn't I think of that," Daniel sneered, shooting a resentful glance at his brother.

"Gaby; why don't you stay with me, while your mom and brothers go up there?" Solange said, looking up at Gaby.

Malou and her two sons turned an inquisitive gaze to the old lady.

"Don't you just stand there, you've got a job to do, and Gaby and I have another."

"Okay, okay, Solange," Malou said, cracking a smile, "We're gone." She turned to Daniel and Stefano. "Alright, boys, let's get up there, shall we?"

Once the three of them were out of earshot, Gaby asked, "What would you like me to do?"

"Let's have a look at the riddle again – the words you've written down. These three sentences are leading me to think there's something more to the words." Solange stretched a hand for Gaby to give her the notepad. "Let me see." She read the riddle aloud.

"Go down the cascade of your memories;
Come to the surface of the pool with the reeds of your father's life.
Victoria falls into a lake of joy when memory trespasses time."

"You see, there's nothing strange about *going down a cascade of memories,*" Solange went on, or *"finding the reeds of your father's life,* but when it comes to the last sentence, *"falling into a lake of joy when memory trespasses time",* I find it odd."

"Why is that?" Gaby asked. "We've all got some good and bad memories, don't we?"

"Precisely, my dear. To me it should read, *"...a lake of joy "and sorrow" when memory trespasses time",* there's no sorrow in those past memories, that's what so strange."

"If there is no sorrow and only joy when you remember your past, wouldn't that mean that you have something to regret?"

Solange stared at Gaby for a moment. "How very clever of you. Yes, I think that's the answer. That's the point of the riddle, Gaby. Your father must have some regrets in his life. I wouldn't know what at this point, but I suggest you all look for a book entitled: "Victory (not Victoria) surfaces (or emerges) from the joy of memories' past."

"Do you mind?" Gaby said, taking the pad from Solange's hands. She wrote it down: *Victory emerges from the joy of memories' past.* "Is that it?" She showed it to Solange.

"Exactly. Yes, yes, that's it. I remember now." Gathering her shawl about her shoulders, Solange suddenly looked much older somehow. Her frail body appeared to be shrinking in the old English chair, and her face shriveled under the age-long lines of her gentle face. "Why don't you call your mother and brothers, dear? I have made a terrible mistake."

"What mistake was that, Ms. Solange?" Gaby queried, observing the old angel curiously.

"Just go, Gaby. I must tell them what we found out."

"Alright then." And with these words, the young woman rushed to the back of the house where she found Stefano looking down from the attic through the hole made by the access ladder.

"Are you ready to come up?" he asked her.

"Not yet; I think you need to come down with Mom and Daniel. Ms. Solange is quite upset. Apparently, she made a mistake in the interpretation of the riddle."

"Oh goodness," Malou said, her head poking over the edge of the banister. "That doesn't sound good." She turned, out of Gaby's sight. "Okay boys, let's go down and hear what Solange has to say."

A few minutes later, Malou and her children had resumed their seats in the living room; their gazes fixed on the old woman.

"I'm sorry; I must apologize to the four of you. I have made a mistake…"

"Anyone can make a mistake, Ms. Solange," Stefano said soothingly. "That's not a problem."

Solange lifted a hand, indicating that she wished to continue speaking without being interrupted.

"Please, let me." She took a deep breath. "When Gaby showed me the riddle written down, I realized that we focused on the description of "falling" or "going down" to a pool of memory, which in itself was correct, yet we should have focused on the word "surface", too, such as you asked, Daniel, "are we drowning or something?" which obviously we are not; on the contrary, we are "surfacing" with the reeds of your father's life. Then, my mistake was to remember the riddle wrongly. I don't know why I honed on the words, "Victoria Falls", while the riddle should read: Victory falls into the lake of your father's memories…, and then emerges with the reeds of his life…, and so forth and so on." Malou was agape. She had a hard time following Solange's reasoning. "In any case, with Gaby's help, I believe we have now the answer to the riddle and probably the title of the book…"

"Which is?" Stefano erupted, visibly impatient.

"Read it aloud, please," Solange told Gaby.

"Okay, here it goes: *Victory emerges from the joy of memories' past.*"

"May I see it?" Stefano asked, extending a hand for Gaby to give him the notepad. He looked at the notes and the entire text and then raised his eyes to his mother. "I think you're right, Ms. Solange, as far as the title of the book is concerned, but the entire riddle deals with much more than just a book title, doesn't it?"

"Let me see," Malou asked. Stefano handed her the notepad. "I'm sure you're right, Stefano. Because, the way this is written reminds me a lot about the tasks' descriptions we had read when your dad and I were first here."

"Exactly, Malou," Solange rejoined. "I think it would be a good thing for you to keep that page of notes tucked away in your pocket, Stefano, so that you could refer to it from time to time while on your journey."

"What do I do now?" Dan asked Gustavo when the two of them came out of the café. "I have no money, I don't know where I live and Fabio will probably not be back until the tenth."

"As I said before, I think we should go to the park where they found you and see if it triggers something else in your mind."

"I guess you're right. But do you know where it is, I mean where that park is located?"

"I don't, but the hospital must have a record of it, besides, they might have the name of the person who found you. Maybe, we should pay a visit to your doctor, what do you say?"

"Okay by me. I'll try anything at this point."

Gustavo smiled at his friend and wrapped an arm around his shoulders in an encouraging gesture. "And once you know where you live, I promise I'll do all I can to find myself a job, okay?"

Dan cracked a grin and looked up. "You've got a deal there, Gustavo. And if it's not a hole in the wall, I'll invite you to crash at my place until you got yourself all sorted out. How's that?"

"Okay," Gustavo replied after a hearty chuckle. "But I'm not easy to live with..."

"Who says?" Dan demanded. "From what I've seen thus far, you're just as easy as a fish in a bowl. You only need a change of water every three days..."

Both men erupted in laughter then.

An hour later, they were facing the nurse on duty at the Key West Medical Center.

"Would Dr. Carson be on duty today?" Dan asked.

"I believe he is, yes, but he's probably making his rounds right now. Is it urgent?"

"No-no, it's just that he asked me to drop by from time to time..."

"And what's the name?"

"Mr. Dan..., I mean Mr. Damianos."

"Alright then; let me page him," the nurse replied. "Why don't you have a seat in the visitors' room while you wait for him, okay?"

"Sure," Dan said, and was about to turn away from the counter when he asked, "Would you be able to tell me where I was found, I mean where I had my accident and who found me?"

"Yes, of course, Mr. Damianos, let me check your chart," the nurse said, getting to her feet and going to the filing cabinets at her back.

Gustavo and Dan watched her while she checked the file folders. When she closed the drawer, she turned and came back to her desk with Dan's chart, which she opened in front of her. "Let's see now..." She flicked through to the back page. "Okay, here we are, you were found at the Bill Butler Park..., but the man who found you didn't want to leave a name."

"That's too bad," Dan said, "I would have wished to thank him..."

"Hold on...," the nurse said, "there's a note here that says that the man apparently takes a stroll around the park every day." She raised her gaze to Dan. "Maybe, you can ask around while you're there...?"

"Well, thank you, Nurse. I'll probably do that. And maybe I'll come back to see Dr. Carson another day. Okay?"

"Sure, I'll leave a note for him to say that you were here."

CHAPTER NINE

It took Dan and Gustavo the better part of an hour to find the Bill Butler Park and then to locate the clearing where Dan had been found.

Dan looked around at the trees surrounding him. There was something about the place that reminded him of another meadow, another location and a small house. Abruptly, he swung on his heels to look in the direction where he thought there should have been a log cabin of sorts.

"Ah, you're remembering something, aren't you?" Gustavo said, walking beside Dan.

"Yes, but there's nothing there." Dan pointed to the edge of the clearing. "There was a cabin there. At least I thought there was. And that's where I saw that shepherd, Damianos. But there's no one here." He sounded dismayed to say the least.

"And do you remember falling from somewhere?" Gustavo asked.

"No, not really. I only remember hitting my head against a tree trunk..." Dan stopped in mid-sentence again. Then shouted, "That's it; I hit my head against a tree when I went down the hill.... Oh God, it's gone again," he blurted, shaking his head. "It's maddening, that's what it is, Gustavo, just absolutely insane."

"And there's no hill anywhere near here," Gustavo added, hoping to be helpful.

"Exactly," Dan agreed. "What I am remembering is a skiing accident. It has nothing to do with this place; and yet, this is where the old guy found me."

"Speaking of the old guy, why don't we have a stroll around that lake – it's called William's Land by the way – and see if anyone knows who he is. What do you say?"

"Okay, let's do that. But who ever he is, even if we happen to meet him, he wouldn't know me and wouldn't be able to add anything..."

"How could you be so sure he doesn't know you?"

"Well, I don't know..., you're right. Maybe I came to this park regularly. I really can't remember anything about this place."

"Would you rather go back to the shelter then?"

"No-no, since we're here, might as well make the best of it," Dan concluded, walking out of the clearing in the direction of the small lake.

"There is not one book here beginning with the word "Victory" in the title," Stefano declared, getting to his feet after crawling on all fours along the bookshelves lining the walls of the attic.

"Same here," Daniel rejoined. He was on the step ladder, examining the spine of every book on the top shelves, while his mother and sister were looking at the books midway between top and bottom shelves.

"And there are books with spines so frayed they're impossible to read," Malou remarked. "I wonder if we should take each of those out and see if it's the right title."

"I don't think so, Mom," Gaby said. "This is a rather new problem, so maybe it would be a newer book, I should think."

"Why don't we ask Solange if the book should be a new one, what do you say?" Malou suggested.

"Good idea," Stefano agreed. "I'll go down and ask her," he added, already on the ladder leading to the hallway on the second floor of the old house.

"Have you found it?" Solange asked, coming down the corridor to meet him.

"No, Ms. Solange, we haven't. But we were wondering if you think it would be a newer book or a very old one."

"Why do you ask?" Solange looked up at the young man. "Your problem is not a new one, yet it's very different to the majority of the goals people have when they come down to revisit their past."

"They usually come down together as a family, you mean?"

"Yes, Stefano. You see, most people come for a visit when they would like to correct or redress something that happened to them years ago, and although they soon realize changing the past is impossible, they learn valuable lessons while journeying through the years that brought them to their present date."

"Okay, if that's the case, we shouldn't have to pull out books that have no legible spine, is that correct?"

"As far as I can tell, yes, that's correct. Besides, I don't recall that particular book being damaged in any way."

"Oh so you've seen it before, have you?" Stefano asked.

"Yes, absolutely, but as I said to your mother once before, my eyesight is not what it used to be, and today I couldn't distinguish one title from the other, unless I put my nose to it."

"But you were able to read the notepad alright, why not the books then?"

"Because, son, the truth of it is that I can't interfere with your search."

"How do you mean?"

"You and your family need to find the book, Stefano; that's part of the task. I can only guide you to finding it with solving the riddle, but I can't actually point you to it."

"I see; *Search and ye shall find*, is that it?"

"Yes, Stefano, that's exactly what you, your mother and siblings ought to do."

Malou, Daniel and Gaby had been listening to this conversation from the opening in the attic.

"Alright then," Malou said, stepping onto the ladder to come down. "Why don't we go to the den downstairs? I seem to remember it containing quite a few war books..."

"What would we want with war books?" Stefano asked as he helped his mom step off the ladder.

"Think about it, Stefano: the title begins with the word "Victory". When there's war there's usually victory, isn't there?"

As Daniel reached the last step after Gaby had come down, he said, "I wish we could use a cell phone or a laptop."

"And how would those things help you?" Malou asked.

"The internet, Mom. It would give us a clue about the riddle's message maybe."

Gaby giggled quietly. "I don't think it's a riddle that you'll find on the internet, Daniel. It's very personal…"

"Yes, dear, you're absolutely correct," Solange agreed. "Every riddle I have ever seen or deciphered in this house has always been dedicated to the people concerned. Such as in your case, you yourself have noted something that I had not even considered, didn't you?"

"You mean about "regret"?" Gaby asked.

"Yes, yes, my dear." Solange looked at her four visitors and before Malou could ask for an explanation, she added, "But let's go down to the den, and I'll let Gaby explain."

Once they were assembled in the den, Solange sat on the chair facing Damian's old desk while the three children sat on the floor, and Malou leaned against one of the shelves.

"Alright then…," Solange began, "Stefano, let's see the page of notes…" She stretched a hand for the young man to give her the sheet of paper he had stuck in his pants pocket.

He handed it to her. Solange looked at Gaby. "When we read the last sentence of the riddle, as I remembered it at first, I noted that something was wrong. The sentence read: *Victoria falls into a lake of joy when memory trespasses time.* To me it should read "…a *lake of joy* — "*and sorrow*" — *when memory trespasses time*". There's no sorrow in those past memories, that's what so strange."

"And then I said," Gaby interposed, "if there is no sorrow and only joy when you remember your past, wouldn't that mean that you have something to regret?"

"And that would mean that Dad must have some regrets in his life," Daniel suggested.

"Precisely," Solange said. "So, even though you'll find the book with the title as we deciphered it, I'm sure you'll need to remember that your father's memories of his past contain something for which he has some regrets."

After walking halfway around the lake, Dan and Gustavo decided to take a seat on one of the stone benches near the edge.

"This is a beautiful place, isn't it?" Gustavo remarked.

"Yes, except it doesn't inspire me at all," Dan replied, another shadow of discouragement passing over his face.

"Did you ever visit a lake with your parents?"

"Yeah, with my wife I did…"

"What did you say?" Gustavo turned to stare into his friend's face.

"I…, I don't know, Gustavo."

"You said that you went to a lake with "your wife"; was that another of these odd images?"

Dan shook his head. "I suppose it was. These snap shots come and go. And if I said "my wife", maybe it was someone else in the car, or maybe I am seeing someone else entirely." He bowed his head. "I just wish somebody would tell me what happened to me."

"Hey, man, I'm sure it's going to come back to you," Gustavo said, punching Dan in the arm. "You'll see that I'm right."

"I sure hope so, because right now it feels like I'm in one of those long tunnels, but there's no light at the end of it and it keeps on veering one way and the other."

"Oh but there will be light at the end of it, I'm sure," an old man said over Dan and Gustavo's shoulders. He was holding a walking cane in a hand striated with the wrinkles of age. His face reflected the joviality of his expression and his smile was inviting and inspired confidence. "I'm sorry to interrupt your conversation, fellows, but I think I recognize you." He rounded the bench to face Dan. "I am the person who found you, son." His amused grin didn't abandon his lips. "May I sit down?"

Quite surprised, Dan blurted, "Please, sir, by all means," his face suddenly lightening up with renewed hope. He shoved over, so to leave space for the man to sit down. Dressed of an elegant summer suit over a white shirt that did everything to enhance the man's natural tan, he took a seat between Dan and Gustavo, putting both hands on the knob of his cane.

"I'm sure you have many questions to ask regarding the circumstances that led me to find you, don't you?" He turned to Dan.

"Yes, absolutely, but before I ask the obvious, could you tell us your name?"

"Nicolas is the name, son. And yours?"

"I found out only two days ago that my name is Dan Politano."

"And I'm Gustavo," the latter interposed with a broad smile.

"Well, I must say, gentlemen, I am very pleased to make your acquaintances. It is not every day that I have the occasion of rescuing, shall we say, someone from an awkward situation." He paused to look into Dan's eyes. "But did you say that you only found out your name two days ago?"

"Yes, I guess I bumped my head when I fell, and the doctor said that I have short-term amnesia."

"And you came here in hope to find out what happened to you, is that correct?"

Dan nodded. "…And to thank you for calling the ambulance for me."

"You must have had a concussion; didn't you?"

"Yes, that's right. And I can't remember most things." Dan threw a glance at Gustavo. "It's thanks to my friend here, that I have been able to piece some of this puzzle together."

"Well, all I could say is that I, too, would like to shed some light at the end of the tunnel in which you're traveling presently, Mr. Politano. You see, Nicolas is not a name given to me by chance or even by my parents. If you recall your saints' history, Nicolas is the patron saint of sailors, merchants, thieves and children. Quite an awkward assemblage of personalities, wouldn't you say?"

"You mean you're a saint?" Dan asked, astounded by his own inference.

Nicolas chuckled heartily. "Oh goodness no, young man, far from it in fact. Let's say I was given this pseudonym because I happen to love people in general and children in particular, and so many have come across my path that perhaps one of them compared me to him. Gift giving is my hobby. I love to see the children's faces when they get their toys from Santa Claus."

"Is that where the name Santa Claus comes from then?" Gustavo asked, apparently interested.

"Absolutely. But Nicolas or Nicolaus actually, is the original name of the saint." He turned to Dan again. "And as for you, Dan Politano, I was most pleased to have given you a helping hand when you needed one."

"Well, Nicolas, I'm sure happy to have fallen at your feet, so to speak," Dan said, laughing quietly. "But Gustavo and I went to the clearing where you found me and I couldn't remember a thing."

"I see," Nicolas said musingly. "In that case, why don't we go back and perhaps I could explain how I happen to come upon you?"

"Of course. If you don't mind, sure," Dan said, already getting up from the bench.

CHAPTER TEN

As they were walking toward the clearing, Nicolas asked Dan, "Do you know a man by the name of Damianos?"

Dan stopped in his stride and turned to look at the old man. "Why do you ask? Do you know him?"

"Not in so many words, no. But since you hollered the name before you passed out, I was wondering if you remembered who he is."

Dan had lost hope again. Nicolas had heard him scream the name Damianos, but he was the only person on Earth it seemed who saw the tamer in his dreams. "Well, that's too bad, because he must have been part of my life before I fell in the clearing and it seems as if I am the only one around here who remembers him."

"Mind you," Nicolas went on, "the name is familiar to me, and not for the reasons you might think. I mean most people know the name in passing, I suppose, but in my case, I had an opportunity some time ago, when my wife was still alive, to take a trip down memory lane, you might say, and meet a shepherd by the same name."

"That's it!" Dan shouted. "You saw him, didn't you?"

The three men had stopped walking. "Please, Nicolas, could you describe him for me?" Dan pleaded.

"Well yes, of course. He sported a long grey beard, bushy eyebrows and wore one of those cloaks that shepherds donned in ancient times."

"What about his hair? Do you recall anything in particular about it?"

"Ah yes, I seem to remember his hair being grey but he had a patch of white just above the hairline." Nicolas looked at Dan curiously. "Is he the same person you saw in your dreams?"

"Yes, sir, that's exactly the same description I would give of him if I were asked."

"And when you said, you and your wife took a trip down memory lane, what did you mean?" Gustavo queried, quite interested in Nicolas's account.

"Oh that's a long story, and one that probably wouldn't help Mr. Politano in the least, not at the moment anyway."

With these words they entered the clearing and Nicolas led Dan and Gustavo to a particular tree. "This is where I found you." He pointed to the base of a tall oak tree. "And I came to you as fast as I could, but since I'm unable to run, you were unconscious by the time I reached you."

"That's a mighty tall tree," Gustavo remarked, shooting a glance upward to its expansive canopy. "You could certainly hurt yourself if you fell from one of these branches..."

"That's one of the first things the nurse told me when I woke up in the hospital. She said I had probably fallen from a tree," Dan added.

"Yes, I could see why someone should arrive at that conclusion," Nicolas said, "when there was nothing else that could have hurt you the way it did."

"You mean there was no one else in the clearing when you arrived, is that it?"

"Yes. Besides, I didn't see any bruising on your skull, as when someone has received a blow to the head. So, I didn't think you had been attacked in any way."

"And where did you find a payphone around here to call the ambulance?" Gustavo asked. He hadn't noticed any phone box anywhere near the clearing.

"Oh, that was a stroke of luck really. As I went back to the path, I saw someone holding one of these portable telephones and I asked him if he could dial 911 for me."

"Wow, that was lucky alright," Gustavo said. "Was he a lawyer or something?"

"He said he was, yes, and he waited for the paramedics to arrive while I returned to sit and wait at your side until they came to attend to you."

Dan was looking down at the spot where he had met his troublesome fate when he asked, "Would you mind very much if I asked you to tell us about that trip down memory lane?"

Nicolas chuckled lightly. "I wouldn't mind at all, but today, I don't think I would have the time, I'm sorry. You see, I have a granddaughter who's punctual to a fault, and missing the dinner bell is a grave sin." He paused long enough to notice Dan's deflated reaction. "But if you would like to come back tomorrow, I would be pleased to tell you all about it."

Dan's face brightened. "I think we could do that?" He looked at Gustavo.

"Yes, absolutely. I'd love to learn about that Damianos fellow, too."

"Alright, gentlemen, I'll be seeing you tomorrow then," Nicolas said, already walking away in the direction of the path edging the clearing.

Getting a little impatient, Malou said, "Alright..., whether Dad has anything to regret about his past, we need to find him first before we could ask him; so, I think our time would be better spent in locating that book. What do you say?" She looked at each of her children in turn.

"Okay, Mom," Stefano said, pulling the library ladder toward the farthest corner of the room. "I'll start up here, if you want to look at the other end...?"

"I guess I'll be the crawling butt again," Daniel said, a grin spreading across his face.

As they resumed their search for the elusive book, Solange got up from her seat and made her way to the lounge room. She felt tired and somewhat restless. She wasn't used to having a whole family traipsing about the house anymore. Those days were long gone and now she longed to return to Damian's side. Although she knew he was observing her every move, it was not the same. She sat in her chair beside the fireplace and prayed silently for Malou and her children to find the book quickly. While her eyes were closed, she saw her beloved husband come to her in her thoughts.

"You shouldn't worry, sweetheart," he murmured, "It won't be long now."

"I guess not, Solange replied quietly, but as you probably noticed I've made an awful mistake..."

"Please don't worry about it; as Stefano said, anyone can make mistakes. Besides, you recalled the right verse in the end, didn't you?"

Solange nodded and smiled.

It was only a few minutes later that she heard a loud scream emanating from Gaby's mouth announcing that she had found the book.

At long last, Solange said to herself. She got up from her seat in time to see Gaby burst through the lounge room's archway – book in hand.

"See, it's the book, Ms. Solange. We found it!"

Malou, Stefano and Daniel came rushing into the room after her.

"But it's got a lock, just like our book did," Malou said, pointing to the side of the hefty volume. "Do you know where this key is?"

"Of course, of course. I remember now. It's the key that I gave you to open the bureau, Gaby. Do you still have it?" Solange peered into the young woman's eyes.

"Well, I…, I left it in the lock of the desk. It must still be there," Gaby said, practically running to the bureau.

And yes, the key was still sticking out of the lock. "There you go!" She grabbed it and handed it to Solange.

"Well then, Gaby, please give the book to your mom and when it's time we'll open it."

"What do you mean "when it's time"?" Stefano asked. "Can't we just open it now?"

"In the morning, will be time," Solange replied sternly. "But for tonight, I think we all need some rest. It's late, and for the journey you're about to undertake tomorrow, I think it's best."

Dan and Gustavo looked after Nicolas as he walked away, and smiled at each other.

"I'm glad that at least you've found someone else who's seen your Damianos guy," Gustavo remarked.

"But isn't that a strange coincidence? I mean, first the man finds me in a place where no one comes often, and then he has dreamed of the same shepherd as I did."

"Maybe he's Santa Claus?" Gustavo said, laughing.

Dan grinned but shook his head. "I wish he was, but he's probably a charitable man who's got a lot of money to go round. That's all."

"Alright then," Gustavo said, "What would you like to do now? Shall we find Fabio's place?"

"I don't know if we have time. It's getting late and as you said, it's near the airport or something…"

"We could take the bus and at least see the place. If you recognize it or if it triggers something in your memory, we could always come back. What do you say?"

"Okay, we can try. And if it's in fact where I live, we could come back in the morning with our bags and get settled..."

"Now you're talking," Gustavo agreed. "Okay, let's get out of here then."

It took them the better part of an hour to make it to the front of Fabio's place. While riding the bus, Dan already had noted a few things that he remembered — a pizza place in particular. They had decided that, on their way back, they would have a bite to eat at that restaurant before returning to the shelter.

"How about it?" Gustavo said, looking up at the building. "Does it tell you anything?"

"Not much, except that I've been here before."

"Well that's a start. Why don't we ring the manager and see if he recognizes you?"

"Sure, but somehow I don't think I live here. It's not my kind of place."

"What do you mean by that? It could be just a temporary arrangement."

"Okay, let's go then."

As they opened the main entrance door, a man came out and paused, looking into Dan's face. "Well, hello there, Dan. How are you? I haven't seen you in a couple of days. Did you go back to see your parents?"

Dan drew a complete blank. He stared at the young man. He was about his own age, well dressed and apparently ready to get to his car, jangling keys in hand. "I'm sorry, I know this is going to sound absolutely insane, but do I know you?"

The young fellow opened and closed his mouth again. "You're right; your question does sound a bit odd. So let me ask another in return: what happened to you?"

Gustavo was quick to interpose; "I am very sorry, sir, but Dan here was hurt over the weekend, and he's suffering from amnesia. I'm just a friend, trying to help him remember as much as he can. The name is Gustavo." He extended a hand for the man to shake.

As he did, he said, "Hi, nice to meet you, Gustavo. I'm Emilio, a neighbor of Fabio and Dan." He looked at Dan who seemed ashamed of his condition. He had his head bowed and was looking at the floor beneath his sneakers.

"Do you think the manager would let us in the place?" Gustavo asked. "We phoned Fabio — he had left a note for Dan; that's how we found his number and this place actually, and we know he's away..."

"I don't think that would be a problem," Emilio said to Dan, who finally raised his head to look at his neighbor.

"I feel like such an idiot right now," he mumbled. "I'm sorry."

"Don't worry about it, man. But how did you happen to lose that memory of yours? Were you in an accident?"

"Well, it's hard to explain, but someone found me in Bill Butler park unconscious..., more than that I couldn't tell you."

"Wow, that's a long ways away from here. Do you know what you were doing there?"

Dan shook his head. "Sorry, I couldn't even remember my name at first — but no, I can't explain any of what happened."

"As I said, don't you worry about a thing. I happen to know the manager pretty well and I'll get him to come down and let you in the apartment." He turned to Gustavo. "What about you, where do you live?"

A little embarrassed, Gustavo replied, "I was traveling and found a hostel not too far from the hospital and that's where I met Dan. We're lodging together for now."

"Okay..., but let's not stand here between two doors and go to the manager — Joe is his name, by the way — and see if he's got a spare set of keys. Shall we?"

Both Gustavo and Dan nodded in unison and followed Emilio to the elevator.

Dan felt ill at ease for some reason; mainly because he could not place Emilio anywhere in his past. He felt as if this was all unreal to him.

CHAPTER ELEVEN

Although it was late into the night, Stefano, Daniel and Gaby couldn't get to sleep. Solange had told the boys to take the spare room on the second floor where they had found a single bed and a pull-out couch already fitted with sheets and blankets. For Gaby, Solange had prepared another room off the landing. It was small, but the bed was inviting enough, and Gaby accepted the accommodation with a gracious smile. As for Malou, Solange had told her to stay in the den where she could sleep on the large sofa comfortably.

"It's better for you to stay here with the book, dear," Solange had said as she had brought the blanket and pillow to her. "I don't think it would be a good idea for the book and its key to get into the children's hands before morning."

A little curious, Malou had asked, "Why would that be?"

"The best way I could explain it is with the old adage: "curiosity kills the cat"," Solange had replied with a hint of a smile.

"Do you think Mom has left the book in the den?" Stefano asked Daniel, turning to look at his brother.

"Or she's sleeping with it under her pillow. Do we even know which room she's staying in?" Daniel asked by way of a reply. "And why do you think we've got to wait till morning to open it?"

"Well, for one thing, it's not a good idea to start a journey during the night like Solange said."

"And for another?"

"I don't know, Daniel. But I sure hope Mom doesn't open it by herself."

"She wouldn't do that." Daniel sat up suddenly. "What about Gaby? Do you think she would sneak downstairs and open it?"

"Come on, Daniel; I know this trip is all in our imagination, but that would be going too far, even for our curious sister."

A knock at the door interrupted their quiet conversation. Stefano was up with a jolt and went to plant himself beside the door, an ear against it. "Who is it?" he whispered.

"Gaby. I just want to talk."

Stefano opened the door and let his sister in. "What about?" he asked, closing it quietly.

"I'm just worried about Mom. She's not upstairs. I think she's sleeping in the den. I saw Ms. Solange take a blanket and a pillow from the linen closet and bringing it down with her."

"I don't think there's anything to worry about; Mom is probably sleeping on the sofa. But why would you worry where she's sleeping?"

"I don't know, but this house is a little creepy. I mean with all these books that are supposed to be related to people's problems, it's not very comforting." Gaby shrugged. "I don't know, Stefano. It would be nice if the morning came right now."

"Okay, why don't you and Daniel stay in this room and I'll take yours." He looked into his sister's worried eyes. "Come here, you silly...," he added, taking her in his arms and hugging her. "Besides, there's nothing to worry about during the night. Remember, we all got a dream catcher around our necks to make sure no bad dream interrupts our sleep."

Gaby nodded and looked down at the amulet as she pushed away from Stefano.

"And if you sleep here, you better not snore," Daniel said jokingly, trying to break the tension.

"I don't snore!" Gaby retorted, grabbing Stefano's pillow and throwing it at Daniel.

"Okay, guys, let's cut it out for now. Okay?" Stefano urged. "I'll just go to your room"—he looked at Gaby—"and you two stay quiet. Okay?"

As soon as the elevator doors opened on the ground floor and Joe came out, a broad smile shot across his lips.

Dan froze. He recognized the older fellow instantly. "Sorry to bother you, Joe," he said quickly before Emilio could place a word in, "but I've lost my keys and I was wondering if I could get a spare from you until I could get a new key cut?"

"Rough weekend, was it?" Joe said, chortling. "But why did you wait so long to come home?"

"Long story," Dan replied. "But since Fabio is away anyway, I thought I'd stay with Gustavo here." He turned to him. "But now, I think I'd like to sleep in my own bed tonight."

"Hi," Gustavo said, cracking a smile.

Emilio observed the exchange in silence, only shooting a quick glance to Gustavo when he saw that Dan had recognized their building manager. "Okay," he said, "I think I better be going, or I'm going to be late for my date."

"Oh sorry, Emilio," Dan said. "Shall we see you later maybe?"

"Sure; I'll drop by tomorrow, if I don't have a hangover." He laughed. "See you then," he added, heading to the door.

"Okay then, Dan, why don't you come upstairs and I'll get you a set of keys."

Dan nodded and he and Gustavo followed Joe back to the elevator.

Once upstairs, the two of them stood in the doorway of Joe's apartment while he fetched a set of keys for Dan. They heard him rummage through a desk they gathered until he came back saying, "I almost forgot: there's a letter that came for you with the wrong apartment number – 304 instead of 309," handing keys and envelope to Dan.

"Thanks a lot for that," Dan said, taking the letter and keys from Joe's hands. "I'll come back with the keys tomorrow as soon as I've got them cut, if that's okay?"

"Sure, sure," Joe replied. "Just don't lose that set; otherwise, you'll be sleeping in front of the door until Fabio gets back." He laughed at the thought.

Dan didn't. *If there had been no other way, I probably would have already,* he mused.

"Where are you, Dan?" Malou murmured as she tried to make herself comfortable on the sofa. She touched her amulet and looked up at the ceiling. "I only wish I knew where to look for you. How far back are you gone?"

When she finally closed her eyes, all she could see was the ocean swell coming up and drawing down around her. She wasn't swimming or scared. The ocean meant something. But what?

"What does it mean; what does it mean?" she screamed as the morning light came streaming through the curtains of the den, startling her awake. Out of breath, Malou sat up and looked around her. It was instant recall. She was sitting on the sofa and the book..., the book was under her pillow. She grabbed it and looked at it. Same as the cover of the first book had been, this one was also embossed of a dream catcher's web. It was very ornate and seemed to be well preserved.

She immediately wondered if she had slept late or if it was early still. Since there was no clock anywhere in the house, she couldn't imagine what time it was.

She got up quietly, went to the door and listened. All she heard were plates being deposited on a table. She smiled. *Solange must be up,* she thought. Opening the door, she was assaulted by the aroma of freshly brewed coffee, baking and bacon.

When she burst through the kitchen door, she found her three children busy preparing a breakfast feast for everyone.

"Hi, Mom," Gaby said with a broad smile, "Are you hungry?"

"Hello...!" Malou replied, still in her bare feet, and coming to the table. "Have you seen Solange yet?"

Stefano shook his head in reply.

"But we've heard someone move upstairs after we came down," Daniel said between mouthfuls of pancakes. "How did you sleep?"

Still a bit dazed, Malou sat down and poured some coffee in the cup in front of her. "I just had a strange dream..."

"What about?" Gaby interrupted, going to take a seat beside her mother.

"Just the ocean. I mean I was surrounded by the ocean swell."

"Were you scared?"

"Oh no, and that's the strange thing, I wasn't scared at all. I just wondered what it meant, that's all." She took a sip of her coffee. "What about you guys; did you have a good night?"

"Well, at first I was a bit uncomfortable sleeping with all these books around me, but when Stefano and I switched, I was fine..."

"And she didn't snore," Daniel remarked, after drinking some orange juice.

"Ah, I see everyone is up and about. Good morning to you all," Solange said happily as she came into the kitchen.

"Wow, that's a beautiful dress," Gaby said, admiring Solange's outfit. The long, white gown was trimmed with soft fur and a string of tiny pearls around the wrists, neckline and hem. "Are you going to somewhere special?"

"You might say that," Solange replied. "But more of that later, my dear. Have you slept well?"

"We did," Malou replied quickly. "Why don't you take a seat and I'll get you some coffee and perhaps some toasts if you want?"

"Oh no-no, dear. Do not bother. I don't need anything for now, thank you." She paused for a fraction of a second before going to sit at the head of the table.

"And before you ask, we haven't opened the book yet," Malou said. "The kids just surprised me with breakfast and as soon as they're done, we can get it open, if you think it's okay." She looked at Solange pleadingly. She and the children were impatient but didn't want to show it.

"Of course, of course," Solange said, "but don't rush through breakfast. I'm sure you'll need all the strength you can muster for the journey ahead."

"I am glad Joe had a letter for me. Since there were no names on the panel downstairs, I wouldn't have known which apartment these keys would open," Dan remarked as he and Gustavo came out of the elevator.

"If you had told him what happened, he probably would have told you," Gustavo said in reply.

Dan smiled. "But do you realize it's actually the first time I recognized somebody? I was so happy about it, and a little surprised I might add, that I just wanted to act normal, if you know what I mean."

"Yeah, I think I do. This whole thing has been hard on you, hasn't it?"

"More than you can imagine, Gustavo," Dan said, as they came to a stop in front of the apartment door. "Okay, this is it – 309 – this is where I live, my friend." He turned the key in the lock and pushed the door open.

They stepped into the hallway hesitantly, yet as soon as Dan saw a red folder on the desk, he smiled. "That's it! That's my mail folder from my mom." He grabbed it as if he had found a lost treasure. "Look…," he said to Gustavo, opening it for him. "I've got photos of my mom and dad…, that's fantastic."

"What about the letter Joe gave you; is that from your folks too?"

Dan shook his head. "No, I don't think so." It was still in his hand. He looked at the envelope curiously and then opened it. "It's from my brother…, his name is Rafael. You remember; he's the one I saw in a pizza shop…."

Gustavo waited until Dan finished reading. "So…, is it good or bad news?"

"Well, I guess it's neither. He's just talking about this girl he met…, not very clear…, not to me anyway." He looked up from the letter to Gustavo, and then dropped it together with the folder on the desk. "Why don't we take a tour of the place?"

Gustavo nodded. "You lead and I'll follow."

One thing that surprised Gustavo a little was how neat everything looked. And then he remembered that Dan and Fabio were on their way to become navy officers, and probably pilots at that, so they would have to be as well organized as he himself once was when he joined the army.

CHAPTER TWELVE

In one of the corners of Dan's room there was a bike helmet and a bag filled with sports' clothes. Dan smiled when he saw the items. "I remember now," he said to Gustavo. "I love bike racing. Dirt bikes, actually." He opened the bag and took out one of his shirts. "Number 4, see?" He put the shirt across his chest and then smelled it. "It's clean. That means I haven't raced in a while." He shrugged, folded the shirt and replaced it in the bag.

"Did you win?"

Suddenly, as if struck by a strange thought, Dan stared into space. "Yes. . ., yes, as a matter of fact I did, Gustavo. I remember racing every Saturday night. . ., somewhere — I can't remember where — but I know I won quite a few races."

"That sounds great. Anything else? I mean does the room remind you of something else?"

"No, not particularly. I think I'll remember a lot more when I talk to Fabio. But in the meantime, let's see if we can find out if I have a car or a bank account." Dan turned to the desk and began looking through some of his correspondence. "Ah-ah, there you go! That's a bank statement." He showed it to Gustavo. "And it's seems that I've got a bit of money in there, enough to pay you back for all the phone calls and bus-passes." He put the statement back in its envelope then looked around for something else. "I can't see anything about car insurance." He looked up at Gustavo. "Do you think I would recognize it if we went to the garage?"

Gustavo chuckled, uncrossing his arms from in front of his chest. "It's like a girl, man. I don't think you're likely to forget your car, even after being knocked over the head."

"You're probably right." Dan laughed and took the bank statement from the table again and put it in his pants pocket. "So, if I have a car, there must be keys somewhere."

"Maybe, you've got them in one of the coat pockets in the hallway," Gustavo suggested. "Since you two guys seem to be neat-freaks, I wouldn't be surprised your keys are on a hook somewhere."

"Good idea." Dan walked out of his room in somewhat of a rush.

He was already looking through the pockets of some of the jackets hanging on pegs near the door when Gustavo joined him.

"I hate going through Fabio's pockets, but since I don't remember which coat is mine, I'll have to look through every one of them."

Gustavo looked around him and went to the kitchen. A moment later he said, "What about these?" He pointed to a set of keys hanging at the corner of the kitchen wall.

"Yeah! That's it! Those are my car keys," Dan exclaimed, taking the set off the hook. "See, I've got that little helmet on the keychain...." He seemed very pleased to have found something that had re-ignited another memory.

"Alright," Solange said when she saw that everyone had finished breakfast and that Malou and the kids had returned from freshening up in the upstairs' bathroom, "Why don't we go and see what your book has to tell us?"

"Lead the way," Malou replied, "and we'll be right behind you."

Once the five of them were sitting in the living room, Malou put the book and key in her lap.

"Now, remember, Malou," Solange said, "The writing may not be what you expected..."

"What do you mean?" Malou asked, frowning. "Aren't they going to be tasks to accomplish in order for us to find Dan?"

"Maybe, maybe not. You see, the first book were filled with tasks that pertained to virtues that your husband needed to uphold or lessons that would be useful for him to remember in the future. However, in this instance, you are searching for him. So, I would suggest that the book will guide you to finding him."

"That makes sense," Stefano remarked. "And what form would these guidelines or tips would take do you think?"

"Are they all going to be riddles?" Gaby added.

"I don't know. Yet, I don't think they'll be difficult to decipher," Solange replied. "But why don't we see what it says?" She smiled at Malou.

"Okay, here we go…." Malou put the key in the small lock and turned it. They all heard the click and saw the latch being released. Then, with trembling hands, she opened the old volume. The first pages were blank, up to the middle of the book. Gaby and Daniel to one side of her and Stefano on the other, peering down at the first writing, Malou began reading aloud:

Find the right key and you will find the cardinal point of his destination. However, do not stray toward the swells of the ocean of your memories, for they will be wasted errands.

And that was it. There was nothing else on that page. The four of them were stunned. Perhaps they had expected a straight forward explanation or something more precise, but the two sentences were nothing like that.

Gaby asked, "May I see the book, Mom?"

"Sure, but the rest of the pages are blank…"

"I know," she said, taking the book from her mother's hands. "How many pages were there before that one?"

"Well, why don't you count them, if you think it means something," Daniel said, going down on his knees and crawling in front of his sister.

"Yeah…, that's what I thought," Gaby said, seemingly excited. "You see there are twenty-five blank pages before this one. Maybe Dad's gone twenty-five years in his past." She looked up. "Would you think that's possible, Ms. Solange?"

"Absolutely. And it's a very good observation, Gaby. These books always start and stop to the important times in one's life. If there are twenty-five pages preceding your first writing, it probably means the number twenty-five describes either a number of days, weeks, months or years before the important span of time."

Malou said, "So, it could mean four things; twenty-five days, weeks or months or years. That's not simple…"

"But it is, Mom," Stefano said. "We all remember what we were doing 25 days ago or even 25 weeks ago, don't we?" He looked at his siblings.

"Yeah, but when it comes to looking at more than two years ago; or 25 years back, we were not even born then," Daniel added.

"Yes, you are all on the right track as far as time span is concerned," Solange said, after listening to their little discussion patiently, "but for now I think you should focus on what the book told you."

"Yes," Malou agreed, taking the book back from Gaby. "Why don't we write the direction on your notepad, Gaby?"

"Sure, I'll get it." She got up, went to the bureau, opened it and took out the notepad, looking at it, agape. "Mom!" she screamed. Every one turned their heads to stare at her. "It's already written down. Look!" She took the notepad to Malou. "See, the two sentences are already written down. How did that happen?"

"I think our journey has started, Gaby," Malou replied, smiling up at her astonished daughter.

"I believe you're right, my dear," Solange said, getting to her feet. "And now I think it's time for you to leave and rejoin Damianos. He'll be waiting for you at the edge of the forest."

Excited to find *his* car, Dan couldn't run fast enough down the garage stairwell. Gustavo in tow, Dan finally stopped in front of a Trans Am Turbo.

"Wow!" Gustavo said, staring at the sport's car. "How old do you think it is?" He bent down to look through the window on the passenger side.

"It's 6 years old. I remember my father buying it new when I was still in High School. It wasn't cheap..." Dan stopped. "It's gone again. I hate when this happens." He unlocked the driver side door, sat at the wheel and opened the door for Gustavo.

When they were about to reverse out of the parking space, Dan turned the ignition off. Gustavo turned to look at Dan. "What's the matter? Did you forget how to drive?"

Dan shook his head and banged his fists against the wheel. "NO, Gustavo. But I haven't got a license, have I? Since I lost my wallet when I fell in that clearing, I lost my license too, didn't I?" He swore under his breath. "You know, it seems like every time I take a step forward, I have to take two backward."

"Okay, I can understand that," Gustavo said reassuringly, "but that's not the end of the world, now is it? Besides, you're not the first guy who's lost his license. All we have to do is drive to the DMV and get you a copy until you can get a new one."

"That simple, eh? And what if I'm caught between here and the DMV?"

"Well, if you're afraid of getting caught or taking the wrong turn, the only thing I could suggest is for me to drive you to the DMV."

"You have a license?" Dan asked, opening his eyes wide. "And you don't have a car?"

"Well, the two things are not mutually exclusive, are they?" Gustavo said, chuckling. "If I had enough money to buy a car, I certainly would have bought one by now." He paused. "Anyway, do you want me to drive?"

"Of course I do. Let's see if I can get that copy before the close of the day, shall we?"

"I don't think that's going to be possible. I've got an idea it's past 4:30 and these guys don't do overtime."

"Shit," Dan swore, "Now what?"

"Why don't we go back to the shelter, get our bags and get back here before Mr. Harrison charges us for another night, what do you say? Unless, you've changed your mind about me staying with you...?"

"Of course not." Dan seemed offended by Gustavo even mentioning this. "Are you crazy? I want you to stay with me, as I said, and besides, you've made me a promise that I intend you to keep, remember?"

"Alright then, and yes, I remember," Gustavo replied, getting out of the car to change places with Dan. "But what about another bed?"

"Don't sweat the small stuff, Gustavo. You'll sleep in Fabio's bed until we get a second bed in my room, okay?"

"Okay then, let's go."

When Solange closed the door of the old mansion on the four of them, she looked up at the ceiling above the hallway. "And it's time for us to join them, isn't it?" she said almost inaudibly.

Going down the hill toward the forest, Malou turned around to look at the old house. "I hope when we come back for a final visit, it'll be with Dad," she said softly.

"What was that you said, Mom?" Gaby asked.

"Oh, nothing. I was just hoping that Dad will be with us when we get back."

"He's got to be," Daniel said. "Besides, he might be searching for us by now."

"Somehow, I don't think so," Stefano interposed.

"What makes you say that, son?" Malou asked.

"Oh it's just that I don't think he can visualize his future where he is, like we can't see our own future right now."

"Yeah, but if he remembered..."

"No, I think Stefano is right, Gaby. You can't remember things you haven't experienced yet." Malou paused for a moment while they continued walking.

"But that's just the thing, Mom," Daniel argued. "In Dad's case, he has actually experienced everything until 2013, so he might remember things."

"Why don't we ask Damianos?" Malou suggested.

"Ask me what, dear lady?" their cat asked, appearing before them all of a sudden.

"I'll never get used to that," Gaby said, "I mean you appearing and disappearing like that. It's scary."

"Ha-ha-ha," Damianos laughed. "Pay no mind to my laughter, Gaby. I just take pleasure in surprising people."

CHAPTER THIRTEEN

As they were about to cross an intersection on their way back to Dan's apartment, they saw Nicolas waving them down from the sidewalk.

"What on Earth is he doing here at this hour?" Gustavo blurted, pulling to the curb.

"No idea," Dan replied, lowering the window on the passenger side. "Hi, Nicolas, what's up?"

"Hello, Mr. Politano. I think we might need to have a talk..."

"But didn't you say we were to meet you at the park tomorrow? Has something happened?"

"Yes, yes, of course. But I believe this is important. It can't wait, really."

Seeing the elderly fellow's anxious face, Dan said, "Okay then, why don't you get in and we'll go to my apartment," opening the door and climbing out of the vehicle. He lowered the front seat to let Nicolas into the backseat.

"I'm very sorry about this, fellows, but you see I had another dream while I took a nap this afternoon..."

"What sort of dream?" Gustavo asked, turning his head to the man before pulling from the curb.

"Oh much too complex to explain in the confines of a car," Nicolas replied. "But once we're settled in more comfortable surrounds, I will tell you everything."

Dan and Gustavo exchanged a glance before Gustavo pulled into the evening traffic once again.

"I assume you have copied the first clue of the directions onto the notepad?" Damianos asked, looking at Gaby.

"I didn't, but someone sure did," she replied, handing the pad to Damianos.

"And what have you deduced from the first sentence?" he asked.

"Nothing yet," Malou answered, "but Gaby thought that since there were 25 pages to turn before we got to the first clue, Dan must have traveled 25 days, weeks, months or years into his past." She looked at Damianos pleadingly. "Does that make sense?"

"Yes, it does," a man's voice replied to Malou's question. He was dressed in a beige suit and stood beside Solange, both radiant and as if peace itself enveloped their presence. "I'm sorry; I must introduce myself. I am Damian, Solange's husband." He smiled in the children's direction. "You do remember, Malou, don't you?"

"Absolutely, Damian. And it's a pleasure seeing you again."

"Same here. But to come back to your question: that your husband has gone back to a time equivalent to the number of pages preceding the first writing, is absolutely possible."

"But could you tell us if these pages meant for us to be counting days, weeks, months or years?"

"I couldn't be precise, Daniel. God does not reveal his plans in such details, and for Him they are minute details, you understand. But I would suggest we forget about days or even weeks. I would prefer saying the pages are to be counted or representing months or years."

"Wow," Malou said much louder than she expected. "Is that even possible? I mean that Dan went as far back as twenty-five years?"

"Yes, my dear," Solange said. "You must remember that anyone's visit into one's past most often is not accidental. Everyone has a desire to return to the scene of some prominent event in his or her life. Yet, and before you ask, Malou, even though Dan seemed to have fallen, literally, into a past unknown to us, subconsciously, it must have meant something to him."

"You mean, even though his return was an accident, he must have gone back to a time and place where he experienced something important?"

"Yes, Stefano. And although you or your siblings wouldn't be able to remember the event in question, perhaps your father talked about it on occasion," Damian suggested.

"What about the clue in these two sentences, are they indications of the event then?" Daniel asked.

"One step at a time, young man," Damian said. "The first clue is most often an indication of the location where the person has landed."

"Let's see this first sentence again," Gaby asked Damianos.

"Yes, of course." He handed her the pad.

"It says: *Find the right key and you will find the cardinal point of his destination.* What do you think that means?" She looked at her mother.

"I believe I should be of some help in that regard, Gaby," Damianos interposed. "The two significant items in this clue are "key" and "cardinal point"."

"How does that help?" Stefano asked. "And when you say "significant items" what do you mean?"

"Ah, I see that you have your father's analytical mind, very good," Damianos replied, smiling. "*Significant items* mean they are words to remember. Since this is only the first clue, we need to remember each of these significant words, if you prefer, until we have received the entire set of directions."

"Okay then," Daniel said, "where do we go based on "key" and "cardinal point"?"

"Let me add," Damian put in, "that some of those words are names of places perhaps."

"Then, it's time to go," Damianos declared suddenly, snapping his fingers.

When Dan, Gustavo and Nicolas arrived at the apartment, Gustavo made a bee line for Dan's bedroom to deposit their bags and the few pieces of clothing he had brought with him, before joining Dan and Nicolas in the living room.

"Would you like a drink or something to eat?" Dan offered, looking at Nicolas who had taken a seat on the sofa.

"Oh no, thank you. I have already eaten and what I have to tell you won't take long."

"Okay then," Dan said, sitting down across from the little man. "What happened to you and how does it concern us?" He shot a glance in Gustavo's direction. He had plopped down in the other chair beside Dan's.

"Well…, let me begin by saying that yes, I have met Damianos as you gathered. Same as you have."

"You mean you dreamt of him?" Dan interposed.

"No-no, I mean not exactly. As I told you, when my wife was still alive, we took a drive to a town by the name of Pahokee at the edge of Okeechobee

Lake." He advanced his body to the edge of the sofa – his cane still between his legs. "Looking at you, Mr. Politano, I can see the place doesn't mean anything to you, does it?"

"No, not at the moment, but a few hours ago I didn't even know I lived in this apartment"—his eyes traveled around the living room—"so don't be surprised if I don't remember anything of what I might have known before my accident."

"Yes, yes, exactly my point…"

"I'm sorry, Nicolas, I don't mean to rush you or anything, but could you tell us why you're here? Or, why you needed to tell me something so urgently that it couldn't wait until tomorrow?"

"Well, let me put it bluntly then, you're not supposed to be here, Mr. Politano."

Gustavo and Dan exchanged a curious glance and then switched their gazes to Nicolas, staring.

"I think you better explain what you just said, Nicolas," Dan stated, still peering into the old man's eyes.

"The thing is, Mr. Politano, I have had the privilege of talking to Damianos on several occasions since I, myself, traveled to my past and could not return to my present."

"Okay, Nicolas," Gustavo said, opening his mouth for the first time since he sat down, "Why don't you start by telling us who's this Damianos guy?"

"Well, yes. I think you're right, Gustavo. As I was saying; my wife and I traveled to Pahokee and there we found an opportunity to take a trip to our past. I won't go into details as to how we did it, but the result was that we didn't come back in due time and both of us remained in our past until we lived our future and subsequently died…"

"Now, now, Nicolas," Dan interrupted, a derisive smile crossing his lips. "I am sure you're quite alive at this very minute, unless you're telling us that you're a ghost. Is that it?"

Nicolas shook his head. "I know you think me a crazy, old fool, as many people would, but I'm neither crazy nor a fool, I can assure you." He paused to look at Dan fixedly. "If you wish to call me a "ghost", it is of course your prerogative, but, in reality, I am a messenger. And I have been sent to you to let you know that you have fallen in a past that no longer belongs to you."

"And who would it belong to, may I ask?" Gustavo interposed, visibly intrigued. "If, on the one hand, you're saying Dan isn't supposed to be here, where should he be? And, on the other, if you're saying this past doesn't belong to him, to whom does it belong?"

Nicolas stood up unexpectedly. "First, I would like you both to believe in my assertion. I am here…, and yet I am not…." He snapped his fingers and disappeared before Dan and Gustavo's eyes.

The two of them sat there, open mouthed. Then Dan said, "Are you sure Harrison didn't slip something in the coffee he served after dinner?"

Gustavo shook his head. "No, I don't think so, Dan. And to tell you the truth, I've seen this sort of thing before when I was in the battle field. But then I thought I was suffering from exhaustion or I was dreaming while I was awake."

"Like hallucinations, you mean?"

"Yeah, something like it. But the personage I saw then never stayed long enough to have a conversation. Anyway, I think we should listen to him, because the other thing is; I've heard of people disappearing unexpectedly around that lake. Everyone thought they'd drowned or something. So, this may be another explanation."

"Well, if you think we're safe listening to this old guy, I'm with you," Dan said, lowering his head and looking down to his lap.

When they landed, so to speak, Malou and her children were standing on a beach facing the ocean.

"Where do you think we are, Mom?" Gaby asked, hanging on her mother's arm, apparently not wanting to let go any time soon.

"This is the first of your cardinal points," Damianos replied from behind them and walking along the water's edge. "We are as far east as we can be without crossing the Atlantic Ocean."

"And what are we supposed to do here?" Daniel asked, watching the waves roll gently onto the sand at his feet.

"Amazing," Stefano remarked, "have you seen how we're dressed?"

Everyone looked at themselves.

They were all dressed for the beach. Their clothes were perfectly suited for the climate and environment.

"Yes, that's one of Damianos's tricks. He loves to dress people for the parts they have to play in their imagination," Malou said.

"What parts are we supposed to play; that's what I'd like to know," Stefano said, picking up a seashell and throwing it back into the waves.

"Simple, Stefano," Damianos replied, a mocking smirk on his face, "Maybe you need to go for a swim and find the key to your treasure."

"Hold on a moment, Damianos," Gaby interrupted, "because the last sentence of the clue is a warning, isn't it, Mom?" She pulled the notepad out of her beach bag.

"Yes, and it reminds me of my dream – remember? I told you about it at breakfast. I was in the middle of the ocean watching the swell..."

"And it says here; *do not stray toward the swells of the ocean of your memories, for they will be wasted errands.* So it might be dangerous to venture off shore to find that "key", don't you think?" Gaby shot a querying glance to Damianos.

CHAPTER FOURTEEN

Not even thirty seconds after Nicolas had disappeared; he re-appeared in front of Gustavo and Dan. They looked up at the "messenger" standing before them, shook their heads and smiled.

"Alright, gentlemen," Nicolas said, resuming his seat on the sofa, "If I have now convinced you that I can help you elucidate this unfortunate interlude in your life, Mr. Politano, I am ready to answer your questions."

"Okay, Nicolas, I'll play..."

"No, Mr. Politano, this is not a game, far from it in fact, but go ahead; don't let me interrupt you."

"Yes, of course," Dan went on, "I guess my first question would be: how did I happen to land in that clearing? Or is that something you're unable to tell me?"

"No-no, it is not a problem. I will tell you what I know. But let me start by saying that what happened to you is not common. Usually, when people travel to their past they have a purpose in mind. You see, most of us have some reason for re-visiting an event we wish to change or enjoy once more before we pass on. In your case, your landing here in 1988 was an accident. However, it is also an indication that you have always had a secret desire, shall we say, to be here."

"You mean I wished to be in Key West?" Dan asked.

"Precisely. You see, as soon as you walked out of the hospital, you went to the naval facilities. Do you know why you did this?"

Dan shook his head. "Not really, no. I felt – if that's the word – drawn to see the aircraft carrier. I didn't know why, but that's the first place I wanted to visit."

"Ah yes, exactly what I thought. You "felt drawn" to something that was niggling at your subconscious, didn't you?"

"I suppose so. And it's only when Gustavo drew my attention to the possibility of my being an officer in the navy that I discovered I was in fact enrolled to take the training on the tenth of this month."

"Good, good. I'm glad to hear that you found out what that secret desire was and that you do know why you fell in this place..."

"Yes, but that doesn't tell me how I happen to fall, does it?"

"Not yet, Mr. Politano, not yet. Have a little patience — all will become clear very soon."

"I'm sorry to interrupt," Gustavo put in, "but could you tell us what sort of messenger you are, Nicolas?" He paused for a fraction of a second. "Because, you see, when I was in the Middle East, I saw a person like you, but at the time I thought I was suffering from battle fatigue and put the whole thing down to hallucination..."

Nicolas's chortle interrupted Gustavo's query. "It was probably not a hallucination, Gustavo, but another messenger like me endeavoring to guide you home in one piece, shall we say."

Putting his elbows on his knees and looking down at his feet, Gustavo nodded. "Yes, and I think maybe I should have listened to my messenger. And maybe I wouldn't have done the things I've done since I've come back." The ruefulness in Gustavo's voice was blatant.

"Perhaps it was, Gustavo, but I have heard you make a promise to Dan here, which should see you out of the woods pretty soon I suspect."

"Thank you for that, Nicolas," Gustavo said, leaning against the back of the chair once again and stretching his arms above his head and then locking his fingers at the nape of his neck.

Nicolas then returned his attention to Dan. "Mr. Politano, I know you're anxious to know how all this happened, so now that we know why you landed here, I think you need to ask yourself where you were minutes before your unfortunate fall. Do you remember?"

"No, I have no idea what I was doing. I only remember being in a clearing very similar to the one in the park and Damianos standing a few feet from me. Besides which, the only thing that I recall was a log cabin at the edge of the clearing — but that's all."

"Very good," Nicolas said, placing both hands on the top of his cane. "Now let me add something to that recollection, and the reason for which you should not be here." Dan returned to his staring at the messenger. "As far as I can gather, you were about to return to your future after an extensive and successful trip into your past, when you missed to abide by one of the rules that would have brought you back safely…"

"Which rule was that?" Dan asked anxiously.

"You forgot to hold hands with your wife."

Dan was flabbergasted. He didn't know if he should jump for joy or cry his heart out. "You…, you…, I mean…, you're saying I'm married?" He got up from his seat and began pacing the length of the living room under Nicolas's gaze. "But why wouldn't I have observed such a simple rule? Was I unable to hold my wife's hand?" He stopped and turned to face Nicolas. "And what's the lady's name?"

"Malou is her name. And you forgot, or shall we say omitted to hold her hand because your arm was in a sling."

"My arm was in a sling, you say? Did I have another accident? Was I riding my bike or something?"

Nicolas shook his head vigorously this time and put up a hand. "No, Mr. Politano, you were not riding a bike, you were skiing…"

"That's it!" Dan shouted, rounding his seat to look at Gustavo. "Didn't I tell you about me falling against the trunk of a tree…, didn't I?"

"You sure did," Gustavo agreed, "And that's when I told you that you must have dreamt it because there was no snow anywhere in Florida…"

"Exactly"—Dan turned to Nicolas once again—"And you're saying that this accident happened in my future, I mean a future from today?"

"Yes, Mr. Politano. And unfortunately, therein lays the problem."

"How do you mean?" Dan questioned.

"Simply because people can travel in their past or visit it, if you like, given the opportunity, but no one is able to visit their future."

"And that means I can't go back, or forward, I should say, to regain my future. Is that right?"

"Absolutely. You see, the only possibility for you to return to your future is for your wife to find you."

"But can't you just go to her and tell her where I am," Dan rushed to ask.

"No, Mr. Politano. Only Damianos will be able to travel with her and your children…"

"I…, I have children too? How amazing is that!"

"Yes, and they are going to try to find you. Since I am not able to travel in the future either, I will only be able to relay messages, such as I did now, giving you an update on their progress."

"But if you can do that," Gustavo asked, "why can't you talk to Damianos and ask him to come to where you are today?"

"Because, I am not supposed to talk to Damianos, and even if I could, I wouldn't."

"But then how were you made aware of all these things you told me about just now?"

"Please, understand me, Mr. Politano, I am only transmitting the messages I receive from God. More than that I don't know."

"I suggest the phrase means that you should not venture in the high seas," Damianos replied to Gaby's question, having regained some seriousness in his voice. "However, there is a key to find on this continent…"

"But is that key an object, or is it the name of a place?" Stefano asked. "Because as Damian pointed out before we left the old house, the first sentence is an indication of the location where my father fell, isn't it?"

"Absolutely," Damianos said, "and as you correctly gathered, the key in question is to be located somewhere at a specific cardinal point."

"But what are we supposed to do on this beach?" Malou asked, looking up to the houses skirting the ocean shore.

"Just ask yourselves the questions that need to be asked, Malou. The answers will guide you farther in your search."

"Yes, Mom, that's what Damian and Solange said. These two phrases are a starting point…"

"And that means, we need to find out where we are and go on from there, is that it?"

"Yes, and without being tempted to err on the ocean swell," Daniel added musingly.

"Okay then, if that's what we need to do, let's go to the town behind us and see where we are," Malou concluded, already walking toward the path that would lead them away from the beach and to the city beyond.

As they arrived to the top of the embankment and stepped onto the esplanade that seemed to stretch far into the distance, Daniel remarked, looking all around him, "And there's no one around here. There's no car, no one walking, did you noticed that?" He looked at his mother inquisitively.

"Maybe it's too early. . . ." She turned her gaze to Damianos. "What time is it?"

"What ever time you wish it to be, Malou. Remember time is of no importance while you're traveling to your destination."

"Yeah, but it's a bit strange, you must admit," Malou countered. "Every place we've ever visited together on our previous journey there was always a time reference, wasn't there?"

"Ah-ah, yes, you're right. However, the previous journey was not dedicated to traveling through time, it was designed to have your husband recall events or visit places that his ancestry had either left or where they had lived."

"Okay, Damianos, but where do we go from here?" Gaby asked, looking down at the note pad again.

"Think of your cardinal points. If the beach to your left was east, then the esplanade runs north-south, so you can choose to go north toward the northeastern states or you can choose to go south. . ."

"And if we cross the street, we'd go west, right?" Daniel interposed.

"Absolutely," Damianos agreed. "However, if you are to read the second sentence again, it asks you not to lose yourselves in the swells of the ocean, which may indicate that you should stay close to the coast."

"Gees, this is worse than the old math problems," Gaby said, shaking her head.

"Why don't we go south then, Mom?" Daniel suggested.

"Why would you say that?" Malou asked.

"Because, Mom," Stefano said, "we've just left Pennsylvania and if there was any reason to believe that Dad had landed north of his initial point of departure, then we wouldn't have landed back in Florida, would we?"

"And how do you know this is the Florida coast?" Gaby demanded. "It could be any coastal town south of Pennsylvania, couldn't it?"

"How about this?" Stefano pointed to a road sign across the street. "Would that be enough to convince you we're in Florida."

"Good Lord, you're right," Malou exclaimed, gazing at the sign, which displayed the Florida State Emblem. She looked at each of her children in turn. "So, do we all agree to go south from here?"

They nodded in unison and began walking along the esplanade. The morning freshness seemed to have opened their eyes to other indications to time and places, for Gaby remarked, "You know, Mom, it shouldn't be any later than seven or eight in the morning..."

"Why do you think that?"

Daniel pointed to the sun. It was perhaps an hour above the eastern horizon. "Look, Mom, the sun is not high enough to be later than that."

"Well," Malou replied, shading her eyes against the light and looking toward the beach, "I guess you're right."

The farther they walked, the more people and their vehicles began to appear. It was as if the city had just woken up to the fact there was another day to be lived and enjoyed under the Florida sunshine.

CHAPTER FIFTEEN

Dan sat in silence for a long while. He crossed his arms over his chest and seemed to reflect on everything Nicolas had told them. He felt a certain detachment from reality. This was definitely not a hallucination or even a wakeful dream. It was real as real can be. Yet, there was an eerie feeling about it all. Nicolas's last sentence before he left the apartment, echoed in Dan's mind: "I am only transmitting the messages I receive from God," he had said. He stood up and kicked Gustavo on the foot. "Hey you; are you asleep?"

Gustavo shook himself out of his own reveries and looked up at Dan bleary eyed. He straightened up but remained seated. "No..., not really. But that talk with Nicolas was probably the strangest experience I've ever had in my life."

"You can say that again!" Dan chortled. "I can't get over what he said..."

"You mean the thing about transmitting messages from God?"

"Yeah, and about me landing in my past because I wanted, subconsciously, to be here."

"Well, that explains a lot, doesn't it? You were already re-living a past incident when you forgot to hold hands with your wife and landed farther back in your life." Gustavo looked up at Dan again, frowning this time. "But if I were to tell this story to anyone, they'd think I've gone completely crazy." He got up and stretched his arms wide and above his head. "I think it's time for bed." He turned and walked in the direction of Fabio's room, then changed his mind and swung on his heels. "So, you're sure it's okay for me to sleep in your friend's bed?"

Dan nodded, stepping beside Gustavo. "He won't mind at all and I'm sure he'd give you his bed if he were here." He padded him on the back. "You go ahead and make yourself at home, okay?"

"Okay, okay. Oh, what about breakfast? Do we need to get anything from 7-Eleven you think?"

"Well, let's have a look at the fridge and cupboards, maybe we still have something edible in there," Dan suggested, taking Gustavo by the arm and pushing him toward the kitchen. When he stood in front of the fridge, he froze.

"What's happening?" Gustavo asked, "Did you remember something else?"

"Yes, yes I did, Gustavo." There was a photograph on the fridge's door. I was standing beside a woman looking at the camera."

"That's probably a photo of your wife..."

"No, Gustavo," Dan cut-in. "Malou has black hair..." He stopped and stared into space. "How did I know that?"

"Well, I'd say that Nicolas did more than give you a name, he's probably transmitted a message to your brain." He guffawed. "I don't believe I'm saying this, you know that? I told you, this is all too weird for this old soldier."

"Yeah, but then who's this woman I saw in the photograph?" Dan asked, finally opening the fridge door. There were eggs and a packet of bacon, some vegetables on the lower shelf, a carton of milk and one of juice in the door. "Everything a man needs for a hearty breakfast," he remarked, shooting a glance at Gustavo. "And there must be some bread somewhere...?"

Gustavo pointed to the counter. There was a bread box on it, near the toaster. "I tell you, you guys are so organized, it looks like you've been brought up by a matron or something."

Dan turned from the counter and stared at Gustavo. "Not a matron, Gustavo, but me and my sister..." He stopped again. "That's it," he shouted, "The woman in the photo – it's my sister, Nicol." His face turned pale suddenly and he seemed about ready to faint when Gustavo grabbed Dan by the arm and led him to one of the kitchen chairs and sat him down.

"Okay, I think you've got enough recollecting for one day, Dan." He patted his cheek gently. "Let's get you to bed before you fall in a heap, okay?"

Dan shook his head. "Something happened to her, Gustavo. She's not with us anymore."

Gustavo looked up at the ceiling. "You know I love you, God, but would you give my friend a break for a bit? He's not moving at your speed, you know?"

"I'd say you're right," Nicolas said from behind them. "You better get to bed, young man," he added, approaching Dan who had put his elbows on his knees and was holding his head between the palms of his hands.

"Just tell me what happened to her, Nicolas?" Dan pleaded. "She's dead, isn't she?"

"Not at the moment, she isn't. But when you find your way back into your future, with Malou's help, you'll be able to know everything that happened to her."

"And may I ask what you're doing here again?" Gustavo asked, looking at their messenger fixedly.

"But aren't you the one who called me?" Nicolas replied, cracking a smile.

"Good Lord, don't tell me, He's listening to me too?"

"Yes, Gustavo, you're on His "radar" as you guys say, for the time being anyway, and that until Malou gets here."

"You mean I'm the babysitter?"

"Let's just say that you've been appointed to watch over Dan, so that he doesn't bang his head again, alright?"

"Okay, okay, Nicolas, I get it. And you've got me for the duration."

As they were walking toward the end of the esplanade, Malou noticed another road sign that, again, was emblazoned with the face of a Seminole Indian. She stopped and looked up at it. "You know, Stefano, this face is strangely similar to our old Seminole man in Pahokee."

"I think you're right, Mom," Daniel agreed, staring at the sign.

"Maybe, we should look for these signs along the way. They might be some sort of guide or indication that we're going in the right direction," Gaby added, she, too, looking at the road sign.

"Very good, Gaby," Damianos remarked, from behind the four of them. "But I also suggest that you notice what the sign itself indicates."

"Such as the name of the next town or the number of miles we've already covered?" Stefano asked.

"Precisely. And I would suggest that some of the signs will give you a choice of path to take."

"You know, Damianos, this sounds much more difficult than the tasks Dan performed during the first journey," Malou remarked. "Because, during our first trip, you always transported us where we needed to go, we never had to decipher our point of landing, so to speak."

"You're right, Malou. And if I was aware of your ultimate destination in time, I would be the first one to take you there. However, as it is, we're searching for the right path to take, nothing more, nothing less."

"How long do you think we've got to continue walking on this esplanade?" Daniel asked.

"As long as it takes for you to find the clues leading you to your next stop."

"What about Chippewa, couldn't he come and give us a hand?" Malou asked suddenly.

Her children's eyes turned to her at once.

"Who's Chippewa, Mom?" Gaby asked.

"That's the actual dream maker," Malou replied, touching her pendant. It felt warm, such as it did when she touched it in the hospital after Dan's accident. "That's it, isn't it, Damianos?"

He laughed out loud. "Yes, Malou, it is. I was wondering how long it would take you to figure this out. You see, the moment you saw the first road sign, you recognized the fact that we were in Florida and then you followed the one-way sign leading you south of here. Ultimately, when you realized that the old Indian's face was none other than Chippewa, I knew you were on the right track."

"But what about our amulets then?" Daniel asked, "Don't they have something to do with guiding us?"

"They will," Malou answered for Damianos. "You see, Chippewa and the road signs will give us directions, but our own dream catchers will enable us to communicate with Dad."

"*Really?*" Gaby practically screamed in her mother's ear. "Why didn't you say so earlier, Mom?"

"Because, I've only remembered about it when I touched my amulet just now. But I don't think it's like your cell phones, or maybe they're very much like it: we're probably going to be in Dad's vicinity before we'll be able to talk to him."

"You mean we don't have enough bars right now to contact him, is that it?" Daniel asked.

"Besides which," Damianos added, "You're not yet in the right time frame…"

"Does that mean we've got to find the year in which he landed first before we could call him?"

"Yes, Gaby, I'm afraid that's you're second step."

"And when are we going to turn the next page of the book then?" Stefano asked.

"When you reach your destination," Damianos replied.

A few minutes later they arrived at the end of the esplanade and immediately Malou noticed the sign. It said: "Fort Lauderdale Embarcadero".

"Damianos, does that mean we've got to go to the marina?"

"No, not a marina, Gaby, the quay where you can embark on your yacht."

"But I thought you said…"

And before Gaby could argue, Damianos snapped his fingers to transport the five of them aboard a luxurious cabin cruiser.

"Good God, Damianos, why don't you give us some warning – so unnerving," Malou said, but smiling up at their cat.

"I'm sorry, Malou, but Damian and Solange are waiting for you down below." He pointed to the stairs leading to the inside of the boat.

"You mean we've reached our first destination?" Daniel asked, visibly surprised.

"Yes, and I thought you would be pleased, aren't you?"

Daniel only nodded in reply and followed his siblings and mother down to the interior cabin. There, they found Solange and Damian seated on the couch facing a small table.

"Welcome to your second étape…"

"Wow! You speak French too? That's amazing," Daniel said.

"I'm sorry, I should have said the second "leg" in your journey," Damian said, smiling at the children as they took a seat beside their mother and facing the angelic couple.

"Do you speak many languages then?" Gaby asked.

"Yes. You see we have quite a few souls in our charge and not all speak English," Solange explained, "And sometimes we forget who speaks what." She giggled at the thought. "But for now why don't we just concentrate on English writing, okay?" She laid the book on the table.

"Thank you, Solange. You have no idea how glad we are to see you both," Malou commented. "It's been such a difficult process, not only to find this place but for me to realize how we were going to accomplish our task."

FORT LAUDERDALE EMBARCADERO

"When you deal with matters that concern space and time, nothing is ever simple, Malou," Damian added. "Yet, I think you'll find this next leg"—he chuckled—"in your journey much more pleasant and recalling many enjoyable events to your attention."

"Alright then," Malou said, looking down at the book. "Shall I open it?"

"By all means, dear, go ahead," Solange replied.

"Here goes it…." When she lifted the cover, they all saw the pages flipping to the 27th pages of the volume as if by magic. "Oh my, I wish I had one of these automatic bookmarks on the side of my bed, I keep losing my page…"

"Perhaps, we should get you a new bookmark when we get home," Gaby said, cracking a smile.

"Right…, thanks. But for now, let's see what it says, okay?"

Everyone nodded and Malou then began reading aloud:

Leaving the Fort behind and keeping the Key in sight will guide you to your destination. Be sure, however, not to travel farther than you are called to do.

"Here we go again," Stefano remarked, "It's another riddle."

"But there's something different about this one," Gaby said, peering down at the writing. "Did you notice"—she turned her face to her mother—"the two words "Fort" and "Key" are capitalized this time. See? Look, Mom."

"Yes, you're right," Malou replied, putting her index finger on each of the words in turn. See, Stefano?"

"Okay then, let's copy the words exactly as they are," Gaby said, taking her notepad out of her bag again.

As she lifted the next page of the pad, she shouted, "Wow! They're already transcribed." She showed the pad to Stefano. "See?"

"I'll be damned," Daniel said, looking at the pad from over his sister's shoulder. "That's so neat!" He looked at their angels. "I guess we won't need any laptop to take notes in school where you are, will we?" he added jokingly.

Damian and Solange exchanged a smile.

"I think we better go and meet you when you reach your next point of landing then," Solange said, retrieving the book from in front of Malou, closing it and taking it as she rose from the couch. She then made her way to the stairwell, Damian in tow.

"Good luck," he said, turning his head before disappearing.

CHAPTER SIXTEEN

Almost as soon as Solange and Damian had left the cruiser, they felt the boat move out of its mooring. Daniel didn't wait. He climbed the stairs up to the upper deck and went to join Damianos at the helm. "Glad you could join me, Daniel," he said, smiling at the young man. "As you're probably aware, cats have this terrible aversion to water, except when it's to catch a fish at the edge of a stream, of course. And since things haven't changed in millennia in that regard, I would much prefer if you took the helm." He turned his head to Daniel only to see a broad grin stretch across his face.

"You've got it, Skipper. I've always wanted to pilot one of these. Thank you!" Again, not waiting for directives or explanation, Daniel stepped in front of Damianos and grabbed the helm. One could say that he was "in his element".

Damianos watched him maneuver the cruiser out of the port and head to sea with the ease of an old seafarer. He then sat down in the seat next to the helm and began examining the weather map, the navigation gauges and radio components. Once he knew they were heading southward along the coast without any problem, Damianos left Daniel to his duty, but not before saying, "Okay, son. You're doing fine. Just keep the same heading along the coast until you're in sight of Hollywood Beach. After that, we'll see, okay?"

"Aye, aye, Captain," Daniel replied enthusiastically. He loved this. The ocean breeze, warm and gently brushing past his face, the smell of the open waters, in fact, everything was perfect. Yet, he knew this was not a pleasure cruise that had a given destination; it was a journey into the unknown with only one objective, to find his father.

Below deck, meanwhile, Malou, Gaby and Stefano were sitting around the table, still analyzing the words of the latest riddle.

"Why writing "Fort" and "Key" in capital letters, that's what I'd like to know," Stefano said, staring down at the notepad.

"How about if Fort meant a place by that name, like "Fort Lauderdale"?" Gaby asked.

"I think you're right, Gaby. We've actually left "Fort" Lauderdale behind already," Malou said and now we've got to find that "Key", right?" She looked at each of her children in turn.

They both nodded. "You're right, Mom," Stefano said, "But which "Key" are we talking about?"

"I think you'll find your answer on this map," Damianos said, laying a sea chart on the table. He tapped a finger on the South Florida coastline. "We'll be stopping in Hollywood"—he pointed to the name on the map—"in a little while to have something to eat and then, if the weather holds up, we'll sail to Miami Beach in the morning."

"That's it – there's the "Key"," Stefano exclaimed, putting his index finger on Key Largo.

"You mean Dad should be in Key Largo?" Malou asked, visibly surprised at the possibility of finding her husband in that town.

"Yes, yes, Mom, that's what the word "Key" means. I'm sure of it," Stefano insisted.

"That fits the riddle in any case," Gaby agreed, sounding unconvinced though.

Malou looked up at Damianos. He was standing at her back. "Do you think that's it?"

"I don't know, Malou. The best way to find out is to go there, I suppose."

"Why aren't you snapping your fingers and transport us there then?" Gaby asked.

Damianos guffawed. "Because it doesn't work that way. For now I only know that we have to follow the coast line. There must be something we should find out while we do that, and that's why I can't snap my fingers right now."

The image of Nicol still encumbered Dan's mind when he went to bed. He was seeing her as he remembered her. But those images were not of a young woman, they were those of a mother with children running around in a garden. Before falling asleep, this time Dan touched his amulet. For some reason it felt warm and comforting. He smiled to himself and said quietly, "Where ever you are, Nicol, I hope you're the happiest woman in heaven. I can't possibly know why at the moment, but I feel you can see me and understand what I'm saying. And since this dream catcher should let you into my dreams, why don't you come for a visit, when you have time, okay?" He smiled and closed his eyes.

A few minutes – or it only seemed to be a few minutes – later, Dan opened his eyes to see a figure appear to him. He recognized her instantly, although she seemed transparent somehow. It was Nicol. Her strawberry blonde curls surrounded her gorgeous face as an aureole of happiness. *She was strikingly beautiful and still is,* Dan thought as he peered at the woman before him.

Her words were soft as a caress. "Dearest Dan," she began, "I have only a few seconds to tell you that I will be beside you always, and that Malou will find you. And now sleep tight, my brother. Be at peace…." And then her image disappeared from in front of Dan's eyes.

He smiled and felt at peace, as Nicol had suggested, for the first time since this whole ordeal had begun. He now knew that Malou would find him. And returning home was just a matter of time.

They were all on deck when Daniel steer the cruiser to its moorage in Hollywood Beach. "Well done, son," Malou said, as they all disembarked on the quay. "I didn't know you had it in you."

"If you mean piloting a boat like this, I didn't, Mom. It just happened," Daniel replied, grinning from ear to ear.

"I bet Damianos had something to do with it, didn't you?" Malou said, looking up at their cat.

"Let's just say it was about time to put him at the helm," Damianos replied, chuckling.

"And you said you found the "Key" in the riddle," Daniel said, shooting a quick glance at Stefano.

"I guess we found a key, but it doesn't mean it's the right one."

"What are you saying then?" Daniel questioned.

"All we could figure out was that "Key" is the name of a town or place along the South Coast. But we haven't got any proof that Key Largo is the right "key"," Gaby put in, as they continued walking toward the end of the quay.

"What would we need to prove to ourselves that Key Largo is the right place then?"

"Memories, Daniel," Damianos replied. "As I said before, your father went to a place that means something to him, and at a time that represented some important event in his life. So, we need to find what that event was in order to confirm the place, and vice-versa."

"But, and again, Damianos, why don't you transport us to Key Largo right now, so that we could find out what happened to Dad," Gaby insisted.

"And again, Gaby, all I have been instructed to do was to take you along the coast, which I am sure will be revealing to you somehow."

"Yes, I think it's best to take it one step, or one port, at a time," Malou concluded, "That way we won't miss something important or something that God wants us to discover in the meantime."

"What about these memories you mentioned, Damianos? Are they memories of what we did around here with Dad? Is that what you mean?"

"Yes, Daniel, the memories you and your mom have of your life or of the time you spent with your dad around here will probably give you the proof you need to pinpoint the place where your father has landed."

"But, Damianos, we were not born twenty-five years ago; how can we remember anything that happened then?"

"I think what Damianos means, Gaby," Malou said, "is that all of us have memories of what Dad has told us about his years in college for example..." All of a sudden, Malou stopped talking and stopped walking.

"What's the matter, Mom, did you remember something?" Daniel asked.

"Yes, yes, I did. It's about your dad in college, and his professor." She steered her gaze in Damianos's direction. "Do you remember us going to visit Professor Hugo when we had to accomplish our last task about "commitment"?"

"Yes, I remember, Malou," Damianos replied. "But what's important here is what you remember of him. So, what is it?"

"Why don't we go to the restaurant and talk about it around a large plate of seafood," Malou suggested, returning to walking out of the marina.

As she did, Stefano, Daniel and Gaby seemed to be at a loss. This was a memory that was way before their time. They exchanged a glance and somehow agreed tacitly not to question their mother until they had eaten something. They were starving actually.

Once they were all seated around a table that afforded them an all encompassing view of the seashore, and in front of a humongous plate of every type of crustaceans imaginable, Malou said, "Okay, here is what I remember of your dad's college days…" She grabbed a prawn, looked at it, dipped it in the tartar sauce bowl and sucked it off its tail. After a visibly delightful swallow, she resumed, "I was introduced to Professor Hugo's son…"

"You mean as in Uncle Fabio, Mom?" Daniel interrupted.

"Exactly. Professor Hugo was your dad's tutor for many years and although Fabio was older than your dad's, both men struck a lasting friendship in college. But what's interesting about this story is that Fabio and your dad wanted more than anything in the world to become navy officers, like Fabio's dad. Professor Hugo had been a navy officer, a captain, I believe, in Venezuela…"

"Did they ever enroll for training then?" Stefano asked.

"Oh yes, but only after they finished college. They actually went on an orientation course in Fort Lauderdale and were supposed to take their training in"—Malou stopped in mid-sentence, her mouth agape—"Oh my God; why didn't I think of it earlier. They had to take their training in *Key West!*" She looked around the table. Damianos smiled and nodded.

"That's it then," Daniel and Stefano exclaimed in unison, looking at each other, chuckling and high-fiving in a noisy clap of their hands.

"It's not Key Largo that we need to go to, it's Key West, isn't it, Mom?" Daniel added.

"That's fantastic, Mom," Gaby rejoined. "And you know, I think you're right, because if you look at the first riddle"—she brought her beach bag to her lap and fetch the notepad out of it—"It said that we should find *the cardinal points of his destination*", which could mean "West" once we found the "Key". Right?" She looked at her mom for approval.

"I believe you're right, Gaby," Damianos said, grinning now.

"But what are we still doing along the South Coast then?" Daniel asked, obviously impatient to get to Key West.

"In my experience, none of God's plans are ever a waste," Damianos replied. "So, there must be something else for you to find or discover before we are to reach Key West."

"Any idea what that might be, Mom?" Daniel asked.

"None at this point, but that's not to say that I won't remember something else on the way, though." She smiled at her children. "But for now, why don't we do justice to that plate. Everything is absolutely delicious."

CHAPTER SEVENTEEN

Following a night spent in a nearby motel, Malou, Damianos and the three children boarded the cruiser once again. Stefano, Gaby and Daniel were apprehensive. They knew where they were going to end their journey but they didn't know how they were going to travel to the time when their dad had lived in Key West. Twenty-five years separated them from the present and the time at which their father had lived in that city. Malou had told them that Fabio and their dad had rented a small apartment before they were due to begin their training as US Navy officers. And that's all they knew, or all that their mother could remember at this point.

As they climbed the few steps separating them from the pier and the boat, Gaby took her cell phone out of her bag. She looked at it for a moment and was intrigued by the fact that none of her friends had left text messages or emails since they left the house. It was a puzzle to her because she knew that although they had left a few days ago and had returned in that time frame, the phone should have rung by this time.

"Have you checked your phone?" she asked Daniel once they were on deck.

"Yeah, I did last night, but nothing doing. It was dead as if someone had taken the SIM card out of it," he said, taking the cell out of his jeans' pocket.

"Same here," Gaby agreed, turning to Stefano. "What about yours? Have you gotten any texts or messages?"

"I wouldn't know. I left mine behind since I gathered that we were not going to be able to use it if we went back to a time it had not been invented yet."

"Oh well, there goes my plan to phone my friends then," Gaby said, shrugging her shoulders. "How did people live without being able to communicate, I wonder."

Damianos had been listening to the exchange without saying a word, but now he felt it was time to remind the three of them of something they seemed to have forgotten in the last day or so. "No need to wonder, Gaby," he said, "we are traveling in a time — at the moment at least — when cell phones and your usual electronics are available, but we are only virtually here. In reality, time has stopped the minute you stepped out of your house in Davie and began your journey. So, none of your gadgets will function until you go home."

"Drat," Daniel exclaimed. "What about my Xbox and my game partners? Does that mean I won't be able to play for *twenty-five years! You've got to be kidding me!*"

"I knew that was going to come up sooner or later," said Malou, who had been watching her children's little debate. "As Damianos said, this is all virtual reality. Such as your dad and I traveled everywhere in our imagination during our first trip, we are now traveling through the past and nothing of what you will experience will exist except in the time-frame and place you visit."

"What about some music?" Stefano asked, examining some of the instruments on the panel of the wheel house. "Do any of those connect with a radio of some sort?" He looked at Damianos.

"Well, I think you're in luck in that regard, Stefano. None of these instruments are going to give you any joy, I'm afraid, but below deck, you'll find a portable radio that will probably capture some of the local stations."

"What about TV, any around?" Daniel asked.

"Unfortunately no, but I think what you're going to experience before we reach Key West is going to be as entertaining as any TV program," Damianos replied, cracking a devilish smile.

"And as for shopping," Malou put-in, looking at her daughter, "I think you'll have to refrain from doing any of it for a while, unless you want to go totally "retro"." She laughed at the thought of seeing Gaby wearing clothes she had worn herself twenty-five years ago.

"And I suppose watching a basketball game anywhere is out of the question, too," Stefano remarked, probably thinking of all the games he would be missing.

"Just think about it this way, Stefano," Damianos said, "You won't be losing any time since you're going to go home the same day you left." He looked around him at the three resigned faces and chuckled.

"This isn't funny, Damianos," Daniel said, "What are we supposed to do to kill time for twenty-five years then?"

"How about we start by getting out of here and out to sea?" Damianos replied.

"Oh alright, that's better than nothing, I suppose," Daniel said, turning toward the helm. "How about untying the mooring lines then?" He looked at Stefano.

"Aye, aye, Skipper," the latter replied, already jumping onto the pier and going toward the aft of the boat.

As soon as they were out of the marina and sailing against the easterlies that seemed particularly strong this morning, Malou and Gaby retreated below deck while Stefano stayed with his brother and Damianos on the upper deck, watching the ever so gentle swell increase gradually before their eyes.

The next morning when Dan woke up, his spirit was up. Nicol's visit had restored his confidence and will power. He knew Malou was on her way, and that's all that seemed important to him. He only had to wait for her arrival, or so he thought.

Once he had showered and was dressed, he went to the kitchen to find Gustavo, his eyes traveling through the want-ads in the paper.

"Anything promising?" Dan asked, going to the counter and grabbing a mug out of the cupboard. "Do you want coffee?" He turned to Gustavo while pouring himself a cup out of the coffee pot.

"Yeah, if you're having one," Gustavo replied distractedly. He lifted his gaze to Dan. "What do you think about me driving a truck?"

"If you like driving, that sounds good," Dan replied, bringing the two mugs to the table and sitting down beside his friend. "But sometimes you'd be on the road for days…"

"Yeah, and I think that would be good for me. It'll be better for me than me staying cooped up in this town." He grabbed the mug nearest to his hand and took a sip. "And since I was driving army trucks during one of my tours, I've got some experience that should count for something." He looked at Dan again. "What do you say?"

"Well, I say you should apply for the job, besides, I don't think your babysitting job will be lasting that long."

"What makes you say that?" Gustavo asked, staring at Dan now. "Have you got some news from Nicolas?"

Dan shook his head. "No, not from him, no." He took a sip of his coffee. "But I saw my sister last night…"

"You did?" Gustavo interrupted, eyebrows raised. "You mean in a dream like?"

"No, not a dream. At least I don't think it was a dream. She appeared to me when I touched my amulet"—he looked down at his dream catcher—"and she told me that my wife will find me. So, I don't think it will be long before I lift off into my future."

"That's great news," Gustavo said, grinning. "But she didn't say when…, or did she?"

"No, but I've got this feeling that it's going to happen in the very near future." He drank some more coffee. "So, if you want to apply for that trucking job, you go right ahead."

Gustavo got to his feet. "How about breakfast while you're still here then?" He laughed and went to the stove. "Bacon and eggs okay with you?" he asked, getting the skillet out of the drawer.

"Sounds great!" Dan said, getting up himself and going to the fridge to fetch the eggs and bacon packet.

An hour after they had left Hollywood Beach, the wind had increased and the waves were starting to lap the boat up to the railings. Damianos had taken the helm out of Daniel's hands and had urged both brothers to go below deck.

He looked at the instrument panels. He knew a storm was coming, but the force of the wind and the swirl of green showing on the screen now were indicative of something much worse – a hurricane perhaps?

"That's not fair," he said, raising his eyes to the sky. You know I don't like water," he shouted. Yet there wasn't a trace of anger in his words. When he returned his attention to the steering of the vessel, Damian and Solange appeared, both standing on the bow of the cruiser.

"Let go of the helm, Damianos," Damian hollered above the noise of the enraged ocean waves. "It's time to get you and the souls in your charge to a time when the calm of the seas would have returned to a tranquil past."

"Do they know?" Damianos asked, letting go of the helm as requested.

"No, they don't," Solange said, seemingly unaffected by the howling wind and pelting rain that had started to lash the vessel mercilessly.

And with these words, the two angels disappeared. Damianos shook his head. He knew this was going to be a rough ride, but didn't want to worry the little family below deck unduly.

He rushed down the few steps and yelled, "Come on, we've got to get out of the storm...!"

Already huddled under the table or lying on the floor, the four of them looked at Damianos, terror in their eyes.

"You mean "this hurricane", don't you?" Daniel countered, getting out from under the table.

"Where or how are you planning to get us out of here? We're in the middle of the ocean bobbing up like a nutshell...," Stefano argued, while helping his mother to her feet.

"You'll soon find out about the power of God, Stefano; and now it's about time for you to obey His command. You come up on deck, all of you, unless you want Hurricane Anthony to swallow you." The tone in Damianos's voice left no doubt in their minds, their cat was serious and in no mood to be questioned.

As soon as the five of them were assembled on deck, holding on to each other and on their knees, a gust of wind enveloped and captured them into a vortex that transported them into space and time.

The ride was rough alright, they sped at incredible speed through a myriad of images, some of which Malou or her children could recognize at a glimpse, while some others, they couldn't place, but most of which were passing before their eyes too fast to catch anything out of their memory. They were then stretched, flying through a veil of fog that prevented them to see or feel where they were going. Gradually the speed at which they were traveling decreased and soon they landed back on the deck of their vessel. The ocean was once again calm and Miami Beach was in sight.

Hesitant at first, they lifted their gazes and looked around them in awe. Their boat was now an elegant cabin cruiser of the mid-1950's.

They rose to their feet and were astonished to see that the deck on which they stood was covered of cedar planks, the railings near at hand was old but polished to a gleaming shine and that the wheelhouse stood proudly at their back, resembling that of an old cabin cruiser of times long forgotten by most sailors.

A half-an-hour later, and as soon as Damianos was alone, having sent the family below deck, he looked around him — they were approaching Miami Beach pier — and a smile appeared on his lips. "It's time to give them a little taste of what they missed," he said to himself, snapping his fingers.

Still stunned by their recent experience and dressed beyond recognition, Malou and the three children emerged from the cabin below. "That doesn't look like the Miami Beach I know," Stefano remarked, stepping on deck first. "What date is this?"

"Don't tell me people dressed like this twenty-five years ago," Gaby said, following her brother. "I look absolutely ridiculous!"

"Oh no, you don't, Gaby," Damianos said, looking at her rose crinoline hat and her very feminine summer dress. "You look perfect actually." He turned to Stefano. "And to answer your question; the date is July 15, 1950."

As she made it up the stairs, Malou cracked up laughing. Her white hat and beautiful pleated dress suited her to a tee. "I love it, Damianos, but do tell, what are we doing so far back in the past?"

"Yeah, I can hardly wait to hear the answer to that one," Daniel rejoined, finally emerging on deck, too.

"I thought you might like to see what sort of entertainment Damian and Solange had planned for you." He paused and smiled. "You see, your dad always had a desire to restore vintage cars and did in fact restore quite a few..."

"You mean like the roadsters we see on TV?"

"No, Daniel. Your dad restored some of the finest cars on Earth. One of these was a Rolls Royce and another was a Bentley. So, we thought it might be fun for you to see where these cars came from and live a few hours of the time when these fine vehicles were traveling the streets of Miami Beach."

"But why are we dressed like this?" Gaby asked again. "Are we going to church or something?"

This time Damianos guffawed. "No, dear Gaby, we are going to have high tea in one of the most elegant tea room in the city. There, you'll also have the chance to dance a few steps with your brothers..."

"You mean like ballroom dancing?"

"Yes, my dear, exactly like it." Damianos seemed very pleased with this little planned interlude. "You three needed to realize there is life beyond electronic games, computers and cell phones, and I thought, in order for you to re-connect with your dad when we find him, it would be good to visit an era that your dad could only imagine when he restored those cars."

"If you're trying to get us to throw our cell phones overboard, Damianos, I don't think you're succeeding," Daniel said, chuckling.

"Not my intention in the least — they won't work anyway as I have explained, but I think you're in for a treat nonetheless."

CHAPTER EIGHTEEN

That morning was one dedicated to running errands for Dan and Gustavo. First, they went to the DMV where Dan got a temporary drivers' license, and after going to the bank to withdraw some money, the two of them drove to the trucking company.

They looked at the warehouse and at the semis lined up in front of it.

"That's a little bigger kind of trucks than those I drove back in Iran," Gustavo remarked. "I don't know if my license will be accepted."

"Well, you won't know until you ask, will you?" Dan said, cracking a smile. He remembered the time he hesitated to enter the recruiting office at the naval base, when Gustavo told him the same thing.

"Right," Gustavo said. "No hurt in trying," he added, getting out of the car.

Dan watched his friend walk toward the warehouse office; he was truly hoping that the big guy would get a break. On the other hand, he wondered if he would ever see Gustavo again after he would leave to return to his future. The thought of the possibility saddened him.

A half-an-hour later, Gustavo was back. He was grinning from ear to ear.

That's a good sign, Dan thought, as Gustavo opened the passenger door and climbed in.

"So, did you get the job?" Dan asked.

"Yeah, and then some!"

"What does that mean?"

"It means that it's going to be a free-ride every time I'm out of town."

"You mean meals and lodging and everything?" Dan asked; all smiles.

"Yep. So, by the time your friend Fabio comes back, I'll probably be out on the road earning my first paycheck."

"That's fantastic," Dan shouted in the confines of the car. It was the first time since they met at the shelter that Gustavo had displayed any sign of true happiness. "And when did they ask you to report for duty?"

"I'll have to go through some training first, starting next Monday, so that I could handle these big rigs. But after that, it should be plain sailing, or "plain driving" I should say."

"Congrats, Gustavo. You've done it!" Dan chuckled. "How about we go and celebrate tonight?"

"Yeah, sounds like a great idea, but I want to ask you something – a favor really."

"Okay, shoot," Dan replied, turning on the ignition. "What can I do?"

"Could you lend me some money or come with me to buy some clothes?"

"You've got it, man. No problem." Dan reversed the car out of the lot. "It would be about time for me to get some new jeans too. I think what Mrs. Stevens gave me has ran its course."

"Okay then," Gustavo said, "why don't we go to the nearest department store and get ourselves re-dressed?" He laughed.

Dan turned his head briefly. His friend was truly happy. He could see it. It was as if he had shed ten years off his age. Silently he thanked Nicolas, because he knew that somehow their messenger had had something to do with Gustavo getting that job so fast.

"A table for five," Damianos said to the maitre d' as soon as they entered the tea room of one of the posh hotels on Miami Beach.

Gaby, looking around her, no longer felt out of place. Most of the ladies wore similar dresses, shoes and hats as she and Malou did. As for Stefano, Daniel and Damianos, their suits could only be described as perfect for the occasion. White linen outfits, white shirts, a cravat or light color tie were all that it took to change their allure completely. Daniel, still feeling uncomfortable, looked at Damianos.

"Are you really going to make us dance in this get-up?"

"Not if you don't want to, Daniel, but I think someone will tempt you enough to have you on the dance floor in no time."

"Like that girl in the red dress," Stefano rejoined, nodding in the young woman's direction and jabbing his brother in the ribs. "She's gorgeous."

"Yeah, well, I don't know....," Daniel said, turning to Gaby. "What about you? Are you going to dance?"

"Let's just wait and see how it goes, Daniel. As Mom explained before, you never know what could happen when in the hands of our cat."

"Your table is ready, sir," the maitre d' told them just then. "Please follow me."

Passing in between a few tables, Malou felt all eyes piercing her back and heard complimentary comments. She felt a bit timid, yet she had no longer any doubt about Damianos's power. He was going to be the perfect host while making sure the children enjoyed themselves. It was nice to be there in fact. She could never have dreamed something like that happening to her and her children before taking her first trip into the past with Dan. Silently, she hoped he was alright.

When tea, in a silver teapot, was served, the cakes and scones tempting everyone on a tree-tier plateau staring at them, Daniel couldn't resist. He took a small cake and put it on his plate. "If that tastes as good as it looks, I'll have a couple or three after this one."

"Take it easy," Malou said quietly. "One pleasure at a time." She threw a gentle smile to Damianos. "Those scones look as divine as they taste, I'm sure," she added, taking one of them and placing it gingerly on the plate in front of her.

A few minutes later, when the children and Malou seemed a little more relaxed, Damianos snapped his fingers and suddenly the back stage that had previously been decorated with flower pots and plants was transformed into a platform with a small orchestra. The music soon permeated the atmosphere and a few dancers took the floor.

Stefano didn't wait to be asked. He got up and went to the young woman in the red dress and bowed politely. "Would you like to dance?" he asked her.

"Oh yes," she replied, getting to her feet.

Malou marveled at the sight of her eldest dancing the fox trot as if he had done it all his life. And it wasn't long before Daniel got up and invited Gaby to dance. His face lit up when he realized that he was light on his feet and that dancing with his sister wasn't that bad after all. She looked gorgeous, truth be told. "You know, you really look good in that dress," he whispered in her ear.

"Well thanks, Bro." She grinned. "And now that I see every girl is dressed like me, it feels good."

Damianos seemed happy about it too. "Would you like to dance," he asked, turning to Malou.

She hesitated. "Do you think it's okay?"

"I'm sure it is, Malou. Dan would be happy seeing you dressed like this and enjoying a couple of steps around the dance floor."

"Alright then," she replied, taking Damianos's extended hand. "I don't know if I'll remember how though."

"It's like riding a bicycle, you never forget," he told her, walking up with Malou to the middle of the floor.

Returning to the apartment, arms laden with bags of clothes and new runners on their feet, Nicolas was expecting them.

"Don't say anything," Gustavo said, looking at their messenger, with a broad grin on his face. "Let us get rid of the shopping before you say a word, okay?"

Dan had to laugh when he saw the expression on Nicolas's face. "Excuse us for a minute, Nicolas; Gustavo has got to settle down before he falls down."

"I'll stay here, sitting on this sofa, until you two are ready to hear the latest," Nicolas said, reclining against the back of the seat. He looked pleased with himself.

A moment later, when Dan and Gustavo were sitting across the little man, he said, "So, I hear you've kept your promise and got yourself a job, didn't you?" He fixed his gaze on Gustavo.

"Yes, I sure did, Nicolas. And it feels great, I tell you. I can't believe I waited so long before looking for a job. It's like I'm twenty again." He paused. "But I think I should thank you for me being hired so quickly, don't I?"

"No thanks necessary, Gustavo, you took the first step and I just pushed things along, that's all."

"But, you know, I've never driven a semi before, and I'm a bit worried that I'm going to mess it up first time out."

"No need for you to worry about anything, Gustavo. It's all taken care of. On Monday you'll step aboard one of those rigs just as if you had done so a million times. You'll see."

"Well, I am glad to hear that one of us is confident."

"Trust in God, Gustavo. He's the one minding this house. So, and as I said, I wouldn't worry about a thing."

"Okay then," Gustavo concluded, throwing a glance to Dan. "But I'm sure you're not here only to reassure me about the driving, are you?"

"Quite right you are," Nicolas replied. "In fact I have some news that may interest the both of you."

"Oh, and what's that?" Dan asked, visibly anxious to hear the latest.

"Well, it's a bit complicated, I'm afraid. But let me tell you what I've heard. Remember, I told you that I couldn't travel in the future, none of us can actually, but all of us can take an occasional trip into the past…?"

Dan and Gustavo nodded in unison.

"Well, it seems that your wife, Dan, and your children are presently having tea in Miami Beach…"

"Wow, that's great," Dan exclaimed all excited. "That means they found the time frame"—he stopped, seeing the somber look on Nicolas's face—"or did they?"

"Not exactly, no. They're actually visiting 1950."

"But why? What on Earth are they doing there?"

"It's a bit complicated as I said, but it seems that the children needed to be reminded of life beyond electronic gadgets."

"What are you saying," Dan demanded.

"Well, you see, in your future, technology would have progressed so rapidly that portable phones and large screen televisions together with home computers will occupy all of the youngsters' time. And our Lord apparently thought it would be a good idea to give them a taste of the past while there was an opportunity to do so."

"And are they going to stay there…, or should I go and join them, since it's in the past," Dan said, pleading almost.

Nicolas waved a hand in front of his face. "No, Dan. There is no plan for you to do that. But there is something that Gustavo will need to do…"

"Me? How? I have nothing to do with Dan's family," Gustavo cut in, switching his gaze from Nicolas to Dan in turn.

"Well, let's just say your warfare experience could teach Dan's youngest son how to fall out of love with war. Apparently, he will need to be shown how war can destroy the souls of people. And I think you know exactly what I mean in that regard, don't you?"

Consternation written all over his face, Gustavo replied, "If I can help one kid out of killing people, you've got me, Nicolas." He turned to Dan. "That is if you're okay with me teaching your kid a thing or two."

Dan nodded. "I seemed to remember something about a town named Sumperk. I don't know what it's got to do with this, but I know I saw people being killed on a road leading to a village where children were dying from the lack of food." He lifted his saddened eyes to Nicolas. "If there's any way I could dissuade that son of mine from enlisting, I would be the first to do it."

"Are you sure, Dan?" Nicolas asked. Dan nodded again. "The reason I asked is because, you, yourself is about to enroll for that training, leading you to become a navy pilot. So, this is the question I need to repeat to you: Are you sure about not wanting your son to take up arms?"

"Yes, I am very sure in a way. To tell you the truth, right now, I don't remember my son, but I would never want him to be on the front line during combat." Dan paused. "But, if his dream was to enlist, I would push him to become an officer only after he graduated from college. And if this question has come up while he was growing up, I suppose I must have been fortunate enough that he always listened to me in the end, and would not make a lifetime decision without asking me first. Being on the front line has got to be one of the most dangerous assignments a young man could be put through. The last thing I would like is for anything to happen to him, and then having to live the rest of my life thinking that I didn't do enough to talk him out of it."

CHAPTER NINETEEN

S ome two hours later, Damianos noticed the couple standing in the doorway of the restaurant before Malou or the children did. "Would you excuse me for a moment, Malou, I have to meet someone," he said, rising from his chair.

Malou nodded. "A secret rendezvous, is it, Damianos?" she teased.

He chuckled. "Something like that, yes. I won't be long," he added, walking toward the foyer of the hotel.

"Good to see the children and Malou are enjoying a well-deserved break," Solange said, as Damianos approached the two angels.

"And you seemed to be taking part, too, aren't you?" Damian rejoined.

"You know cats; agile as they come," Damianos replied, smiling.

"Very good," Damian went on, "but now, the task is going to be a little more taxing than first expected, and we need you to take Daniel out for a sortie of another kind, Damianos."

"You mean separate him from his mother and siblings?"

"Yes. However, we thought it will be better if you do it under the cover of night."

"How's that?" Damianos asked, somewhat puzzled and a little worried.

"Let's not go into details, Damianos, not for the moment anyway. Suffice to say that a friend of his father has seen battle in Iran and Daniel would do well to accompany him for a while."

"It's got something to do with his war games, hasn't it?"

"Yes, Damianos," Solange replied in turn. "He's destined to accomplish a lot more than we are even aware of at the moment, and going to war or take up arms should be a choice he makes in full knowledge of the consequences that could befall him if he did."

"Alright then, where do I bring him and what year?"

When Damianos returned to the table, Malou looked up into their cat's worried face.

"What was that about?" she asked, as he sat down.

"Damian and Solange were here with a message," Damianos replied.

"Oh? What about? Why didn't they come and sit with us?"

"When we return to the boat, they'll have a chat with you before Daniel leaves."

"Daniel? What would God want with him?" Malou demanded, thinking the worst obviously.

"Calm down, my dear. Nothing is going to happen to him. You know that as well as I do. But it's time for him to face some reality."

"What sort of reality?"

Damianos didn't have time to answer. Daniel, Gaby and Stefano were coming back to the table.

"Would it be possible to stay around here for a few days, you think?" Stefano asked Damianos, throwing a smile to his mother. "I'd like to take Lyana on a date," he explained, still smiling.

"Have you forgotten why we're here?" Gaby interjected, visibly incensed by her brother's suggestion.

"No, Gaby, I have forgotten nothing, but since Damianos"—he threw him a glance—"is always telling us that time has stood still since we left the house, a day or more over here in this era wouldn't hurt, now would it?"

"NO, Stefano, is my answer," Malou interjected adamantly. "Damianos has given us a few hours of enjoyment and now it's time to go back to finding your dad."

"Besides, since you've now had a taste of what ballroom dancing can do to your love life," Daniel sniggered, "you can use what you've learned here when you go home."

"Alright, alright, I know when I'm outnumbered," Stefano replied, shaking his head. "Are we returning to the boat then?"

"Yes," Damianos said, finally opening his mouth. "We need to get back before nightfall."

Malou and the children exchanged a quizzical glance before getting to their feet and following their cat out of the restaurant.

Malou seemed lost in thought when Gaby asked, "What is it, Mom? Did you feel something about Dad?"

"Oh no, it's not that," she replied, "but I think we could expect to have another visit from Damian and Solange tonight."

Standing on the sidewalk now, Damianos turned to the little family. "Are we ready?" he asked.

Everyone nodded, and in a moment the five of them were flying through space and time, going through a series of images that seemed to have been extracted from an era and a place they couldn't recognize.

"Alright, Nicolas," Gustavo said, "What will I have to do?"

The three of them were still sitting in the living room of Dan's apartment; Dan pondering the suggestion Nicolas had made about his son going to face battle with Gustavo. "Are you comfortable with this?" he asked his friend.

"Sure am, Dan. It's not like I'm going back to another tour of duty; it's only to have a show-and-tell with your son, isn't it?" He shot a glance at Nicolas.

"It will be a bit more real than show-and-tell, I'm afraid," Nicolas replied, his hands clasping the knob of his cane.

"What do you mean?" Dan blurted, visibly worried.

"Well, in order for Daniel – that's your son's name – to understand what he would be facing if he were going into battle, Gustavo will need to revisit a place and time that has left a mark in his mind."

"You mean the warehouse incident in Tehran?"

"Exactly, Gustavo," Nicolas replied, fixing his gaze on the army man. "And I don't know if you have the strength to revisit that hour of your life. Do you?"

Gustavo bent his head and seemed pensive for a moment. Lifting his gaze to Dan, he said, "Maybe it's just what I need to do. And maybe it will help me erase that memory from my mind for ever."

"But what if it doesn't?" Dan asked. "You'll be back to your nightmares and your drinking. It's like sending you to a bar saying you can't drink anything but juice or water." Dan was serious, but Gustavo cracked up laughing.

"Glad to hear you comparing me with one of those winos, but when I drank it was to forget, not to get drunk per se. But now, it's different. I've got a purpose for going back out there, and that's to teach your son a thing or two about killing people." He paused. "And that, in the end, is something I wouldn't want to forget."

"Well said, Gustavo!" Nicolas declared, rising to his feet. "And now that's settled, you and Daniel will meet near the warehouse tonight…"

"What about me going with him?" Dan asked.

Nicolas shook his head. "No, Dan. This is not a father's job, I'm sorry. Just remember, your son will not be hurt, neither will Gustavo, and very soon your family will join you, all safe and sound."

The year was 1979; Miami was showing all the signs of a city undergoing changes. Their boat was also different – neither old nor new – it had the clean lines of the newer vessels roaming the harbor and being moored at the marina. Landing on the top deck, Stefano immediately noticed that their attire had also returned to jeans, t-shirts and runners, which seemed to please him no end. "Feels definitely better than shirt and tie," he remarked, a broad grin coming across his lips.

"Yeah, I'll have to agree with that one," Daniel said, looking down at his t-shirt and again noticing his amulet. "And throughout all the changes, our pendants still around our necks, have you noticed that?"

"Yes, Daniel, and this is what will keep you safe in all circumstances," everyone heard Damian say from behind them. "Why don't we go below deck, and talk about your next step," he added, smiling to Malou.

"Good to see you, Malou," Solange said, as soon as they were all sitting in the small lounge room of the boat.

Malou only smiled in reply. She was still wondering what Daniel venturing overnight alone had to do with them finding Dan.

"Alright then," Damian began, "you're probably wondering why we're here, since you have followed the directions implied in the writings of your book and that you now are aware of your dad's location and probably approximate time of landing. However, as you now know, there is always a reason for people visiting their past. And in this instance, God has seen fit to give you, Daniel, an opportunity to visit a past you have not had the privilege to know."

"Me? Why me?" Daniel erupted, looking at everyone around the table in turn.

"You, because, you are an important person in your dad's mind at the moment, and because, God has made the decision," he said, smiling.

"Perhaps, why neither Stefano nor me, would be a better question," Gaby ventured.

"Again, Gaby, because God decides and we abide by His decision is the simple answer."

"Okay then," Malou interposed, "what is Daniel asked to do?"

"Only to follow instructions during a visit of a war-torn city," Damian replied quietly, knowing the impact his answer would have on the family.

"Are you saying God wants him to go into battle?" Malou uttered, disbelief written across her face.

"No, not entirely. He wants Daniel to witness first hand what he sees on the screen every day while playing with his Xbox."

"You mean it?" Daniel exclaimed. "God is sending me into my war-games?"

"Not games, son," Damian corrected, "reality is what you are going to face." Silence fell over the family like a pall of foreboding thoughts.

"I can't let you do this, Daniel!" Malou uttered with all the determination she could muster.

"But, Mom...," Daniel tried arguing.

"Listen, Mrs. Politano," Damian interposed. "Your son will not be in any danger. You can rest assured God is watching and will be watching his every move."

The quiet and persuasive tone of Damian's voice touched a chord in Malou's heart. She knew she couldn't deny God's decision. "May I go and watch him?" she murmured, her voice almost inaudible.

Damian looked up at Damianos. He shook his head. "I don't think it would be a good idea, Mrs. Politano. Remember what happened on that road leading out of Sumperk? You and Dan escaped the Messerschmitt's bullets because of Damianos's advance knowledge. In this particular task, Damianos will need to be looking after your son in the same way, so I think it's best if you stay here until Daniel returns."

Malou simply nodded, and lay her head on Stefano's shoulder, who had remained utterly silent throughout this conversation. Both he and Gaby were now feeling what they would be sure to feel if their brother decided to enlist and was called into battle.

"Hi," Gustavo said when he first saw Daniel standing by the Landrover and looking a bit disoriented. "I'm Gustavo." The two men shook hands.

"Hi. . ., I'm Daniel." He looked down at his boots. "I really don't know"—he raised his gaze to Gustavo—"what I'm supposed to do here, where ever 'here' is."

"Why don't you climb in and I'll explain a little of what I know, okay?"

Daniel did and hopped in on the front passenger seat. Once the doors were closed, Gustavo turned his upper body toward Daniel. He, too, was now a younger man, but he displayed the assertiveness of a man much older than his years. "I've seen a few actions already, but this one was, or I should say is going to be a bit different."

"Different, how?" Daniel questioned, looking at Gustavo fixedly.

"Well, for one thing, my platoon has been ordered to search this warehouse"—Gustavo nodded in the direction of a building in the near distance—"and to take down anyone lurking about the place."

"Why?"

Gustavo chuckled and shook his head. "If you were ever to enlist, you'd soon learn that a soldier's place is not to ask why and to execute orders without question."

"But that's dumb," Daniel objected.

"Maybe it is, but in this case, I didn't even know why. So, I couldn't give you an answer even if I wanted to."

"Okay then, and what am I supposed to do?" Daniel asked again.

"You just follow me or follow the orders that are given to you. Clear?"

"Okay. When do we start?"

"Right now," Gustavo replied, turning on the ignition.

CHAPTER TWENTY

They drove slowly toward the warehouse, which was surrounded by a high chain-linked fence. The eerie quietness enveloping the place was indeed ominous.

"Maybe we should drive to the back," Daniel suggested.

Gustavo threw him a puzzled glance before penetrating the enclosure through the ripped fence until they reached the corner of the yard facing the warehouse and the back entrance. In the dark they could still see that the yard was littered with debris of all sorts. When Gustavo switched the engine off, he turned to look at Daniel.

"Are you sure you want to do this...?" he asked the young man.

"Let's just do it," Daniel replied firmly.

With these words, the two of them got out of the car and strode toward the building.

Hiding in the shadows, Damianos was watching them.

Daniel ran up and looked around him. He and Gustavo cautiously walked over the collapsed gate and crossed the courtyard to get to the opened doors at the back of the warehouse.

All of a sudden Daniel stumbled over something. "What the ...," he muttered under his breath. The two of them stopped to look at what had obstructed their path. They could only see the man's eyes, staring at the starlit sky. His chest was covered with clotted blood. Daniel turned away, retching and about to vomit at the sight and smell of the corpse.

"Come on," Gustavo said, patting Daniel on the back, "we've got to get on with it, okay?"

Daniel nodded and straightened up without a word.

As they continued walking, they could see the shapes of men littering the courtyard. Apparently unaffected by the sight of these human remains, Gustavo began running toward the open doors, Daniel in tow. They slammed their backs against the wall, looked around and slipped through the entrance one after the other.

The place had been plunged in darkness with only moon-rays slipping through the cracks of the crumbling walls and corrugated iron roof. It was strangely silent.

Daniel turned his head to Gustavo and whispered, "What do we do now?"

Gustavo didn't answer, yet Daniel heard a voice in his mind, saying, "Just do as you're told, Daniel. Everything will be fine."

"Damianos?" Daniel said in a hushed voice, laced with surprise.

"Don't talk, Daniel," Gustavo told him. "Just listen for any sound that..."

His comments were abruptly cut short by a volley of gun shots outside the warehouse. Inside, they heard people move and rifles being loaded.

"You go that way," Gustavo ordered, "and keep your back to the wall..."

"Where are you going?" Daniel demanded, his voice quivering with anxiety.

"To the other side," Gustavo replied, already rushing in the opposite direction.

Finding the wall behind him, Daniel slammed his back against it, and was about to edge his way toward the corner, when a hand grabbed him by the scruff of his neck and dragged him into a small storage room.

Adjusting to the dimness, Daniel counted at least ten American soldiers assembled in that room. They were all armed to the gills. On one of the storage racks lining the walls only a few machine guns were left unattended. Without a word, the man who had grabbed him pointed to one of the weapons, nodding. Daniel looked at it – an Uzi. The man took it off the shelf, handed it to him, together with a box of ammunition, saying, "Load it! Quickly!"

Daniel struggled for a minute until he realized the man had handed him the wrong ammunition. He looked around him, not really knowing what would happen after he loaded his weapon. Apparently ready to exit the room, one of the men nodded and rushed out, followed by his companions. A minute later, Daniel, left alone in the storage room, heard shots being fired. The shooting had resumed. Silently he wondered where Gustavo was.

Undeterred in his purpose, he grabbed a couple of boxes of ammunition off the shelf, knelt down, his breath audible. He tried to fit each of the ammo, which he had found scattered along the shelves, inside the weapon's chamber with hands trembling. To no avail. "Try these," Damianos murmured from over his shoulder, handing him another box of ammo. Daniel smiled up at him, took the box and loaded the Uzi. A minute or so later, he joined the other men at the door of the warehouse.

There were at least twenty men that had taken cover behind large wooden boxes and other objects placed in front of the opened doors. Daniel positioned himself beside the wall next to the door. He pressed his back against it and carefully poked his head around the corner. As soon as he saw light flashes coming from the left of the courtyard, he began firing his Uzi in that direction. At the first few shots the strong kickback of the weapon threw him off balance.

Gustavo then jumped next to Daniel and pushed himself against him in order to stay under the cover of the wall.

He shouted, "They are on the tall building ... on the left, but not for long...!"

They endured fire for a few more minutes until silence seemed to permeate the whole warehouse abruptly.

Curious to see what happened, another man moved slowly in front of the open door and aimed his weapon at something. Daniel followed him, his Uzi aimed at the invisible target. Without warning, a shot blasted the silence and blood sprayed everything and everyone behind the man. He had been hit. His body fell at Daniel's feet. Horror stricken, he fell to his knees and folded his arms over his head. When he raised his gaze and looked around him, all he could see were pieces of skin and bones glued to the doorframe, or hanging from the crates behind him. The man's face, his eyes, nose, and teeth were littering the ground.

All of a sudden a gust of wind pushed a veil of fog in front of Daniel's eyes. He cried out, "Please, God, stop! Stop, please..."

"It's alright, son," he heard Gustavo say as he came to stand beside him. He helped him to his feet and peered into his eyes. "You'll be okay now. Just remember war is not a game. Death is the only reward you can expect from warfare, whether in the battlefield or later when your memories will not let you rest."

Tears coursing down his cheeks, Daniel bent down and placed his hands on his knees. "I just want to find Dad and go home," he hiccupped between sobs.

"And that's what we'll do, Daniel," Damianos said, having joined the two men. He turned to Gustavo. "Thank you. Perhaps one day you and Daniel will meet again. But for now, I'll take him back." And with these words, Damianos snapped his fingers to transport them back to their boat.

If 1979 had been a year fraught with troublesome moments and indelible images of war for Gustavo, so had it been for Dan. While Gustavo had gone to relive the warehouse incident with his son – a young man he didn't know – Dan had gone back to the depth of his memories while unable to sleep that night.

1979 was the year he had arrived in Florida, having left home behind in Venezuela. He first finished high school, and went to college to get his Batchelor of Science. All was going well until a reversal of fortune hit his father, and the loss he sustained, drove Dan to having to fend for himself. He had to get a job and start his life with the promise that what happened to his dad would never happen to him.

In the past nine years, Dan had managed to raise himself out of the proverbial gutter and, after getting his engineering degree, was now well on his way to becoming a navy pilot. The thought put a smile on his lips in the early hours of the morning when he heard the door of his room open just a crack and Gustavo poke his head inside.

"You awake?" he asked.

"Yeah, couldn't sleep," Dan replied, kicking the covers aside and getting to his feet. "How did it go? How is he?" he rushed to ask.

Gustavo opened the door wide. "He's as stubborn as you are, man," he replied, a broad smile coming across his lips.

"Come on," Dan said, walking out of the room. "I'll put some coffee on."

"Let me get that pack off my back and I'll be right with you." He looked down at his hands and blood-splattered clothes. "I think I better take a shower, too."

As the two of them were sitting at the kitchen table sipping on a cup of freshly brewed coffee, the silence between them was only broken by Dan asking again, "How is he?"

"He's a fine young buck, Dan." He drank some more. "You know, what amazed me the most about him was his lack of fear. He was disgusted at the sight of a few dead men, yes, but when it was time to face gunfire, he didn't hesitate. He planted himself square across the enemy and began firing his Uzi."

Dan was agape. "And you let him...! He could have been killed..."

"No, Dan, he couldn't have. Remember you can't change the past. And he only took my place and when the moment came, the guy in front of him got his head blown off and his body spattered at Daniel's feet."

"Oh God!" Dan shouted. "He's too young to have seen that, Gustavo, how could Nicolas let that happened?"

"No one decided of this happening the way it did, Dan. Only God wanted your son to experience the horrors of war first hand. And His decision was final – not to be questioned."

Dan riveted his gaze on his friend, still having difficulties accepting what had occurred that night. He wondered how Daniel was going to survive the impact of such a horrific display. "How did he react?" he asked finally.

"He cried his eyes out, which was a good thing by my way of thinking."

"Why do you think that?"

"Because, he didn't keep the hurt bottled up, like most of us did at the time. He still knew how to cry, unlike us. See, we were all numbed by war; we couldn't cry anymore, and that's why many of us got to drinking when we got home. We couldn't face our memories. And as for me, I tell you, having to relive the incident is the best thing that happened to me since I came home."

"I wonder what he's feeling right now," Dan said musingly.

When they returned to the boat, no one was asleep. Malou got up from the chair on which she had been sitting for most of the night when she heard footsteps on deck.

"How did it go?" she asked in a rush, hugging Daniel tightly as he came down the stairs. "I've never been so frightened in my life..."

Stefano and Gaby were up and out of their chairs like a shot.

"How was it? What did you do?" Gaby shouted.

"Did you handle any rifle...?" Stefano asked in turn.

"It was okay, Mom," Daniel replied, pushing his mother away gently. "Let me get out of these clothes," he then said, looking down at his army fatigue, and then threw a stern glance to his siblings. "Sorry to have kept everybody awake..."

"Will you just tell us what happened?" Stefano insisted, regaining his seat.

"Yes, Daniel..., please...," Malou pleaded.

"It's not something I would want to go through again, I can tell you," Daniel replied, sitting himself down beside Gaby. "I had seen something like it on the screen of my Xbox, but this was as real as it could be. It was like an ambush. We were all kept at bay in this warehouse. There were about twenty of us in there trying to get out. Outside, there were these Iranians firing at anyone trying to get out..."

"What happened next...? Did you finally get out?" Stefano asked.

"I don't know for sure...," Daniel replied, returning his brother's questioning gaze. "When I fired my Uzi..."

"You fired an Uzi...?"

"Yes, and when I first handled it, I practically fell backward on my butt. That thing has got such a recoil, you wouldn't believe it."

"And what did you do...?" Malou asked.

"Well, we were about to have these Iranians licked, when the guy in front of me got hit..." Daniel stopped; the words unable to escape his mouth.

"What, Daniel, what happened?" Gaby asked.

Daniel looked around the table, tears at the rim of his eyes menacing to fall. "He was killed ...right in front of my eyes... That's all!"

"You mean the man died instead of you?" Malou asked, visibly horrified at the thought.

"Yes, Mom. He gave his life, so we could all get out of there safe."

"Oh God!" Malou cried out. "Why, why did you have to go and see this?"

"Because, Mom, I didn't know what I was playing at when I was playing with my Xbox. I thought that all I was seeing on the screen was just fun and games. I thought nothing of it could ever happen in reality, but it did and it does, Mom. And now, believe me, even if I play another game, I will know the difference."

"And that's exactly what God wanted to hear out of your mouth, Daniel," they all heard Damian say as he and Solange came down the steps to join them.

"But that was such a hard lesson for my son, Damian," Malou said.

"Yes, it was, Malou, but now, I'm sure if Daniel ever wanted to enlist, he will do it in full knowledge of what may be the consequences of his decision."

CHAPTER TWENTY-ONE

Once they were all back on deck enjoying the glorious morning sunshine, Malou asked Damianos, "Could you just explain one thing to me…"

"What's that?" Damianos queried, turning briefly in his seat at the wheel of the cruiser.

Malou got up from her lounge chair and went to stand beside their cat. "If you were able to get Daniel out there in Iran in 1979, in the middle of the war, and he met this friend of my husband, why is it that you can't just transport us to the date and place where Dan is at the moment?"

"Very good question, indeed, Malou. But you see, Dan's friend didn't say where he came from, or the date he left behind to rejoin Daniel in Tehran. Even if I had questioned him, I don't think he would have been able to give me an answer."

"You mean his memory was temporarily erased?"

"I believe so, yes…"

"Not quite, Damianos," Daniel interrupted, coming up to join his mother. "A couple of times he mentioned that Dad was worried about me. So, he must have had some memory of my father, didn't he?"

Damianos nodded, keeping his eyes on the stretch of ocean ahead of them. They were on their way to the Keys. "Yes, you're right, Daniel. Gustavo could remember your dad such as you do when he's around. But when Nicolas — that's the name of the messenger who's looking after Dan, by the way — was ordered to send Gustavo to Tehran, he obliterated the date and place from his mind."

"Okay," Malou said, "but that still does not explain how you or this Nicolas person could not tell us where Dan is. Obviously, you both know this by now, don't you?"

"No, Malou, each of us do not necessarily know what the other does." Seeing that both Daniel and Malou were a little lost at this point, Damianos explained, "You see, I know where we are at this minute and where we're heading, but I have no knowledge of what Nicolas knows. He, in turn, same as I do, can decipher or guess the path we've taken to join Dan, but we're not able to share this knowledge."

"You mean you depend on God or Damian and Solange for direction?" Daniel asked.

"Each of us do, yes, son. Such as Damian and Solange give you clues and directions as to what we should do next, so does Nicolas where your dad is at the moment."

"Does he have a book to guide him too," Gaby piped up from behind the three.

"I don't know, Gaby. But somehow, I don't think so. Since your dad has fallen into his past by accident and not by his own will, it's likely that he hasn't had the chance to re-visit the house where his book is located."

"But will he be able to remember what he learned during his first trip with me?"

"I don't know, Malou. Perhaps he might be allowed to open a few doors into his future, but I couldn't be sure."

Stefano was the last to come up to the wheel house. "Why is God playing games with us?" Everyone turned to look at the young man who stood his back against the back paneling. "What I mean is that God knows where Dad is, obviously, but why doesn't he just allow you"—he directed his gaze to Damianos—"to transport us where ever he is now?"

"Because, Stefano, I am not able to do anything else than what I am allowed to do. On the other hand, it is my experience that every accident has to turn out into a learning experience, which in turn will make you better human beings."

"You mean like me going to war to teach me what I would be facing if I ever decided to enlist, is that it?"

"Yes, Daniel, that's exactly what I believe is happening now. You see, as you rightfully concluded, God knows exactly where your dad is, but nothing of what God does should be a waste. So I believe each of you will be facing an experience during this trip that will benefit you in the future."

"And that includes me, too, I suppose," Malou suggested, lowering her gaze.

"Somehow, I don't think so," Damianos replied, throwing her a smile. "In your case, you have lived through unforgettable ordeals and events during your first trip with Dan; these should be enough to guide you through your future once you and your family return to 2013."

"I don't know, Damianos, all that is a blur at the moment, to tell you the truth. I'm only thinking of Dan and how lost he must be feeling."

It was another Sunday at the beach for Dan and Gustavo. They had decided to spend as much time together as they could, given that the next day Gustavo was due to start his new job. They were on their way to get a drink from the vendor standing on the sidewalk beside his cart when Dan noticed a 924 Porsche pull up and stop not ten feet from him.

"Wow! That's my sort of car," Dan exclaimed, staring at the magnificent vehicle.

"If I had their wallet," Gustavo put-in, chuckling, "I'll probably get myself one of those too."

They watched as the tall man came out and, while he helped his wife out of the passenger seat, Dan stared.

"I know them," he said to Gustavo. "I mean I've seen them both before... Somehow I have met them."

"You did? You do keep some rich company, don't you?" Gustavo looked at the couple and couldn't help but admire their handsome demeanor.

"Dear Dan," the woman said, stepping toward the bewildered young man. "How good it is to seeing you here."

"It sure is a pleasure to meet again," the man rejoined, a broad grin draping over his lips. "And you must be Gustavo," he added, extending his right hand for him to shake.

"I am very sorry, ma'am, but I don't remember where we've met...," Dan blurted, quite embarrassed.

Gustavo, meanwhile, shook hands with the man and fixed his gaze on him. "Same here, sir, I don't think I've met either of you before."

"Quite, quite," the man said, "So, why don't we walk along the beach and have lunch together at the Plaza"—he nodded in that direction—"and we'll explain our intrusion."

Falling in step with the couple, Gustavo and Dan exchanged a questioning glance while Dan tried to retrieve any bits of information he would have on this striking couple from his muddled brain.

"I know!" Dan erupted, stopping dead in his tracks. "You're Solange and Damian, aren't you?" He shot a glance to Gustavo. "These are my guardian angels, Gustavo. They know … everything about me!"

Damian guffawed. "Right you are, Dan. And very good of you to remember." He bowed slightly to Gustavo. "We are delighted to meet you, Gustavo. We have been looking forward to meeting the man who's looked after Dan since he fell in the clearing."

"I…, I really don't know, I mean what do you say when you meet angels?" Gustavo was obviously taken aback by the sudden encounter. "I had no idea that it was possible… I mean… Let me rephrase that…"

Solange giggled. "Yes, we both know what you mean, Gustavo. No need to rephrase." Her smile was mesmerizing. Gustavo's gaze couldn't leave the angel's face.

Regaining some of his composure, Dan said, "But why have you come? Has something happen to Malou and the children?"

Damian shook his head as they resumed walking toward the Plaza Hotel. "No, Dan, nothing has and nothing is likely to happen until they get here."

"Why then?"

"Your impatience hasn't been tamed yet has it, Dan?"

"Oh God…!" Dan exclaimed. "Of course, *The Twelve Herculean Tasks of the Shepherd* – I remember now."

"Glad you do, son. So, why don't we provide you two with a delicious lunch while Solange and I explain why we're here? Would that suit you?" He looked at Gustavo in particular.

"Lead the way, sir. I'm all for a nice lunch any time, thank you." Gustavo still couldn't believe what was happening, but he figured if God had decided that he should be in His good grace for a day, who was he to argue?

After they had delighted in a three-course meal comprised of a soup, seafood and a scrumptious dessert, Dan asked, "I know it's probably inconsequential to what brought the two of you here, but whose Porsche was that – the one that's parked in front of the hotel now?"

"Yours," was Damian's one word answer.

Gustavo and Dan exchanged a glance and then stared at the angels.

"Mine?" Dan blurted, incredulity written across his face.

"Yes, Dan," Damian went on, "This splendid vehicle is yours. You have been restoring old cars for sometimes now, partly for the sheer pleasure of it and partly to earn some extra money for college." He let that sink in for a minute. "Your nickname is "MacGyver", after a television character who had the knack for turning a dire situation into a way to escape his many troubles, thanks to his talent for fixing anything with what ever he found at hand."

Dan had his eyes riveted on Damian's face. "How come I can't remember the things I did then?" He paused. "I remember what I went through with you two and Malou and Damianos after my skiing accident, but none of what you just told me has yet come to my recollection?"

"That's because, your brain is still controlled by your body, Dan. If you recall one of the tasks demanded acceptance of the situation in which you found yourself, and together with acceptance, Damianos forced you into bringing your brain back to controlling your body…"

"Yes, I remember that," Dan said, nodding, "And it was not until I told my body to follow my orders that I was able to get up and walk again after he whacked me in the legs."

"Precisely, Dan. In this instance, though, what you need to do is to cast your predicament aside, accept it for what it is, and take the pieces of the puzzle in your mind and match them one to another until the picture of your life is complete."

"But the problem, as I see it," Gustavo put-in unexpectedly, "is that Dan only remembers things – or your puzzle pieces if you like – when his mind is triggered by one event or another, or by an image that means something, much like the Porsche you're driving."

"Yes, Gustavo," Damian agreed, "But in order for these images to become the trigger, you need to be in front of them or search for them."

"Like what I did when I went to the naval base, is that what you meant?"

"Yes. You were driven to go there, because your mind was in control. You let it guide your steps. However, now, you've become pre-occupied by other matters, which, although very important, have served as a shield in front of your memories."

"Such as my going with his son to Tehran, you mean?" Gustavo asked.

"Exactly like that, yes," Solange answered. "You see, both of you have now entered a new phase of your lives and your mind, Dan, is waiting for Malou's arrival. You know she will be here soon; so your only preoccupation is waiting."

"What else could I do?" Dan asked. "I don't know what my future holds; I only know that I will be leaving as soon as she arrives."

"Ah yes, and perhaps that's where you need to re-examine your decisions – those decisions that are leading you to accomplishing your dream."

"You mean like going for the naval training to become a navy pilot?"

"Yes, Dan. You need to remember what happened for you to decide on that career choice."

"But that was because of Professor Hugo; he was a captain in the navy in Venezuela…"

"Precisely my point, Dan. You did remember an important fact from your past when you were presented with a similar eventuality."

"But I remembered other things as well, like me leaving Venezuela, my high school days, the college and my father's troubles…" He paused. "But wouldn't I remember all those things once I return to my future?"

Solange and Damian turned to each other and nodded.

"Unfortunately, you will not remember much of your past to this date," Damian said, "if you don't recall *all of the events* that furnished your life before you go back to your future."

"It's like not remembering when you first scraped your knees, Dan," Solange added. "You need to remember what happened since infancy before you venture back into your future, I'm afraid. Since you wouldn't have any recollections of those experiences that have forged your life, you would be liable to make the same mistakes in your future."

Dan was dumfounded. He thought everything would be alright, with his memory intact, once he returned to his future with Malou and the three children. "Will you help me?" he asked in a whisper.

"That's why we're here, Dan. And Gustavo, although busy with his new job, will assist you as well."

Gustavo, who had been sitting beside Dan, passed an arm over his friend's shoulders, saying, "Don't you worry, buddy, we'll have these memories of yours back in no time. That's a promise."

CHAPTER TWENTY-TWO

There was very little they could see through the fog that had gradually enveloped their boat. Damianos had lowered anchored as soon as they were in sight of Key Largo's marina and had lit the fog lights throughout and around the decks before he had joined Malou and the children in the cabin.

Gaby was rummaging through the contents of the small fridge with an air of disgust marring her lovely face. "Haven't you got anything decent to eat in this boat?" she asked Damianos, turning her head up to him. "There isn't even one stick of celery or a tomato in here – just bread, sausages and something that looks like a soup of some sort..."

"Sorry, my dear," Damianos replied, chuckling, "I forgot to do the shopping last time we were ashore."

"What about the freezer?" Malou asked. "There might be some fish we could fry in some oil...," she suggested.

"Maybe there's a pizza too," Daniel said helpfully. "I sure could eat something."

"Since I see that you're all hungry," Damianos went on, "Why don't I take you all to the restaurant for a bite?"

"Grand idea," Stefano exclaimed. "How about we return to the tea room...?"

"Oh, stop it!" Gaby flared. "You know I love you to death, dear brother, but I don't think I could stand another session of tea and cakes tonight. Thank you very much!"

"Well, Damianos, what is it going to be then?" Malou asked, throwing a glance at their grinning cat.

"I think you might enjoy the place, Malou." And with a snap of his fingers, the five of them were sitting around a table at the terrace of a restaurant in Carita at the edge of the Indian Ocean.

"Good Lord!" Malou exclaimed. "This is the place where we stayed after our horrible trip aboard that old sampan." She fixed her gaze on Damianos. "Why here? I hope you're not thinking of having us relive that tempestuous journey, are you?"

"No, nothing of the sort, my dear..."

"But this is gorgeous, Mom!" Gaby said, standing up to look out at the crab-like structures erected in the water near the beach with their fog lamps burning brightly under the moonlit night.

"What are those for?" Daniel asked.

"They look like giant spiders," Stefano remarked, coming to stand beside Gaby.

"They're lobster and crab traps," Malou explained, while pointing to the lamp at the top of the structure closest to them. "The light attracts the crustaceans to the structure and they get caught inside some creels at the foot of each of those bamboo legs." She returned her attention to Damianos. "So, why have you brought us here?"

"Well, since you like fresh seafood, and I quite like fish myself, I thought this would be the perfect place to enjoy both in a natural setting, away from the tea room." He threw a glance to Gaby. "Would that be okay then if I ordered a plate of seafood, some bread and fruit for dessert?"

"What are you waiting for?" Gaby said, laughing. "I can't wait. It sounds like a meal fit for a king, or a princess I should say."

Once they regained the apartment later that afternoon, Dan's attitude was one of frustration. "I can't remember anything else," he said for the umpteen times, as Gustavo brought him a beer from the fridge and sat down across from him. "I can see a few images of Venezuela, where we lived before coming to America, and then going to high school, and of course, college. But restoring that Porsche is like I've never done something like that before. Could you imagine you doing something that complex and then not remembering it?"

"I think you're closing your mind to the possibilities, Dan," Gustavo answered.

"What do you mean by that?" Dan asked.

"Just because you're surprised to see what you obviously have done, doesn't mean you couldn't do it again or even remember what you've done."

"Are you telling me that I should start restoring another car?"

"Perhaps not another car, no, but going to a restorer or some garages that do that sort of thing could help you in recalling what you've done or how you did it." Gustavo drank a long gulp of his beer.

"But I wasn't living here when I did..."

"No, but I'm sure you're not the only person around here who's been into doing that kind of thing, are you?"

"I suppose not."

"Well then, why don't you venture to one of these garages and see what they're doing." Gustavo paused. "I won't be able to help you on that one tomorrow, but I'm sure Nicolas could be on hand if you call on him nicely in the morning." He chuckled.

"Why are you laughing?" Dan asked, still a bit annoyed.

"It's because I can picture our St. Nicolas going to get his hands dirty and his white suit all blotchy while working with you on a car."

Dan had to laugh too. Indeed, seeing Nicolas sliding under a vehicle was an image to behold.

"Yeah, I guess you're right. I'll check the phone book and see where they've got a restorer's garage around here." It was Dan's turn to start relaxing a little. He drank some beer. "But I wish I could see some other things I did..."

"Well, that's my department," Nicolas said, suddenly appearing beside Dan on the sofa. "I think you and I will have a few places to visit in the morning," he declared, reclining to the back of the seat.

"How do you feel about getting your hands dirty?" Gustavo asked, hiding his grin behind the lip of his bottle.

"Now, now, Gustavo, I'll have you know, I used to get my hands into everything when I was a lad..."

"That's it!" Dan erupted all of a sudden. "Getting my hands into everything — that's one of the things my dad used to tell me when I wanted to fix something around the house."

"And you did, didn't you, MacGyver?" Nicolas said to Dan, smiling. "I saw you getting your hands into house plumbing — do you remember fixing faucets and plugged drains?"

"Absolutely," Dan answered, excited now. "I couldn't stop searching for things to do."

"Exactly. And you did most things very well, I must admit."

As the five of them were walking along the beach after dinner, Gaby was the first to notice a fog bank advancing toward the shore.

"Look, Mom," she said, pointing at the seemingly impenetrable veil, "it's like a cloud coming to take us away."

Malou turned her head in the direction of the ocean just before they were all transported to some other shore, to another time.

Hanging for dear life onto Stefano's arm, when Gaby dared open her eyes, they were all assembled in a lavishly decorated boudoir inside some old house they surely didn't recognize.

Before they could ask Damianos what they were doing here, a door opened and a woman walked decisively toward them. Her long brown hair was tied in a pony tail and her casual allure didn't give away the fame that accompanied her everywhere she went.

"Ah, my dear child, there you are," she exclaimed with flourish, her voice laced of a strong Italian accent. "I was afraid you wouldn't find your way in this horrible fog."

Malou looked at Damianos inquisitively while the children stared awkwardly. "Let me introduce Ms. Cecilia Bartoli to everyone," he said, beaming.

"Oh yes, yes, of course," Cecilia said, "I am so sorry, where are my manners?"

"This is Mrs. Politano, her daughter Gaby, and her two sons, Stefano and Daniel," Damianos went on.

"My pleasure," Cecilia replied, bowing slightly. "And has Damianos informed you why you're here?" She looked at each of them in turn. "I guess he has not," she added, seeing the blank look on their faces. "No matter"—she extended an arm in the direction of the door from which she came out—"why don't you follow me to the studio?"

"Who's she?" Daniel whispered in Gaby's ear.

She shrugged in response.

Malou, who had recognized the name, answered instead, "She is a famous opera singer, Daniel."

"And now I'd like to hear that voice of yours, Gaby? Would you mind singing something for me?" Cecilia asked, as she sat down at the grand piano in the middle of a very spacious room.

"But Ms Bartoli," Gaby objected timidly, I've never sang opera..."

"I've heard that you have a beautiful voice, no matter what tune you're singing. So, if you would indulge me and sing a few bars for me. You choose the tune, and I'll accompany you."

Gaby, who had advanced to the side of the piano, turned to look at her mother. She wished she was back on the beach....

"You go ahead, Gaby. You won't have another opportunity like this one when we go home," Malou replied encouragingly, while she and her sons sat down in the chairs lining the far wall.

As soon as Gaby began singing, she felt as if transported on stage somewhere and facing an adoring audience. She was no longer afraid. All shyness seemed to have abandoned her. As the saying goes, she 'let her hair down' and sang her heart out. She was absolutely magnificent.

Her mother and brothers had never heard her sing like that. They were simply in awe.

Once she finished the song, Gaby bowed and turned to Cecilia. "Thank you so much, Ms. Bartoli. That was fantastic."

Cecilia got up from her seat at the piano and went to take Gaby's hand. "You know, I was a timid child like you when I started singing. I was always afraid people would not like my voice and demean my talent with acrimonious remarks, and it's only when my music teacher told me to sing for God and not for the audience that I began to understand and accept my talent. You see, God has given you a tremendous voice, a gift not to be denied or hidden. So, and if you're grateful for what He has given you, sing your joy to Him, without restraints." She smiled and embraced her.

Gaby was overwhelmed. She began letting the tears course down her cheeks and only nodded when Cecilia released her.

Turning to her mother and brothers, she looked up at Damianos. "How did you know?" she asked him.

"I didn't, my dear, but someone knew and told me you needed a friend of the Arts to let you know how gifted you are."

After thanking Cecilia for her time and the advice, Gaby and her family made their way out of the building to find themselves transported to their boat.

Once they were back in the cabin below deck and getting ready to spend the night aboard the cruiser, Stefano asked Damianos, "And what do you have in store for me?"

"No need asking me, Stefano," Damianos replied, "God only knows what plans He has in reserve for you."

"Maybe some beauty is waiting for you at the marina in Key Largo," Daniel said, jabbing his brother in the ribs.

"Oh stop that, Daniel," Stefano said. "Besides, I'm not the flirt you think I am…"

"Oh no? And who wanted to return to the tea house to meet Lyana again, eh?"

"Well, that's different. She reminded me of someone I knew. That's all."

"Okay, kids, it's time to quit for the night I think," Malou declared. "Let's go to bed and see what tomorrow will bring us, okay?"

CHAPTER TWENTY-THREE

That night, Dan couldn't get to sleep. He tossed and turned until he had enough. He threw his legs out of bed, stood up and tousled his hair. Shaking his head, he went to the bathroom to splash some water on his face. When he looked up at his reflection in the mirror, he didn't see his face but the one of the shepherd. "Damianos?" he whispered. "What are you doing here?"

"Come to the beach with me, Dan," was Damianos's answer before he disappeared.

Still wondering if he was dreaming awake, Dan touched his dream-catcher and asked, "God, please tell me what I should do?" and stood looking at the mirror, waiting for an answer. When none came, he dried his face with the nearby towel and walked out of the bathroom. In the corridor, he looked in on Gustavo – the man was snoring the night away. Smiling, Dan went back to his room, got dressed and walked out to the front door. He grabbed the house keys and went out, shutting the apartment door quietly behind him.

In the elevator he hesitated. He knew the beach was only a short distance away and decided not to take his car. He pressed the button for the lobby and went to the ground floor. As he came out, he looked up at the sky. *I hope I am not walking into one of your traps, Damianos,* he thought, remembering the many times the shepherd had tricked him into going somewhere he didn't really care to go.

Ten minutes later, Dan found himself walking along the ocean's edge, hands in his jeans' pockets. When he reached a rocky ledge, he sat down. "Okay, Damianos, I'm here. Now what?"

It wasn't long before the shepherd appeared to him, a broad smile adorning his old face. "Glad to see you accepted to meet me, Dan. How are you?"

Not in a mood to be civil, Dan replied, "Cut the crap, Damianos, and tell me why I'm here." He looked up at the man. "Okay, okay, please?" he added, finally cracking a smile.

"Yes, the magic word will do it every time," Damianos said, sitting beside Dan. "And to answer your question; I'm here because, once again, you need help…"

"But Nicolas said that he would help me remember things I've forgotten…"

"Yes, Dan, I heard him say that last night, however, he's only a messenger and can't do much for you." He paused. "You need to do more than just remember events; you need to strengthen your mind and will, Dan. And that Nicolas can't do for you."

"And you can?"

"I think you should throw your mind back to the twelve tasks we've accomplished together, and then ask yourself how you could apply everything you've learned to the present situation. Can you?"

"You mean it's up to me? Nicolas can't make me remember; is that it?"

"Yes, Dan. As Gustavo rightly remarked during your lunch with Damian and Solange, you remember things when images or fragment of speeches trigger your memory. So, I'd like you to look at some of the images I'm going to throw in front of your eyes to help you remember those events that you should never forget."

"Can you do that?"

Damianos's eyebrows shot up. "After you've witnessed some of my deeds, you still have doubts?"

Dan started laughing. "You're right. I shouldn't have any doubt, should I?"

"And that's another thing that will help you; cast all doubts aside, Dan. You can and did restore cars. You can and did many other things in your life…"

"Okay…, what else did I do then?"

Damianos erupted in loud chuckles. "That is something you haven't forgotten, is it?"

"What's that?"

"Impatience, Dan. You give way too easily to impatience and frustration. Remember the blind man, who could only "hear" the distance separating him from the chair where you had invited him to sit?"

"So?"

"So, he had the patience to calculate the distance he had to travel to reach the chair before he took the first step. And such as you should do now, arm yourself of patience to revisit the images I will show you. Then let your mind be your guide — patiently."

When morning came, no one was astir aboard the cruiser. But not for long. Damianos stepped down to the cabin and began cooking breakfast. The smell of bacon and eggs had everyone up and about in minutes.

"Where were you last night?" Stefano asked, stretching and yawning as he came into the lounge room. "When I got up to take a breath of fresh air on deck, you were nowhere to be found."

Keeping his eyes on the skillet, Damianos smiled. "I think you should remember that I am still a cat and cats do not sleep indoors generally."

"Yeah, but you were not on deck either..."

"No, you're right..., I had a few errands to run actually..."

"What sort of errands?" Daniel asked, coming to stand beside his brother. "Boy does that ever smell good!" he added, sniffing the aroma above the stove.

"Never mind that, boys," Damianos replied. "How about you set the table instead, while your mother and sister have their showers?"

"Okay, okay...," Daniel said, already looking for dishes and flatware in the cupboards and drawers, while Stefano cleared some of the magazines from one of the benches.

"What's that?" Stefano asked, lifting one of the issues and putting it under Damianos's nose. "Are we going bike riding or something?"

"Or something, yes," their cat replied, putting a plate of bacon and eggs in the middle of the table. "Any objection?"

"No, I'm just surprised, that's all," Stefano said. "And where is that likely to happen?"

"Oh that's for me to know and for you to find out later today."

"Let's see?" Daniel said, grabbing the magazine out of his brother's hand. "But isn't that a dirt bike race, like the ones we did with Dad?" He pointed to the cover picture.

"Yeah, that's why I was asking Damianos..."

"What were you asking Damianos?" Gaby asked, emerging from the sleepers' part of the cabin, a robe wrapped around her, and wiping her hair with a towel.

"About dirt bikes and the races we did with Dad a while ago. Do you remember?"

"How can I forget? You guys always came home dragging mud and dirt all over the house…"

"Okay, why don't you sit and have breakfast before it all gets cold," Damianos demanded, grinning.

"Quite a little housewife, aren't you?" Stefano said, snickering. "You should get Mom's apron…"

"Don't push it, son," Damianos replied, returning his attention to the serving of pancakes he was now putting on the grill.

Staring at the magazine they had placed on the table, the three children began eating in silence.

"Well, isn't that a nice sight to wake up to," Malou said, coming to join the four of them. "How are my kids this morning?"

"Good morning, Mom," the boys and Gaby said in unison.

"Good morning, Malou," Damianos rejoined. "Did you sleep well?"

"As the proverbial log, thank you, Damianos. What about you?"

"He spent the night out," Stefano cut in, "and hasn't told us where he went yet."

"I had a nice sleep on the beach, if you must know, Stefano, and I'm well rested, thanks," Damianos replied, smiling and putting some pancakes on each of the kids' plates.

"That looks and smells absolutely delicious, Damianos, thank you," Malou said, taking a seat beside Gaby. "So, what's the plan for today?"

"We're going bike riding," Daniel replied for Damianos.

"Oh no you don't, young man…"

"Actually we do, Mom, according to Damianos, that is."

Malou looked up at their cat. "Is that right?"

"Something like it, yes."

"What do you mean by that?" Malou demanded. Then turning her head to the kitchen counter, she added, "How about some coffee or juice, Gaby?"

"Humm," Gaby said, munching on a piece of pancake, "Sure. Sorry, I forgot."

"You mean the "maid" forgot," Stefano put in, chuckling between mouthfuls and looking at Damianos.

"Alright, enjoy your pleasure at my expense, while it lasts," their cat said, returning to the last of his cooking tasks. "Next time, I'll bring my apron and chef's hat...."

Laughing and continuing to eat, the family didn't notice when Damianos switched the burners off, snapped his fingers and disappeared quietly. He had to arrange for the family's next trip. And this was going to be tricky.

That morning, Gustavo was up before first light. He had slept well – too well, in fact. He felt heavy and unable to wake up it seemed. So, to clear the cobwebs out of his muddled brain, he took a cold shower and was about to turn the water off when he heard a knock at the bathroom door.

"You up?" Dan asked.

Laughing, Gustavo opened the door and said, "What does it look like?"

"Sorry..., of course you are," Dan replied, turning to go to the living room. "I only slept a few hours and I don't know where my mind is going this morning."

"Same here," Gustavo said, "except that I slept so soundly, I couldn't wake up."

"What time do you have to be at the warehouse?"

"Seven. But I want to be there way before time to have a look at the rig I'll be driving." He looked down at Dan, who was now sitting on the sofa, his head down and his elbows on his knees. "What's the matter with you? Are you okay?"

Dan lifted his gaze to his friend. "Yeah, I'm fine. But I still can't believe what happened last night."

"What's that?" Gustavo was slowly getting worried. On the one hand he didn't want to be late for his first day on the job, and on the other, he didn't like to leave Dan, if his friend was still depressed.

"It's just that I traveled through my early past with Damianos..."

"You mean that shepherd was here?"

"No, not here exactly. I met him on the beach and he took me on an incredible trip through my memories. I still can't believe the powers of the man. It was like going on a ride in Disney Land – you know the one you go in at the one end and then come out at the other – as if you've lived an entire different lifetime in ten minutes." Dan shook his head. "I tell you..., it was quite something."

"Sounds like it," Gustavo said, coming to sit beside Dan. "But what about Nicolas, is he still going to show you some of those things you couldn't recall?"

Dan shook his head. "No, actually, I think he's going to be on hand somewhere else this morning."

"And where's that?"

"Maybe he'll be there at your job site."

"I guess we'll just have to wait and see." Gustavo sat silent for a minute. "What about Damianos, will you see him again?"

"I think so. He said something about bike riding, I think."

"Now you've lost me," Gustavo said. "Did you ever ride a bike?"

"Like everyone does, yes, but I rode dirt bikes. Remember, I showed you my helmet and shirt..."

"You mean the one you've got in that bag in your room?"

"Exactly."

They were silent for a moment before Gustavo asked, "Do you want me to go with you, wherever it is you're going today?"

"No-no, Gustavo. I'll be fine with Damianos..., I should be okay."

"But tell me something; wasn't Damianos supposed to be accompanying your wife and children on their trip to find you. So, how come he's here? Does that mean your family has arrived?"

"I don't know, Gustavo. It would be logical to think so, but I don't really know what's going to happen. Everything is happening so fast now; I've got a hard time keeping up."

"Well, I'm sure it'll turn out just fine. God is watching. Of that I'm sure."

CHAPTER TWENTY-FOUR

This was Damianos's old stomping ground – *Big Cypress*. Perched on a branch of a tree, he was looking at the track with its intricate circuit and danger lurking at every turn for the inexperienced rider. Yet, he knew once Dan was going to be on the track, he would remember how to handle himself and his bike without any trouble. Climbing down, he noticed the riders preparing themselves for the next race. *It's time to get father and sons to the starting line,* he thought.

"Okay, are you boys ready for a bike race?" Damianos asked, stepping down the stairs of the cruiser.

"Do we have to go too?" Gaby asked, visibly in no mood to get close to dirt and sweat this morning.

"Up to you, my dear," Damianos replied. "You could spend the day shopping with your mother, if you prefer?"

"No, I don't think so," Malou interjected. "For some reason, I think we better go all together to the race, Gaby."

"Oh alright, I suppose we could," Gaby replied resignedly.

"Alright then, if everyone is ready, we shall go to Big Cypress," Damianos said, snapping his fingers.

Big Cypress? Malou thought, *why on earth are the boys racing all the way up there?*

By the time she would have thought of answering her own question, Malou and the three children were landing by the race track. The boys were already dressed and saddled on their bikes when their mother opened her eyes.

"Okay," Damianos said, "I think you ladies should stay in the shade and relax. This is going to be a boys' race."

As soon as Gustavo had left for work, Dan felt, rather than saw, Damianos's presence in the apartment. "Come on, you darn cat, show yourself. I know you're here," he yelled at the top of his lungs.

"What you felt and didn't see was me, yes. But I can't appear to you at the moment since I'm someplace else."

"And where is that?" Dan asked, speaking in undertones now.

"I want you to relax and follow the images I will show in your mind, Dan."

"What does that mean?"

"Just close your eyes, relax and look ahead of you."

"Okay," Dan replied, shutting his eyes tightly. He knew there was no use arguing with their cat.

Once he was sufficiently relaxed, he saw a dirt road ahead of him. He didn't recognize it right away, but it looked familiar. He felt as if he was floating just above the ground and going down the road at incredible speed. At one point he thought he was going to collide with a tree around the bend, but didn't. The trip lasted only for a few minutes and when Damianos told him to open his eyes, he found himself astride a dirt bike – his own bike – dressed in his own gear and wearing the helmet he had found in the apartment. He looked down at his shirt and smiled when he saw the number "4" in decal in the front of it.

Dressed as a race official, Damianos appeared beside him and said, "I hope you can complete the race and maybe remember someone you know among the other racers."

"But they're all wearing helmets," Dan objected. "And I can't concentrate on the race and try finding people at the same time."

"We'll see," Damianos replied evasively.

Within minutes the racers heard the horn signaling the start of the race. Ignoring everyone around them, the boys literally flew off the starting line and began heading the pack. They rode for about thirty seconds of the two-minute race ahead of everyone else and that until some other rider caught up to them. Daniel felt the guy close behind him, and try as he might he couldn't keep the lead. Stefano, for his part, tried not to fall back, but it was no use, he soon fell back and swore under his breath when he saw *Number 4* pass him.

At the finish line, Dan swerved and stopped. He felt elated, invigorated and as if he had never raced as well in his entire life. Taking his helmet off, he looked around him to watch the other riders cross the finish line. There was a sense of deja-vu when he observed the two young men taking their helmets off. He had seen them before, but where? He couldn't place them.

Having watched the race from their vantage point, Gaby and Malou applauded the winner as soon as he crossed the finishing line and then, all of a sudden, Malou exclaimed, "That's Dan, that's *Number 4...!*"

In that same moment, Damianos snapped his fingers and transported Malou and the boys back to the cruiser.

"What did you do that for?" Malou demanded, visibly enraged. "We were right there, a few feet from him and you took us away – why?"

Damianos shook his head under the staring gazes of the family. "He is not ready to meet you. Your husband, Malou, has lost his memory when he fell into a clearing in Key West. He saw you both"—he turned his gaze to Stefano and Daniel—"but couldn't recognize you. So, that's when I decided to take you back."

"But why?" Gaby screamed. "We could have taken care of him...!"

"No, child, you can't restore what God has not decided to give you back yet."

"Does that mean we'll have to take it one step at a time, again?"

"Exactly, Malou. Dan's mind is very fragile at the moment and the shock of seeing you or the children – if he's not ready – could send him back to the darkness from which he emerged only a few days ago."

"You mean he's starting to remember now?" Daniel asked.

"Yes, he is. But until God tells me otherwise, I can't send you to him."

"All in God's time, isn't it?" Malou concluded, dumfounded.

"At least we know he's alive and well," Daniel rejoined. "And he's still beating us..." He smiled at the thought of *Number 4* roaring past him.

"You know, I didn't put two and two together when I saw that guy past me," Stefano added, "And when he took his helmet off, I still didn't recognize him."

"That's because you remember your dad the way he was when he left you," Damianos explained. "And keep in mind he's about your age now – twenty five years younger than he was." He turned to Malou. "And you recognized him, even if it weren't for the *Number 4* on his shirt, because you would know him anywhere, isn't it?"

Malou lowered her gaze. "Yes, and it was some sort of a shock seeing him so young." She looked up at the children. "And now that begs the question, how will he feel when we meet him?"

"If you're wondering if he would prefer to remain where he is right now in time," Damianos answered, "That's a question he will have to answer for himself, I am afraid."

"What if he doesn't want to go back with us?" Gaby asked, already dreading the answer.

"God has given all of us the liberty to choose, Gaby," they heard Solange say from behind them. They all turned to her and Damian who stood at her back. "And in your father's case, the choice might be more difficult. Nonetheless, it is there for him to make."

"Remember God's love is all-encompassing," Damian added, "and your father loves you very much. All of his current plans will take second place to his love for his family. Yet, as Solange said, we will not be interfering in his choice of future."

When Dan was propelled back on the road to return to Key West and to the apartment, he hardly took notice of the track or of anything around him, for his mind was encumbered with the images of the woman who had yelled his name and the young girl beside her. *Could they have been my wife and daughter,* he asked himself as soon as he landed in the kitchen.

"Oh there you are," Gustavo exclaimed when he realized Dan was back. "How was your day? Did you go to a race?"

"I saw them," Dan answered, staring blankly out the window by the kitchen sink.

"Who did you see?" Gustavo asked, raising his gaze from the couple of potatoes he was peeling.

"My family. Or at least I think it was them."

"But that's wonderful. Why the long face then?"

"Because I don't know them, Gustavo. My wife — if that's her — is a gorgeous woman, and so is my daughter. But I can't really remember them." He paused. "It's like they're somebody else's family... I really don't know how to explain it."

"Did you see your sons, too?"

"Yeah, I raced with them, without even knowing who they were. The taller of the two, is my age, Gustavo. Do you realize what I'm saying?"

Gustavo went to the fridge, took out two bottles of beer, handed one to Dan and grabbed him by the arm to lead him to the living room. "Come on; let's have a chat about this, just you and me and the four walls."

Dan nodded and followed his friend. Plopping down on the sofa, he said, "How am I going to cope with them, Gustavo?" He flipped the cap of the bottle and drank a long swig of beer. "It's like I am my boys' age. How can I return to my future, without knowing them or even remembering anything about them?" He took another sip. "I would have to be in love with my wife all over again, and then relive the birth of each of my three children." He paused and stared at the wall behind Gustavo's head.

Sitting down and stretching his leg in front of him, Gustavo replied, "I think you need to understand something, Dan. They will come here to take you back, but they'll only be able to do that if you choose to accompany them. No one will force you to go back. God and love will be able to do that. Nothing and no one else could do it for you."

"You mean I will have to decide whether I stay or go back?"

"Absolutely, Dan. You have a career path traced ahead of you. You want to become a navy pilot. You want to climb the ladder of the Navy. And if you don't want to take that path, you may choose some other future, but it's your choice entirely."

After a long moment of silence between the two men, Dan said, "I guess, I'll have to wait until they get here." He paused. "What about you, how did you cope on that first day?"

Gustavo guffawed. "I wish you had been there, man. They got me this guy to show me around the warehouse, I met the guys and gals in the offices, and then the manager took me on a ride with this semi. What a rig that was! I couldn't get over it. Everything is at your fingertips...."

"Did you get to drive it?" Dan asked, unable to refrain from grinning at his friend's visible joy.

"Oh yeah. And that was a surprise and a half, I tell you. I didn't hesitate; everything I had to do was easy. Even doing reverse parking of the beast in this corridor type of thing was a cinch." He drank his bottle empty and smiled. "I'll have to thank Nicolas when I next lay eyes on that little guy. I don't know how he did it, but my mind was clear as bells. I couldn't believe it."

"When do you start hauling things then?"

"Not for another couple of days, Bill said – that's the manager. He wants me to be there every day to get the routine down, sort of thing, but I won't be on the road until the end of the week I gather."

"Sounds like you've made it, man. And I am really happy for you." And Dan meant it.

CHAPTER TWENTY-FIVE

That night Dan lay on top of his bed and turned his thoughts to the day's events. He was sure the woman who called his name after the race was his wife. He smiled when he saw her face in his mind's eye. However, he couldn't come to terms with that sense of distance — something separating them. He couldn't imagine how he was going to leap over the chasm of time that was keeping them apart. He imagined himself standing on the one side of the Grand Canyon and she on the other side. Only the echo of their voices would carry their words. If only he could see himself the way he was, or would be, twenty-five years later. Perhaps it would make it easier for him to choose whether to stay or to leave with them.

Yet, another thought returned to his mind; something Gustavo had said. *"You have a career path traced ahead of you. You want to become a navy pilot. You want to climb the ladder of the Navy... But it's your choice entirely."* The question was: Was he a navy pilot twenty-five years hence? Perhaps he was, and yet Dan didn't think so. But then why wasn't he? Could he have chosen not to take the training? Could he have resigned after a while? And what about the children — all grown-up and handsome kids they were. Why...? "Why...?" was the last question that remained in the forefront of his troubled mind when he finally fell asleep.

It must have been a couple of hours later when his dreams took him on a journey through a troublesome moment in his imagination. He was sitting on a sofa, a hand holding that of his wife. A strange book was on his lap. Then all of a sudden as he was about to open the book, a ball of fire emerged from the fireplace and tore its way through the living room. The old woman who had been sitting across from them was thrown out of her chair and was crawling out of reach as he and his wife tried to escape the fireball. He screamed, "Malou! Malou!" before he woke up.

He had no idea whether the dream was a recollection of something that really happened or simply a nightmare. He sat up and then realized that he was still dressed. He looked around him for a moment before getting up. He shook his head and went to the bathroom to splash some water on his face. In the hallway, he threw a glance to the kitchen and, out of the corner of his eye; he noticed a newspaper on the table. He couldn't recall reading the paper at any time during the previous day. His curiosity peeked, he went to grab it. It was opened at the classifieds' page. His eyes traveled down the section of engineering positions advertised and his gaze rested on one particular ad. For some reason, he couldn't take it all in fast enough. This was exactly what he would be looking for, if he were not going to take the training. He sat down, dismayed.

"So, you think this would be an alternative to the Navy?" Damianos asked him quietly as he came to stand beside Dan.

Dan looked up, and then returning his gaze to the paper, nodded. "But why would I do that?"

Damianos sat down across from him. "Listen to me, son. You have all the qualifications required to take that job." Dan frowned. "Yes, you do, Dan. What's more the Navy will be a dream that you have already lived in your imagination. You have lived on the aircraft carrier day after day, taking flight from time to time to troubled spots in the world, waging wars against an enemy, shooting down a young pilot or two – boys the same age as you." He paused. "And then you came home to the base to an empty room, where only sleep could reconcile your desire for excitement and those for a family. You felt the joy coursing through your body when lifting your bird to the firmament and you felt the emptiness of your life and the remorse for having killed another human being every time you landed. Are you sure you want to make that dream a reality?"

"What about Fabio?" Dan asked. "We are going to take the training together..."

Damianos shook his head, lowered his forearms onto his knees and folded his hands in front of him, while still looking at Dan. "Maybe he will follow in his father's footsteps or maybe he will decide otherwise."

"Does that mean I might be alone when I take the training next week?"

"It might, son. And then again, you might both be someplace else at that time." He peered into Dan's eyes. "But what ever the choice, Dan, it should be yours and yours alone. Don't ever make the mistake of following in someone's footsteps or stand by a friend when you're not sure that you could do the job or enter a career by yourself." He smiled. "Friends disappear, Dan, but loneliness and regrets, once they set in, never do."

"What about my love of flying – do I give that up too?"

"Why should you?" Damianos retreated to the back of the chair and crossed his arms over his chest. "God never leaves you without alternatives, Dan. If you wanted to get your pilot certificate, or what ever is required for you to take a seat in the cockpit of an aircraft, He would be there to help you, the same as he did with Gustavo."

"You think Gustavo wanted to drive these big trucks..."

"Ever since he was a boy, yes. Yet, he only drove trucks in the army and saw the horrors of war as a reward for following a dream that nearly got him killed in the process. If he had had the same opportunity as you have today, he would never have been to Iran, or have found himself divorced and on the brink of losing himself to drugs and alcohol."

"So, you're saying I should apply for that job?" Dan tapped his finger on the advertisement. "Is that it?"

"No, Dan. If you had been listening more closely, you would have realized that I have made your options a lot clearer for you. I have shown you where each choice could lead you. Yet, I will leave the decision entirely to you."

Both men fell silent.

Then Dan looked up. "What about my family? Those people I saw – they were my family, weren't they?"

"Yes, Dan, and when you feel you're ready to meet them and return to your future with them, you shall."

"But I'm ready right now!" Dan objected a little louder than he expected.

Damianos shook his head. "No, Dan. You can't go back with regrets lacing your heart. You need to make a decision and accept the consequences of that decision before you are ready to face them."

"What about them? Are they ready to take me back?"

"Yes, they are. But God doesn't want to precipitate your reunion before they, too, accept the fact that you have alternatives and a choice to make."

Dan turned his head to the window and by the time he returned his gaze to Damianos, the man had disappeared. He cupped his head in the palms of his hands and began crying in earnest.

Aboard the cruiser, Stefano and Malou were sitting alone across the table in the small living quarters. Gaby and Daniel had gone to bed.

"There's something I don't understand, Mom," Stefano began.

"What's that?" Malou asked.

"Everyone is telling us that Dad is not ready to meet with us. Why would that be, do you think?"

"You heard Solange and Damian didn't you?" She looked into her son's eyes. "They both told us that your dad had a choice to make..."

"Yes, yes, I know, Mom. I know what they said, but what is this really about? Dad has recognized us, at least he recognized you. Of that I'm sure. So, why does he have to choose between staying where he is and going back with us?"

"There is more to it than that, Stefano," Damianos said as he came in to sit beside Malou. "You see, your dad is at present at a crossroad in his life. When he fell, he unconsciously wanted to return to this particular place and at that particular moment in his life."

"Yes," Stefano said, "I remember you saying something about that. But it's different – he's revisited Key West, he's probably seen what he wanted to see. So, what's keeping him from choosing to return with us?"

"Think about it, Stefano," Malou interposed, "your dad is at a point in his life when he has to make a decision. If I recall, he was about to take his pilot training when he changed his mind." She turned her head to Damianos. "Isn't that right?"

"Yes, Malou. And the reason he wanted to go back to Key West when he fell was because of the decision he made at the time."

"You mean he would have preferred taking the pilot training?" Stefano threw a glance at his mother. "So why didn't he? Did you make him change his mind?"

Malou saw the accusatory look in Stefano's eyes.

"No, Stefano. I have never interfered in your father's decisions and never will. Yet, I can feel that he has unresolved issues or even regrets with that decision."

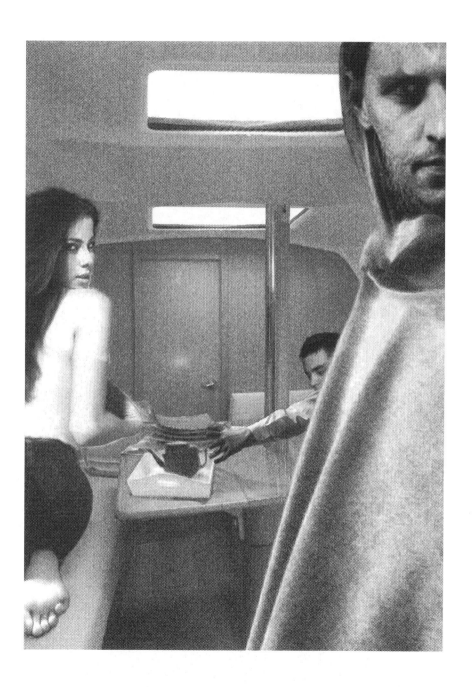

"And that is why, Stefano," Damianos added, "that we need to give your dad time to come to terms with the decision he will make."

"What happens if he decides to take the training after all; where does that leave us?" Stefano asked, fearing the answer.

Damianos smiled. "Remember, Stefano, no one – not even God – can or will change the past. What has been done; what has past stays in the past. Yet, everyone may wish they had chosen another path in life, and these regrets often need redress. They need to be quashed in order to "move on", as you often say in today's vernacular."

"So, you're saying that Dad will make the same decision as he made twenty-five years ago, but will no longer rue the day he made it?"

"Yes, Stefano, that's exactly what I meant. Your dad won't be able to change the past, but he needs to make the decision in full knowledge of the alternatives and knowing the reasons for which he chose not to go through with the training."

"But if he regretted not to have taken the training why didn't he choose a related career then? I mean there are plenty of careers available for an engineer…"

"Because the opportunity didn't present itself at the time, son," Damianos concluded.

Gustavo woke up the next morning, and was on his way to take a shower, when he noticed Dan's bedroom door wide opened and the bed looking as if no one had slept in it. He looked into the kitchen. It was empty and silent. Wondering where Dan was, he went to the hallway and looked at the peg where the car keys used to hang. They were gone.

Suddenly, fear dropped at the pit of his stomach. *Where is he gone in the middle of the night?* He then noticed the newspaper on the table and his gaze rested on the ad that had attracted Dan's attention the previous evening. Gustavo shook his head and thought his friend had perhaps gone to apply for that job. *But why would he do that,* he wondered. *He was so keen on taking that navy training.*

Unable to come up with a reasonable answer, Gustavo dropped the paper back on the table and went to take his shower.

Meanwhile, Dan, after driving along the beach for a while had parked his car and had gone to sit on the sand. He couldn't reconcile the idea of going to an office and start a career, with the opportunity he had to train as a navy pilot. Everything Damianos had told him was right; nevertheless, he knew he couldn't just walk away from the Navy. He was young, full of life and *nothing could stop me. . .*

"And that's where you're wrong," Damian said, coming to sit in the sand beside Dan.

Dan turned his face to the angel. "Why is that wrong?"

"Because you can't change your past, Dan. You've made the decision once, and although you have regretted it, you now need to reconcile yourself with it. Cast your mind forward to the time you had a skiing accident, will you?" And before Dan could argue, he found himself at the top of the ski slope, trying to decide whether to leap out onto the run.

Damian was beside him. "You are free, Dan, free to decide either to hop off onto the descent or remain here. What did you do?"

"I went down and nearly lost my life," Dan replied.

"Exactly. Taking the training will lead you to the top of this hill, Dan. And then, the only way to return to the lodge is to leap off the ledge and ski down to your death."

"You mean I could be killed?" Dan asked as if the thought never occurred to him.

Damian nodded as he brought them back to the beach. "It is an alternative worth considering, Dan."

CHAPTER TWENTY-SIX

When Dan returned home, Gustavo had already left for work. He sat down at the kitchen table and read the advertisement once again. The company in question was well known throughout the States. It was a large outfit with hundreds, if not thousands of employees. And that was one of the things that bothered Dan. He didn't want to be a number on a paycheck. He wanted to be his own man. Yet, there was one aspect of this proposition that could be attractive — he could make a lot more money being employed in that company than he would ever make in the Navy. And with that money, or what he could save, he could open his own enterprise. On the other hand, he wouldn't have the training the Navy offered him, nor would he have the benefits, such as free housing. And then there was the temptation of traveling to all those places...

"...which travels you would do aboard an aircraft carrier," Nicolas said as he came in the kitchen and sat down beside Dan. "And if you have ever been aboard one of these monsters, they lodge up to two thousand men for weeks on end."

Dan looked at the little man and smiled. "Yeah, that's perhaps not the best way to see the world, is it?"

"Besides, you would leave your lovely Malou on the shores of Florida and spend countless days waiting to return home. Not the way I'd like to live my life in this day and age." Nicolas shook his head.

"And if I could save enough money, I could travel with Malou anywhere we please, couldn't we?"

"Absolutely, son. There is nothing stopping you from making the choice you actually made already, the difference being that now you know and will remember why you made that decision."

"How's that?" Dan asked a little puzzled.

"You are now in full possession of the knowledge that you will not be given the opportunity to kill another young pilot or enemy in the course of duty, and that you have a brilliant opportunity to carve a future for yourself."

"And I could even become a licensed pilot if I wanted to, couldn't I?"

"Yes, Dan. So, please stop thinking of flying a navy aircraft when there are so many other doors you could open right now."

Pondering Nicolas's remarks for a moment, Dan then asked, "Do you really think I would be killing some other pilots during these missions?"

"With the rumors of war roaming the Heavens today, Dan, I wouldn't be surprised that you would do so, very soon in fact." Nicolas paused. "However, it is not for me to convince you one way or the other…'

"Yes, yes, I know. It's my choice entirely," Dan finished for Nicolas. He paused. "By the way, shouldn't you be watching over Gustavo today?"

Nicolas shook his head and sniggered. "That boy doesn't need me, Dan. He's got an innate talent for driving these big semis. But, don't you worry; I'll be there when you leave to rejoin your future."

"Do you know when that is likely to happen?"

"When you made the decision you're required to make, and act upon that decision, I should think Damianos will be here for you to take the trip."

"I thought I would go back with them…?"

"Perhaps you will. Frankly, I don't know. Maybe, you'll go back alone to join them in 2013."

"I guess I better get my act together and go to that company, don't I?" Dan pointed to the ad again.

"I think it would be a grand idea, son." Nicolas smiled, got to his feet and in an instant disappeared.

Aboard the cruiser, Malou and the three children were having a leisurely breakfast on deck, trying to wait patiently – if that were possible – for the moment Damianos would announce their departure, setting sail for Key West.

Malou said, "Why don't we take a trip along the coast and stop at some marina or other on the way? What do you say?" She looked at Stefano.

"That's sounds like a great idea, Mom," Daniel rejoined. "I'm getting a little antsy waiting for our cat to come up with Dad's answer."

"Do you think that's a simple decision for Dad?" Gaby objected. "If I were him, I would do what my heart tells me to do, but I'm not him."

Stefano chuckled. "No, you're not Dad, that's for sure."

"What do you mean by that?" Gaby flared. "I'm as much Dad's daughter as you're his son!"

"Glad you think so," Stefano retorted, "and no, I don't think any of us would have an easy time with a decision such as the one Dad has to make."

"Besides, I don't think it's the decision itself that is important here," Malou interposed, "it's the fact that he needs to make it and never regret having made it."

"That's what Damianos said," Gaby agreed, "Dad couldn't change the past by making a different decision than the one he made, but he has to make it knowledgeably this time."

"So, you think it was a rash decision originally, do you?" Daniel asked.

"I wouldn't say it was a rash decision, no, but I don't think he was fully aware of the consequences of it back then."

Malou had listened to her children attentively. She smiled. They seemed to articulate her thoughts perfectly.

They were already several miles out of Key Largo and in sight of Islamorada when the clouds started gathering to the east. The wind picked up gradually while Daniel was at the wheel of the vessel.

"Do you think we should worry about these?" he asked his brother, while pointing to the bank of clouds to the port side of the cruiser.

"I shouldn't worry about them," Stefano replied, "we'll be at the marina before they get anywhere close to us."

"It's getting a little stuffy up here," Malou said, getting up from the lounge chair on the aft deck." She looked at Gaby. "Why don't we go down and get some lemonade ready? I think everybody will be thirsty..."

"Good idea, Mom," Gaby replied, "It's getting hot." She bent down to fold her chair, when a wind gust grabbed her scarf from around her neck and took it away. "Oh no! That was my favorite one," she cried out, annoyed and horrified all at once.

"Let's get downstairs, Gaby. I think we're in for a storm," Malou suggested, abandoning the folding of her own chair and grabbing her daughter's hand.

"Look out there." She pointed to the grey clouds advancing rapidly toward the coast. "Those are a bad sign."

"Are you okay?" Stefano asked when he saw his mother and sister rush down toward the stairs.

"Sure, but I think you and Daniel should either get that boat anchored somewhere quickly or get down here on the double."

"But we can't just leave the wheel, Mom," Daniel shouted.

"Then do what you think is best, but do it quickly." Malou had stopped at the top of the stairs, watching the storm clouds approach rapidly. "These are a bad omen, son."

Malou, who had lived the better part of her younger years in Haiti, knew exactly what she was talking about. She had learned to recognize tornadoes, and these clouds looked very much like one of the storms you either remember or die trying.

Stefano knew his mother was right. He looked at his brother and hollered over the now howling wind, "Let's you and I get her as close to shore as we can, okay?"

Daniel didn't reply and only nodded.

As the two boys tried to maintain their course, directing their vessel toward the nearest beach, the rain began to fall and the swell started to bloat as if the waves were inflated with more water with each wind gust, making their progress very difficult indeed. They couldn't lower anchor anywhere – no time for that. As the rain pelted down and lashed their boat tirelessly, the clouds soon enveloped it of a strange darkness. Night seemed to have replaced day in a matter of minutes. The drape of water falling in front of the vessel seemed impenetrable.

They didn't know where they were or where they were going anymore.

Time and space appeared to have taken over the vessel and its occupants. At a loss to know what else to do, Daniel and Stefano hung on to the wheel, staying their original course, while each wave seemed to lap over the railings of the boat with every swell they climbed.

"How long do you think it's going to last?" Daniel asked, shivering in his wet clothes.

"I have no idea, Bro. I only hope the wind will push us onto a beach somewhere."

"Where's Damianos when we need him?" Daniel sounded annoyed.

"I don't know…, and maybe we shouldn't have come this way alone."

"If you mean God is trying to stop us from going to Key West, He's doing a great job of it!"

Stefano couldn't help but laugh at his brother's rejoinder. "You're right at that. He's probably showing us what He could do if we don't follow His guidance."

"Yeah, but what I'd like to know is when we're going to touch land," Daniel said, raising his eyes to the blackened sky. "Just let us know before we crash, okay, God?"

And all of a sudden as if God had decided to give none of the warning Daniel asked for, the vessel slowly but surely carved its way onto a deserted beach.

"We've hit ground!" Malou yelled, while rushing up the steps. "Where are we?"

"Not a clue, Mom," Daniel replied, looking around him.

"Wow, this is gorgeous," Gaby exclaimed, as she came to join her mother and brothers. "Look at the rainbow!"

The rain had stopped as abruptly as it had started and, now, as the clouds parted, a beautiful arc of colors adorned their departing backdrop.

"But where are we?" Stefano asked, looking ahead of him at the stretch of sandy beach in front of a jungle-like forest.

Dan hurried to turn the keys in the lock when he heard the phone ring insistently inside the apartment.

Panting a little, he grabbed the receiver and said, "Hello!"

"Hey, Dan, how are you?"

It was Fabio.

"Hi, Fabio, how you doing?" Dan asked, happy to hear his friend's voice.

"I'm fine. What about you?"

"Just great…, but I'm glad you called…" Dan hesitated. "I don't know…"

"Hold on, man, before you say anything. I've got something to tell you…"

"What is it?"

"It's about meeting you at the hangar on the tenth." Fabio paused. "I've changed my mind. I don't think I'd want to take the training…"

"Me neither," Dan said to Fabio's audible surprise.

"You mean, you've decided to do something else?"

"Yeah. I've found an ad in the paper yesterday and they're hiring engineers."

"That's exactly what I was thinking, man. I wanted to take that training because of my dad mainly, you know that, but I don't think I'm cut up for it."

"And I've had a long talk with someone I met recently – a nice guy, you'll like him – and since he's seen what the war can do to a man, he suggested that I think about enlisting."

The line went dead for a moment.

"Are you there?" Dan asked.

"Yeah, yeah, I'm here," Fabio replied. "But tell me; did you apply for that job then?"

"Sure did. I just came back from there actually. And the good thing about it is that they asked me if I knew anyone else who would want to apply…"

"And what did you say?"

"Well, since I didn't know you'd changed your mind, I only said that I would ask you."

"That's great," Fabio said. "But could you ask them to put my name down on the list? You know my background – maybe better than I do myself even – and you could fill out an application for me…?"

"Way ahead of you, man," Dan said all smiles now. "I've taken an application form with me and I'll fill it out for you."

"Fantastic!" Fabio blared at the other end of the line. "Thanks, man. I'll owe you one."

"And when are you coming back then? Is it still on the tenth?"

"Maybe a couple of days before that. I don't know. But you'll see me when I get there…"

"Hold on…" Dan didn't know how he was going to explain Gustavo's presence. "It's just that I've got that friend I told you about staying in your room…"

"No problem, man. We can always find another apartment or a house for the three of us. Don't sweat the small stuff, Dan. Life's not worth the worrying."

"You're getting philosophical on me now?"

"Not really, but I'll explain why I've changed my mind, when I see you."

"Can hardly wait to hear that one," Dan concluded.

And after a few more parting words, he hung up and exhaled a sigh of relief.

CHAPTER TWENTY-SEVEN

"Okay," Malou said, after gazing at the coastal forest, "you kids need to dress with long pants, long-sleeve shirts and grab your shoes to walk through that forest." She sounded adamant.

"But, Mom...," Gaby protested.

"No buts, young lady. The three of you are going to do exactly as you're told," Malou added, going down the stairs and toward the sleeping quarters.

Stefano and Daniel exchanged a glance, shrugged and then followed their mother and sister.

"Can I ask why we need to be dressed like that?" Daniel asked, slipping into his long pants.

"This is a tropical forest, son, and trekking through it is not as simple as you think. You've got to worry about insect bites, snakes and spiders, all of which will attack you unexpectedly." Malou shook her head. "And I have no desire to see any of you die from a bite from these nasty things. Understood?"

"What about water, do we need to take some of those water bags I saw stored at the back of the cupboard?" Stefano suggested.

"Yes, that would be an excellent idea," Malou agreed.

"What about Damianos, do you think he's going to appear anytime soon?" Daniel asked.

"I don't know, but knowing him, he's probably the one who organized this little excursion."

"So why are we getting all dressed up?" Gaby asked. "Doesn't he usually do that?"

"That's exactly why I'm asking you to get dressed up. He hasn't shown up and I'm starting to wonder who got us here..."

"But didn't you just say that he's probably the one who led us here?"

"I know what I said, Daniel, but I don't know anymore than you do, so it's better to be prepared."

Once they had filled the water bags, had climbed over the boat's railing and had jumped onto the sand one after the other, they made their way silently toward the luxuriant forest. Before taking the first steps through the bordering plants and trees, Malou touched her dream catcher — it was warm to the touch — and prayed. *Dear Lord, I know you are watching over us, and I thank you for your vigilance. Could you also take us safely to where you have decided to lead us? Amen.*

As soon as Dan hung up the phone from talking to Fabio, a pang of regret hit him. He slumped into the kitchen chair and touched his dream catcher. "God, I just want to be a pilot," he cried out, his gaze raised upward to the ceiling of the apartment. "Why couldn't I change the things I have done?"

Fury now lacing his mind, Dan brushed the newspaper aside and put his head in the palms of his hands. "It wasn't right then, and it isn't right now," he hollered.

"No need to yell," Damianos said quietly, "I know what you were going through and although you cannot change the past, there might be a way to alter it, so that your dream could become a reality for you and your family."

Dan lifted his head to look at Damianos sitting across the table from him. "What do you mean by "altering" the past?"

"Do you recall the time you were at the top of the ski slope?"

"Not that again! I don't want to think about it right now."

"Why not, Dan?"

"Because, I should never have gone down that hill…"

"Exactly my point…"

"What do you mean?"

"I mean you could not change the fact that you went skiing on the day, but you could have chosen another slope and alter the course of your history without changing your future."

Dan had his eyes riveted on the old shepherd's face now. "You really think I could take that training then?"

"No, Dan, that is definitely not what I am saying."

"What then?"

"You can't change the fact that you did not take the navy pilot training, but you can certainly choose another slope to reach your future — or even a better future — if you so wished."

"But how? I've already applied for the position at Seagate, how can I back out now?"

"In the same way as you could have backed out from the treacherous hill and choose another one."

They had been walking for nearly a half-an-hour when Malou stopped, looked up through the trees' umbrella and said, "We're nearing a clearing. Let's follow the light."

"It looks all the same to me," Gaby said, wiping the sweat dripping from her forehead. "It's hot, sticky and it smells like a compost bin around here..."

"That's because you're in a natural compost bin, dear," Malou said to her. "Why don't you have a drink, and get some water in you?"

"So that I could sweat some more? No thanks!" Gaby objected.

"Come on, Gaby," Stefano said, "you're not on your way to a beauty contest or even on *Survivor*; you need to replace the water you keep losing..."

"And if I don't?" Gaby snapped back, obstinately.

"If you don't, you'll soon pass out from hypothermia," Daniel put in.

"This is intolerable, you know that?" Gaby said, taking a swig of water from her water bag. "Are you sure there's a clearing up ahead?" she asked her mother.

"As sure as I can be, Gaby. It's much lighter directly ahead of us and that means there is a spot open to the sky — no trees to block the sunrays."

"How come you know that much about this kind of forest, Mom?" Daniel asked.

"Well, when I was a little girl, my dad used to take me to the rainforest near Boutillier back home, and he taught me how to find my way in and out of it. And it's like riding a bike, I never forgot it. All that he taught me was coming back to me as soon as we stepped into this forest."

"What do you think we'll find when we get to that clearing?" Stefano asked.

"That I don't know, son. But a clearing in this type of forest is surely man-made. And it would take the constant cutting back of re-growth."

"How fast can it grow back then?" Daniel seemed very curious.

"It depends on the rain. If it rains regularly, the growth can be as quick as a month or two."

"These lianas are getting thicker," Daniel said, as he continued fraying a passage for his siblings and mother to follow the narrow track he was creating behind his steps.

"Let me help then," Stefano said, walking past and ahead of his mother and sister.

Yet, as he did so, he didn't realize that one of the lianas was not a liana at all but a snake slithering up one of the low tree branches. The reptile fell at his feet, frightening Gaby who jumped back with a screech.

"Oh no," she then screamed as she lost her footing and fell backward against a tree trunk, scaring a bunch of small spiders out of their nest.

Malou didn't hesitate. In a bounce she went to her daughter's help, grabbed her hand and pulled her to her feet. The raucous had awakened more than the spiders for the entire forest was soon invaded by the sounds of quacking birds, yapping monkeys and the shuffling of invisible animals escaping into the undergrowth.

Still whimpering her disgust and brushing the small beasties from her arms and legs, Gaby sounded enraged now. "Whose idea was it to have us go through this horrid place," she bellowed, glancing upward at the tree canopy. "If that's your idea, Damianos, you and I will have a serious talk when you next show your face, you know that!"

"Has it bitten you?" Malou asked Stefano, totally ignoring her daughter's obvious resentment toward this state of affair.

"No, Mom. I think that poor thing was more surprised to being pulled by its tail than I was frightened of it," Stefano said, shaking his head.

"Okay then, we better move on, before anyone else takes an interest in us," Malou said, grabbing Daniel's arm and moving ahead with him.

"What about me?" Gaby demanded, flustered and tears running down her cheeks. "What if I have been bitten by one of these spiders? Anyone cares?"

"Come on," said Stefano, taking her hand and squeezing it tightly, "we're almost at the clearing. It will be fine then." He looked at her red face. "And it doesn't look like you've been bitten either. But I also think another drink of water would be a good idea."

"If that keeps up, I won't have to go to the spa when I go home," Gaby remarked with a smile now, "I would have had the best thermal bath on Earth."

"Maybe we should buy this island and build a spa, so you could invite all your friends to experience such a heat," Stefano replied, while both he and Gaby continued walking behind Daniel and their mother.

"Where are they now?" Dan asked after a few moments of silence had passed between the two men.

"If you mean your wife and children, I believe they're on their way to my house."

"Your house?" Dan asked, baffled. "What house is that? I thought you lived no where, or everywhere you were needed."

"Precisely. But whether a cat or a human being or even a messenger such as Nicolas, we all need a place where to rest our heads when the toils of the day are done."

Dan shrugged. "And where's that house of yours then?"

"Where ever I need it to be."

Dan glowered at the old man. "Enough, Damianos! I don't care where you sleep, I care about my family. I want to see them. Now!"

"I'm afraid your impatience is again getting the better of you, Dan. You know very well that your family is safe, otherwise I wouldn't be here trying to talk to you, now would I?"

Dan grunted. "But why all this rigmarole? Why can't I join them now?"

"We live in God's time, Dan. It's not up to you or me to decide. Besides, you still have a dream to "catch", don't you?"

"What on Earth do you mean? If I can't take that navy training, what then? What am I doing here?"

"Good question. And I believe you will find the answer when you and I take a little trip…"

"Oh no!" Dan yelled. "You're not taking me anywhere. Just tell me what this "alternative" you talked about is, and I'll do what ever it takes to make it happen."

"Very noble of you, Dan. But nothing is ever as simple as that when you are the only one who should know the alternative that will fulfill your dream and make it a reality."

"If you're saying that I have to choose the alternative myself, then I'll have to think about it, because right now I don't know what I should do."

Damianos shook his head. "I know that stubbornness is another one of your traits of character, but in this instance you need not to think of what *you should* do, but of what *you want* to do…"

"You mean other than taking the training, right?"

"What dream do you really want to catch, Dan? That's my question, and it should be yours from now on end."

"Okay," Dan agreed, nodding. "And where did you want to take me on that little trip of yours?"

"To a house where you spent a great deal of time searching for a book..."

"Oh, you mean the book I saw in my dream the other night?"

"Yes, the very same."

"But I saw a ball of fire going through the living room. What about that? Did you try to kill that poor old lady?"

Damianos guffawed. "No, Dan. That ball of fire wasn't mine. I don't dwell in the haunts of Lucifer."

Dan was staring now. "Are you saying it was of Satan's doing?"

"With everything that happens in life there are always two sides to the same coin, Dan. If you experience something good, you can be sure there will be something bad to accompany it."

"How's that?"

"Let me see if I can explain this clearly for you," Damianos said reflectively. "With birth comes death; with sunshine you will have rain and with rain plants and flowers will grow." Dan frowned. "So, you see, God maintains a balance in all things. You know what could happen if the rain would stop falling on your garden or if the sun could not shine, don't you?"

"Of course, all things would die," Dan replied.

"Exactly. And when you've accomplished a good deed, such as finding your book, there had to be a downside to the find. Lucifer had to make his presence felt, just as a warning for you and Malou to stay on the path that was traced for you. And if you had strayed from the road on which you were traveling at the time, there would have been consequences to befall you."

"And I guess, Malou and I didn't stray, did we?"

"Not quite. At least you did stay on the straight and narrow, but forgot your instructions at the last minute..."

"And that's why I fell in my past, isn't it?"

"Yes, Dan. Yet, your accident became an opportunity for you to redress your past or choose an alternative to your future."

"There is always two sides to the same coin," Dan repeated and smiled, finally.

CHAPTER TWENTY-EIGHT

As they were approaching the edge of the jungle, Malou came to a dead stop. Her children crowded her to see what had interrupted her decisive advance.

"What's a matter, Mom?" Daniel blurted. "Is there another snake somewhere?"

"No, nothing like that. Just take a look...," Malou replied, pointing to a gap through the brush of tree branches and lianas.

"Oh wow! That's no ordinary clearing," Stefano piped up, peering at the sight over his mother's shoulder.

"Let me see," Gaby demanded, pushing ahead of her brothers. Her mouth fell agape.

"It looks like Hans and Gretel's house – like in the story book," Daniel said, still staring through the tall bushes.

"It's actually more than that, Daniel; it looks exactly like the clearing from where your dad and I left to return to 2013."

"And like the one where we landed when we started our trip," Stefano added.

"Does that mean Damianos is sending us back without Dad?" Gaby's frustration with the whole thing was returning at a gallop.

"I don't think so," Malou answered. "I think this is the departure point..."

"Departure to where?" Stefano demanded. "I thought we had reached our destination. We already saw Dad, so why should we leave now?"

"Yeah, Mom," Gaby insisted, "We've done everything we were supposed to do, so why this?"

"We'll soon find out, I'm sure," Malou replied, taking the next steps that would lead her and the children out of the forest and onto the gracious and refreshing meadow. "Alright, kids, just follow me and be very quiet."

Only the noise of the jungle birds and animals could be heard behind the four of them as they made their way to Hans and Gretel's house. When they were half-way to its door, Malou stopped again.

"There's something wrong," she said. "Damianos should be here. He never let anyone enter the house by themselves – as far as I know anyway."

"What do you think it means, Mom?" Gaby asked quietly.

"I really don't know, but I suggest we don't go any farther for now." Her gaze traveled to each of her children in turn. "Let's sit down and wait for a bit. We've been walking quite a long ways, so a rest would do us all a world of good I think."

"What if we returned to the boat and wait there?" Daniel asked. "Maybe Damianos was supposed to find us in the cruiser and not out here."

Malou shook her head, while the four of them sat down in a circle. The grass was soft and dry. The sun rays were gentle on their skin, and the tranquility of the place soon invited them to lie down. In a few minutes they were asleep.

When Dan and Damianos landed in the old house, Dan recognized the lounge room, the bookcases reaching upward to the ceiling and lining the walls on either side of the fireplace. He also recalled the high-back chairs, the coffee table and the tattered settee – everything was the same.

"You know, it feels like coming home somehow," he told Damianos, before sitting himself down on the sofa.

Damianos only smiled in response.

"I'm glad you think so," a voice emanating from somewhere near the fireplace said. Dan hadn't seen the little old lady sitting in the winged chair, the back of which was facing the settee.

"Oh God, you're here too?" he blurted, getting up in a bound to go to the lady, who was standing up now.

"How are you, Dan?" she asked, taking a few steps to round the seat.

"I am fine, Solange. And truth be told, very glad to find you here."

"Good, good," Solange said, going to stand in front of Damianos. "The book is back in its place in the basement, dear; would you mind getting it for Dan?"

"Of course not, milady. I'll be right back," Damianos replied, already disappearing down the hallway leading to the steps to the basement.

"But I don't understand, Solange," Dan began, "why opening the book again? Haven't I done all twelve tasks already?"

Solange, with the help of her cane, turned to face him. "Why don't you sit down with me and we'll have a chat, shall we?"

"Okay...," Dan said, going back to the sofa with Solange. "And why are you not an angel, I mean you're supposed to have departed by now, haven't you?"

"Oh no, Dan. You forgot that you are twenty-five years younger than the last time you came to this house, and my departure, as you call it, had not occurred yet. Besides, your last visit here was simply geared by your imagination, whereas now, you have an enormous task ahead of you and not quite as imaginary as you may perceive at present."

"You mean choosing an alternative for my future...?"

"Yours and that of your family, yes."

When Gustavo came home that night, and as soon as he opened the door of the apartment, he noticed Nicolas waiting for him – he was sitting on the couch. He smiled when he saw Gustavo plop down on the chair facing him.

"Good evening, Gustavo. How are you on this fine day?"

"Just peachy, Nicolas, but what are you doing here and where's Dan?"

"All very good questions, my friend. And all of which deserve an answer."

Nicolas paused, resting his hands over the knob of his cane.

"Well?" Gustavo said. "What are you waiting for? I'm tired. I need a shower and I'm hungry. So, what's happening?"

Nicolas shook his head. "I think it would be better, given that you're tired, in need of a shower, and that you're hungry, for me to wait until you've taken care of your body before I clutter your mind with the news."

"I appreciate your concern, my friend, but could you at least give me the headlines?"

"Alright then," Nicolas agreed, "Dan is gone on a long journey with Damianos; Fabio will be coming back next week as planned; and you may remain here for as long as you like."

Gustavo stared at the messenger before he said, "Yes, you're right; I better get cleaned up and eat something before you explain what you've just announced." He got up, went to the kitchen, dropped his lunch pale on the counter and disappeared in his bedroom.

Clad only of a towel around his waist, Gustavo reappeared in the kitchen a few minutes later, and went to the freezer. He took a Pyrex plate of spaghetti out of it and placed it in the oven. He switched it on and turned to see if Nicolas was still there.

"I'll be back in two ticks," he said to the messenger, "don't you dare move an inch, okay?"

"Take all the time you need. I'm not going anywhere," Nicolas said, chuckling.

"Ah, here is your answer, Dan," Solange said, as Damianos reappeared in the living room with a wooden box atop his extended arms.

"But, that's not..."

"Hush, Dan. Your book is in that box. Damian had it made especially for it."

"But why?" Dan asked as he took the box from Damianos and placed it in his lap.

"A question you shouldn't have to ask, my dear boy," Solange told him. "Remember the dream catcher embossed on the cover?"

"Of course, and you couldn't touch it if it weren't for being in this box, now could you?"

Damianos only nodded and smiled.

"Alright then," Solange said, turning to Dan, "Why don't you open the box and get your book out of it."

For some reason, Dan hesitated.

"What's the matter?" Solange fixed her gaze on him. "Is there something wrong?"

"No-no, it's not that. I just don't know that I'm ready to learn what's waiting for me..."

"Don't worry about a thing, Dan. No one could hurt you while you're here with us."

"Oh no? What about that ball of fire that crossed this very same living room the last time I was here with Malou and ready to open the book?"

Damianos guffawed. "No need to worry, Dan. This time, you have already opened this book once and you need not to fear Lucifer at this point."

Dan looked up at the old shepherd and perhaps for the first time since they met, he trusted his word.

"Why don't you sit down, Damianos, you're making me dizzy standing there," Solange asked.

"Alright," he replied, turning the high-back chair to face the sofa. "Is that better?"

"Much better indeed," Solange said with a nod. "And now, Dan, open the box and take the book out..."

"What about the key; do you still have it?"

"Yes, of course I do. And this time, I have it with me." Solange took the small key out of her cardigan's pocket. "See, it's right here."

Again Dan hesitated. "I wish Malou was here to help me..."

"Why on Earth for, Dan?" Solange demanded. "Your decisions are yours to make. And the book will only give you directives, you know that."

"Yes, but our entire future hangs in the balance, doesn't it?"

"Not yet, Dan," Damianos put in. "Remember, the book is not Pandora's box where all that remained was hope after all the other human traits came out of it. This book will only assist you in finding your alternate future. God has already given you a choice; whether you take the navy training or not. And now He's going to guide you in opting for a better future – there shouldn't be any fear in your heart or mind, Dan."

"Well said, Damianos," Solange remarked all smiles. "You're becoming very wise in your old age, aren't you?"

Dan swore he heard their cat purr for a moment. He smiled.

"Okay, let's get this show on the road then," he said, opening the latch of the wooden box.

Once dressed, Gustavo reappeared in the kitchen, took the spaghetti out of the oven and scooped a couple of serving spoonfuls onto a plate. "Do you want some?" he asked Nicolas as he carried the plate to the table.

Nicolas got up and went to join Gustavo. "No thanks, I no longer have to eat to function," he remarked, sitting across from Dan's friend.

"Yeah, must be nice...," Gustavo said. "So, you'll have to excuse me if I dig in while you tell me all about this news of yours, okay?" He went back to the counter, took some rolls out of the bread box, a fork out of the drawer, poured himself a glass of water, and returned to the table – his hands full.

"Alright then. Let's start at the beginning," Nicolas said, pointing to the newspaper still lying on the table. "That ad was quite an eye opener to Dan"—Gustavo nodded—"and as you are probably aware, he went to apply for the job."

"And did he get it?"

"He probably would have..."

"What do you mean by that?" Gustavo asked, between two mouthfuls.

"Simply that he realized that if he was indeed hired, it meant that he wouldn't be taking the navy pilot training."

"Yeah, we talked about that a couple of times. So what happened?"

"Well, when he came back from Seagate — that's the company hiring engineers — he heard the phone as he came in and picked it up just in time to hear Fabio on the line."

"Oh, I see"—Gustavo swallowed—"and what did his friend have to say?"

"Fabio wanted Dan to make an application on his behalf, so that both would be working at the same company."

"Does that mean Fabio had a change of heart about the navy training too?"

"Yes, Gustavo. It seemed that he was no longer ready for the strenuous training and wanted a more stable job."

Gustavo drank a long gulp of water and returned his attention to Nicolas. "What about Dan being gone on a long journey with Damianos; where does that come from?"

"Ah yes. That stems from the fact that Dan didn't want to be working for that company or for any company, in fact. He wanted the pilot training, fly the skies and never look back..."

"But he can't change his past, or can he?"

Nicolas shook his head. "No one can, Gustavo, not even God could."

"So what happened?"

"Well, since the navy training is out and the position at Seagate remained an uncertainty at this point, Dan could choose an alternate route to reach a better future to the one he has now in 2013."

"Is there anything wrong with the life he's got now?" Gustavo asked, wiping his plate clean of the left over sauce with the last bread roll.

"Everything is fine with what he has now, except for one important item..."

"He's not a pilot," Gustavo interposed.

"Exactly. So, Damianos, from orders on high, has taken him to visit a place where he could perhaps find an alternative future."

"What about his family?" Gustavo asked, getting to his feet to carry his dish and glass to the sink.

"They're fine. They will probably join him on their trip toward their new future, and so will you!"

Gustavo turned from the sink in a jerk to face Nicolas. "Could you repeat what you just said? I don't think I heard you correctly."

Nicolas chuckled and shook his head. "My dear Gustavo, did you think for one moment that your meeting and ensuing friendship happened by accident?"

"I don't know. But now that you mention it, it always seemed strange. The way we met, the way I was lead to help him, and then you appearing on the scene..."

"Yes, Gustavo — all of it was God's design. And what ever happens from now on end will also happen under God's guidance. Nothing left to that so-called chance or Lady Luck."

"Well, I'll be darned!" Gustavo exclaimed and then paused before returning to washing the dishes. "What about Fabio saying that I could stay here as long as I'd like. What do I make out of that?"

"Well, you have a choice. Should you wish to remain here and not to accompany Dan in his voyage, you could stay here with Fabio and continue working at the trucking company."

His back turned to Nicolas, Gustavo said, "Yeah, could do I suppose. But I know me. I'll soon be missing the guy and go back to my drinking." He pivoted on his heels. "You can tell the Boss right now — He's got me. I'm not staying here any longer than I have to."

Nicolas laughed. "I'm sure He'll be most pleased with your decision, my friend, most pleased indeed."

CHAPTER TWENTY-NINE

Gaby was first to open her eyes. She looked around her and immediately felt the freshness of the fog enveloping the clearing. She sat up.

"Mom?" she uttered quietly at first. "Mom?" she repeated a little louder now.

"What is it...?" Malou asked, raising herself on her elbows. "Where's the house?" She bolted upright. "Where's Damianos's house?"

Upon hearing their mother's voice, Daniel and Stefano woke up. "Where are we?" Daniel asked.

"Still in the clearing, but I can't see Damianos's place."

"That's because of the fog," Stefano suggested. "Why don't we go in that direction and find out if it's still there," he added, getting to his feet.

"This is the same clearing but it's not in the same place," Gaby said. "Look"—she pointed in the direction of the jungle—"the forest isn't there anymore."

"This is getting weirder by the minute," Daniel said, switching his gaze from where Hans and Gretel's house used to be to where the jungle was once.

"I suggest we stay put until someone tells us what to do," Malou said, looking upward to the sky. All she could see was a dome of white fog. She raised herself to her feet with Gaby's help.

They were suspended in time and place it seemed.

Unable to decide what the best course of action would be under the circumstances, Malou sat down again and so did the children.

"What does it all mean, Mom?" Gaby asked, getting visibly frightened.

"Nothing, sweetheart. Just put your faith in God and He'll soon give us a sign or some indication as to what we should do next."

As soon as Dan took the book out of its box, his heart began pounding rapidly into his chest. He was truly afraid of what he would find out.

"I think it's time for you to be alone with your future," Solange said unexpectedly. "You will need help..."

"Please, Solange," Dan pleaded suddenly, as Solange was about to get up. "Don't leave. As you said, I will need help..."

"Yes, Dan, but this old body of mine will not be able to assist you in what you are about to do. So, I better rejoin Damian and leave you in the care of someone who will be traveling with you." She stood up.

Dan was stunned. "What about you?" He looked at Damianos. "Where are you going?" he asked, seeing that the old shepherd was leaving his seat, too.

"I will follow your progress, Dan, and look after your family, while you examine the options for your future."

"And who's that someone you mentioned just now, Solange?"

"Just open the book, Dan, and you'll soon find out," Solange replied, already in the hallway.

Staring at the two departing figures, Dan felt as alone as ever. As Solange and Damianos had told him on many occasions, he was going to be the one to make the decisions that would change his future for ever.

Within a few minutes of being sitting down again, Malou and the children heard a faint whistle, similar to a breath of insistent wind filtering through the gap of a slightly opened window.

"What's that?" Gaby blurted, nestling in her mother's arms.

"That's probably Damianos," Malou replied soothingly.

"Did you call?" Damianos said, appearing before them with a broad smile on his face.

"You bet we did, you old buzzer," Daniel erupted as he got up. He was about to lunge a fist of frustration in Damianos's face when he was stopped short. The shepherd had extended his forearm and had stopped the young man in his belligerent assault.

"What the...?" Daniel blurted when he realized he couldn't advance a step.

"My dear Daniel," Damianos said calmly, "you should learn to control that temper of yours. Attacking me will not bring you the desired result, I assure you."

Stefano grabbed his brother by the shoulders and pulled him back while their mother and sister stood up and gathered to face Damianos.

"Where are we, Damianos?" Malou asked, curious as ever.

"At the moment nowhere in particular, milady. But I suspect it won't be long before we will begin following your husband in his travels."

"What travels?" Stefano asked. "I thought we were supposed to bring him back to 2013 once we found him."

"That was the original plan, I agree," Damianos replied. "However, your dad chose to *alter* his future and yours."

"Alter his future – how?" Malou demanded. "But we were happy the way things were…"

"Yes, you were, Malou. Nevertheless, and as I explained on a couple of occasions, Dan came down to Key West to revisit his past, and although he could not change the fact that he opted not to take his navy training, God is offering him an opportunity to *alter* his future and yours in turn."

"So, that's it then, he's forcing us into a *new* life," Stefano remarked, showing his annoyance.

"No, Stefano, not a *new* life as much as a more exciting one."

"Why is that?" Gaby asked. "He's always seemed happy with whatever he did."

"Yes, to the onlooker, your dad was happy, but his regrets managed to supersede that happiness. He enjoyed doing new things, explore new business opportunities, yet he needed something else."

"But we've got a beautiful house, a lovely family, and we have no want for anything," Malou interposed.

"Yes, Malou, and Dan has never failed to provide for his family, however his desire to fly the skies, to stretch his wings, as it were, never died."

"But didn't you say that even God couldn't change the past?" Daniel queried, having calmed down now.

"And I meant what I said, Daniel. Yet, there is always a possibility to alter the path you have chosen in order to attain the same result."

"How?" Stefano asked, slightly baffled.

"Let's take an example. You, Stefano, have chosen to go to university and have chosen several courses to obtain your degree at the end of the road. Although, you could not change the fact that you chose to go to university, you could opt to take other courses along the way to either become what you want to become or become something entirely different. The outcome – getting a degree – would not change, but the path you've chosen could be altered at any time, couldn't it?"

"Yeah, but once I got my degree, how could I go back and alter the courses?"

"Once you've obtained a degree, Stefano, it's not the end of the road, but the beginning of another one, isn't it?"

"You're not answering my question," Stefano argued.

"Oh yes, I am. That degree of yours could be improved in many ways, couldn't it?" Stefano nodded. "Well then, improving the results does not mean that you've changed your past, but that you've *altered* your ultimate choices."

"It's like if I wanted to be a nurse," Gaby put in, "and once I had my certificate, I went back to school, took different or improved courses to become a doctor. Is that what you mean?" She looked up at Damianos.

"So that means Dan is trying not only to alter the path he had chosen originally but he's also endeavoring to improve our future. Is that it?"

"Yes, Malou, that's exactly what he will be trying to do."

"Will he have help? Are Solange and Damian going to help him do all that?" Gaby asked.

"Absolutely," Damianos replied. "Although most of the assistance will come from someone you met already, Daniel." He fixed his eyes on the young man.

"You mean Gustavo?"

"Precisely. God has put Gustavo in your dad's path by design. And the man is on his way to meet with your dad at the beginning of his journey."

"What about us; what are we supposed to do in the meantime?" Daniel asked.

"I believe, as I mentioned, that we will be asked to follow your father. Yet, at this point, I would not be able to say for sure."

That night, after Nicolas had left him to ponder the news he had brought him; Gustavo asked himself, "I should have asked that old goat when I'm supposed to go. How am I supposed to get where ever Dan is right now?"

"A question I am here to answer," a voice replied from behind him.

"Who are you?" Gustavo uttered in disbelief, for the man who came round his chair to stand before him seemed to be surrounded of a strange aura.

"I'm Damian. Perhaps you remember our meeting at the beach and our lunch at the Plaza?"

"Of course, sir…. I am sorry, but I was lost in thought for a minute there. Have you got some news from Dan?"

"Not exactly, Gustavo. Since you have accepted to accompany him, I am here to take you to Dan. The two of you have a journey to start."

"You mean right now?" Gustavo sounded surprised.

"Is there a better time than the present?"

"But what about my job? Don't I need to give notice or something?"

"I don't think that will be necessary, Gustavo, these Earthly concerns will be taken care of, not to worry."

"How? I was supposed to take a semi to Atlanta…"

Damian shook his head and smiled. "Actually, you have been called away and a phone call to someone who needed that job has accepted to replace you." He paused. "I know it might be difficult for you to comprehend, but whenever a decision is made in Heaven, an appropriate action ensues on Earth."

"Isn't there a saying about that?" Gustavo asked, trying to recall the old adage.

"Yes. I believe you meant, "Man decides and God disposes," is that the one?"

"Exactly," Gustavo said, rising from the chair. "So, shall I follow you, or how does that work?"

"You know how it works — you've already taken a trip to Iran, didn't you?"

"Yes, yes, sorry…, I'm not quite with it tonight."

"Okay then, shall we go?"

Gustavo nodded and in the space of a second he landed in the living room of Solange's old house.

"Good Lord!" Dan exclaimed. "Are you the one who's going to travel with me?"

"I guess so, buddy." Gustavo looked around him. "Gracious me, I've never seen that many books in one room before. Is this a library?"

"No, it's Solange's house. You remember Solange, don't you?"

"Yeah, and it's her husband who got me here actually," Gustavo replied, going to sit down beside Dan.

"Did he say anything about my family?"

"No, it was first Nicolas who came to tell me that you were gone, and then he told me that I had a choice; I could either stay put or go with you to alter your future, as he put it. And when I was asking myself when all of that was likely to take place, Damian came to get me and brought me here."

All the while Dan had been looking at his friend's profile. "And why on Earth did you accept to come with me? You had your future all traced out for you now that you've got a job and you're not drinking..."

"Hold it right there, buddy," Gustavo cut in, "I didn't know if I could make it on my own yet – and that's a straight an answer as you're gonna get – I wasn't sure that I wasn't going back to the booze, truth be told. Too many unknowns actually."

"But you could have stayed with Fabio..."

"No, Dan. As Nicolas explained it, we were thrown in each other's paths because of God. He planned it all. So, who am I to say the opposite of what the Boss has decided, eh?"

Dan nodded and finally smiled. "I'm happy that you're here, Gustavo. I think I couldn't have tackled this task on my own either."

Gustavo looked down at the book in Dan's lap. "What's that? Is that the book you mentioned when we met Damian and Solange the first time?"

"Yes, you see"—Dan pointed to the title—"it's *The Twelve Herculean Tasks of the Shepherd*. And it contained twelve tasks, mostly related to behavior or character traits that were designed to help me in my future. But since I came back to my past again before I had time to use any of the things I saw or learned, I guess God has decided for me to open it again."

"Like a refresher course, you mean?"

"I suppose so. Well, let's open it then, shall we?"

CHAPTER THIRTY

"I think it would be a good idea for us to return to the boat," Damianos suggested.

"What for?" Daniel argued. "It's beached somewhere beyond that jungle..." He pointed to where the forest used to be.

"And it isn't there now, is it?" Damianos said, chuckling.

"Of course not. You've taken it away, haven't you?"

"Daniel, will you stop arguing?" Malou said, berating him. "Damianos has other things to do than answering your questions. Besides we're not here to stay, we're here to join your father in his quest for a better future for us, right?"

Daniel nodded, apparently resigned to his fate.

"Okay then, everyone, let's get back to some more comfortable quarters, shall we?" Damianos said with a snap of his fingers.

In a fraction of a second the little family was back aboard the cruiser, which was now moored at the Key West marina.

Malou looked at the sign atop the front door of the yachting club facing her. "Why are we back in Key West? I thought Dan had left this place already. Isn't that what you said?"

"Yes, Malou," Damianos replied, sitting down at the wheel. "He left Key West to go back to Solange's house in Bethlehem..."

"What on Earth would he be doing there?" Stefano asked, taking a seat on one of the lounge chairs near the wheel house.

"Do you remember your father's book?" Damianos looked at the four faces staring at him.

"Yes," Malou replied. "But why getting that book open again?"

231

"Did your husband have any opportunity to use what he learned while accomplishing all of his tasks?"

"No, of course not. He fell back into his past..."

"Precisely, my dear. He needs to re-open the book now — not to accomplish the tasks, but to remember what he learned."

"But I thought you said Dad had regained his memory now?" Gaby questioned in turn.

"He has regained memories of his past from the time he was twenty-three years old, but after that — his future actually — he only remembers prominent events and not the details he will need to advance in his new life."

"And how long is that going to take?" Daniel asked, sitting down beside Gaby in another lounge chair.

"How long is a piece of string, Daniel?" Damianos replied, smiling. "Besides, all of us now, including your dad, will be navigating in God's time and space. That means there will be no clock to watch, no days or night to account for, and no space for you to recognize at first sight."

"What do you mean?" Gaby asked, intrigued now.

"Remember, you three kids are not born yet. What you are experiencing right now and what ever is to come will only become memories when you return to 2013."

"And why did you send us through that jungle and to that clearing?" Stefano inquired.

"It was decision time for your dad, Stefano. While he was making up his mind, I thought it best to occupy your time with a little experiment of my own." Damianos chuckled again.

"But why, Damianos? Did we really need to face these slithering beasties and spiders?" Gaby demanded.

"Life is full of obstacles, my dear. And what you are going to face while following your dad in his progress may be much more annoying and perhaps even more frightening than a harmless snake or a bunch of trotting spiders."

"You mean that was only a sample of what you've got in store for us?" Daniel seemed more bothered than ever.

"Precisely, Daniel. You have seen war now, but your siblings have yet to face harsh realities."

Seeing that their discussion was going to lead nowhere tonight, Malou nodded and said, "Okay, why don't we get downstairs and change our clothes before we have something to eat?"

"That's the best idea I've heard all day," Daniel shouted, already rushing down the stairs to the cabin. "I'll be the first in the shower," he added, running to the back of the boat.

Dan looked positively ill at ease. He turned to Gustavo. "Are you absolutely sure you want to do this with me?"

"Listen, Dan, solitude is one thing, but loneliness is something entirely different. It drives you to all sorts of misdeeds. As a human being you need to belong somewhere. And me, I don't belong anywhere else but with you. I have made a commitment to stay at your side, and it is a promise I intend to keep." He gazed into Dan's eyes. "So, why don't you stop stalling and get on with it!"

"Well said," an old fellow, sitting in the chair Damianos had left moments before, said, grinning from ear to ear.

"Who are you?" Dan blurted, staring at the man.

"Ah yes, you don't remember me," the latter remarked. "The name is Chippewa, the Dream Maker." He chuckled.

Still stunned, Gustavo opened his mouth at last. "Chippewa you say? Are you here to help Dan?"

"Oh yes, Gustavo, and much more in fact."

Dressed in cotton trousers, a plaid shirt, leather boots and a tattered hat plopped over a full head of white hair, this ageing man looked all goodness and amiability. His smile and his striking blue eyes inspired trust and joviality.

"What about the book here?" Gustavo asked, pointing at the unopened volume in Dan's lap. "Is Dan going to find the answers he's looking for?"

"No, Gustavo. The book will give him the tools he needs to forge the future of his choice." Chippewa turned his gaze to Dan. "Let's not waste anymore time, and open it, will you?"

Dan nodded, put the key in the small lock at the side of the book, and as soon as he heard the click indicating the release of the latch, he lifted the cover. The first page was blank but the second wasn't.

"Why don't you read the paragraphs aloud, Dan?" Chippewa suggested, advancing his body to the edge of the chair and placing his forearms on his elbows.

"Okay, here it goes," Dan replied.

You have been proved worthy of opening this book to this first chapter. Therefore, you are now at liberty to receive the powers of the dream-maker, those powers that will enable you to reach the future of your choice and assist you in reaching your goals for you and for your progeny. The first of your tools will demand that you turn your mind toward understanding and tolerance which will free you from the sin of obsession.

"What powers is this paragraph referring to?" Gustavo asked, lifting his gaze to the Dream Maker. "Is it like magical powers?"

Chippewa burst out in laughter. "No, Gustavo. Nothing you and Dan will read in this book or all the things that Dan will be required to do, will have anything to do with magic."

"What are these powers then?" Dan asked, his eyes still traveling along the lines of the paragraph.

"The powers that I will bestow upon you will enable you to use the tools you are receiving while you read the book."

"Could you give us an example," Gustavo queried.

"Sure. In this first paragraph, God demands that you turn your mind toward understanding and tolerance and away from obsession, doesn't it?" Chippewa fixed his gaze on Dan.

Dan nodded. "But I believe I am tolerant and understanding," he argued. "And I don't think I'm obsessed with anything."

"Do you now? Interesting. You have been obsessed, Dan, and more so than you want to admit..."

"How?" Dan flared.

"With becoming a navy pilot, for example."

"That wasn't an obsession," Dan countered, "It's been a dream of mine."

"No, Dan. Your dream was to fly an aircraft, not necessarily becoming a navy pilot."

"Okay, you're right. I thought it was the cheapest and easiest way to get the training I wanted."

"Exactly my point. Obsession can drive you to using any means possible to attain the desired result."

"What about being tolerant and understanding?" Gustavo put in. "I haven't known Dan for very long, but I've not seen any intolerant behavior in him."

"Ah yes. Tolerance resides in direct opposition to intolerance. And the fact that you, Dan, wanted to become a navy pilot at all costs, proved that you wouldn't tolerate any hindering factors coming your way or crossing your path."

"Could you explain what you just said," Dan asked, getting a little mystified.

"Okay, when you enlisted to take the training, you saw only one road ahead of you, becoming the pilot at the control of a fighter jet, right?" Dan nodded. "Yet you ignored the consequences of the choice you were about to make and became intolerant toward anyone obstructing your path."

"Is that why you placed the newspaper on the table that night?"

"I personally didn't do it, Dan, but someone had to suggest an alternate route for you. And that someone was well aware of the consequences that could befall you if you persisted in your chosen career."

"Who was that?" Gustavo asked innocently.

Chippewa looked at him and smiled.

"Oh..., you mean the One up there?" He lifted his gaze to the ceiling.

"Yes, Gustavo. The "One up there" had to stop Dan in his decisive path." The three men fell silent for a moment.

"What about these powers then," Dan asked again.

"When ever you will be faced with a choice, I will make sure tolerance and understanding of the consequences that could follow each option will be your only guiding tools. Your mind will no longer be obsessed with attaining your goal without acknowledgement of what hindrances could cost you or your family."

"So, I'll have the power to make wise choices from now on end, is that it?"

"Yes, Dan. Should you, at any time, refuse to see the light or the forest for the tree, you will be recalled to attention instantly."

"And what will I do in all this?" Gustavo asked Chippewa.

"Give Dan a nudge when he's about to jump off the cliff," the Dream Maker replied, chuckling.

Damianos, having decided that it wasn't an evening for Malou to start cooking, took the family to the marina's closest restaurant. The décor suited the place perfectly. The blue drapes and white tablecloths reminded the patrons of the color of the ocean and beaches skirting it. The wooden trims around each of the window set the stage for the view beyond the palm trees fronting the restaurant. It was a comfortable place and a quiet one. Looking around her as she came in, Malou wondered in which year they had landed when they had returned to the cruiser, for the restaurant certainly didn't seem to be a modern one. But soon recalling what Damianos had mentioned about traveling in God's time and place, she instantly dismissed the thought of questioning him.

Of course it wasn't long until their conversation returned to the subject in the forefront of everyone's mind.

"You said that we were supposed to follow Dad in his progress," Stefano began, "but how are we supposed to do that if we're to stay here?"

"Very good question," Damianos replied. "You see, and as I mentioned earlier today, your dad is revisiting Solange's house to read his book. While he's doing that, we will be waiting for him to finish his reading right here."

"Is it likely to take days?" Gaby asked.

"Didn't I tell you that we are navigating in God's time from now on end?"

"Yes, Damianos, I understand that," Gaby went on, "but what I wanted to know was if we needed to prepare ourselves for the trip."

"No, my dear. There will be nothing to prepare. Once your dad will have read all twelve paragraphs and once he would have..."

"Which twelve paragraphs are you talking about?" Daniel demanded, finishing his ice cream.

"Let me answer that," Malou interposed, looking at Damianos. He nodded. "You see, the book your father is reading right now, as I explained to you when I first returned home, contains the description of the twelve tasks he had to accomplish while we were revisiting our past."

"Okay," Daniel said, nodding. "And why aren't we reading the same thing, since we'll need to follow him...?"

"That's the point," Damianos said, "You and your family will *follow* your dad in his progress. You won't be able to intervene..."

"What if we don't like what he's doing?" Gaby asked, getting a little annoyed.

"Your father will make all decisions in full knowledge of the consequences, Gaby. However, you will be able to express your opinion, such as every one of you will be able to do."

CHAPTER THIRTY-ONE

"I suppose everything I will do will also depend on my family's cooperation," Dan said, following a moment of reflection.

"Not necessarily, Dan," Chippewa answered. "Your family is ready to follow you in what ever path you choose to take. Your wife Malou will have no need to cooperate in your desired pursuit. She and the children will simply be spectators..."

"But won't they have something to say in the matter?"

"There will be times for explanations and learning, of course. They will need similar tools to yours while they tread in your steps. They will, for example, need to arm themselves of understanding and acceptance."

"That may be a difficult one," Gustavo remarked. "Children are self-centered a lot of times, and understanding what ever happens to their parents is not often something they can contemplate."

"Again, well said, Gustavo," Chippewa said. "However, Damianos will be there to monitor their progress and will ensure that they don't fall into the traps of rebuke or annoyance."

"That'll be easier said than done," Dan argued. "I don't know my children yet, or I don't have any recollection of them, of course, but as Gustavo said, kids are not so cooperative when they don't – or won't – understand what's going on in their lives. I know. I was one of those kids."

Chippewa looked at Dan for a moment before he said, "Yes, you were a recalcitrant child, but your character was forged on the basis of goodness and love, the same as your children were."

"But I had to accept a fate that I was not prepared for," Dan objected. "When my father lost everything, a future I didn't want fell at my feet and I had to accept it. I had to climb the ladder once again and that pretty much on my own."

"And did you resent your father for his loss of fortune?" Chippewa asked.

"No, I never resented him for anything that happened, let alone blame him. A reversal of fortune could happen to anyone, even the most astute of business man. I do believe he did the best he could and I simply had to accept the situation and move on."

Chippewa nodded. "And I think this is a good time for you to turn to the next page of your book, Dan."

The latter threw a glance to Gustavo before he returned his gaze to the book.

"Go ahead, Dan," Gustavo said, grinning. "I'm sure you're not going to turn into a frog, now will you?"

Dan had to chuckle at the remark. He turned the page and read:

Since you now understand what tolerance involves, your future endeavors will call for you to find acceptance of all that occurs to you and around you. However, accepting your situation or the circumstances surrounding the event doesn't mean fatalism should invade your mind. Should you be able to accept all things for what they are or have become, you should also be able to fight for truth and knowledge. Therefore, you should now be able to accept what happens to you, deal with the consequences and fight to achieve your goals.

"How come it always seems to refer to the questions that we just discussed?" Gustavo asked, reading the paragraph from over Dan's shoulder.

"That's because Dan's mind is very much attuned with his character traits, Gustavo. There's a progress in all trains of thoughts and Dan's book was written in accordance with his way of thinking."

"I seem to remember something about this paragraph," Dan said musingly. "Damianos described one of the tasks I had to accomplish…" He stopped in mid-sentence. "No, wait. What he said had to do with patience. But this one also triggers something in the back of my mind."

"Very good of you to remember, Dan. Yet, in this particular instance, we're here not to recall any of your past but to give you a future. So, let's go over that paragraph again. Shall we?"

"It says that I will have to accept everything that occurs to me. I suppose that means the circumstances in which I may find myself might be difficult to swallow, right?"

Chippewa nodded again. "Yes, Dan. Not all is what it seems. Perhaps I could give you an example." He waited for Dan to show his assent. He did with a silent nod. "Okay, when you woke up in that hospital in Key West, those were not the best of conditions, were they?"

"They certainly weren't," Dan agreed with a smile. "I felt totally lost, to tell you the truth."

"Precisely. But with time and a little patience you found your way and landed in the shelter with Gustavo here. Didn't you?"

"And you were the strangest bed-fellow I ever had," Gustavo put in, chuckling. "You woke up in the middle of the night screaming after Damianos, and even went to get your amulet out of your bag. Anyway, I was glad to have a new mate."

"Yeah," Dan added, "accepting all of what was happening to me was not easy, but once I realized that I had a friend at my side, and that I was there for a purpose, it became a lot easier."

"That's the point, Dan," Chippewa went on, "You always need an anchor to secure your boat and this time, acceptance of what happened enabled you to move forward."

"What about this fatalism the paragraph is referring to; what does that mean?" Gustavo asked, throwing a querying glance to Chippewa.

"Well, there is a little bit of fatalism in all of us, Gustavo. For example, when you believe that some things are inevitable, you express a form of fatalism. When you left your umbrella at home and it starts raining, you might say it was inevitable; I forgot my umbrella, therefore it had to rain." Chippewa chuckled at the thought. "But there is a more serious aspect to fatalism that should be avoided."

"Which is?" Dan asked.

"Which is the fact that you feel that all things that happen to you were the consequence of bad fate. It was your destiny for you to fall in that clearing for example, and you did nothing about it. That would have demonstrated fatalism on your part."

"But it was Dan's destiny to land in that clearing, wasn't it?" Gustavo argued.

"Yes, absolutely, Gustavo, but Dan accepted the fact and went about to redress the situation, didn't he?"

"At least I tried understanding it, yes," Dan agreed.

"Precisely. You wanted to see the whys and wherefores, and that is avoiding a fatalistic attitude."

When they returned to the boat, Malou and the children were surprised to find Damian and Solange waiting for them.

"Well, hello there," Malou said as she climbed aboard ahead of Damianos and the children. "Nice to see you."

"It's nice to be here," Solange said, "And how are you holding on, my dear?"

"Oh wow, you guys are here," Daniel said, as he reached the deck. "Is Dad ready to go?"

"Daniel!" Malou interjected a little louder than she expected. "Couldn't you say hello before you lunge head long into your questioning?"

Daniel bowed his head. "Sorry, Damian, Solange. How are you?"

"Hi," Stefano and Gaby piped up in unison as they joined the little group.

"Hello to all of you," Damian said with a broad smile and returning his attention to Daniel. "And to answer your question, Daniel, no, your dad is not ready yet. But we would like to talk to all of you before that happens nonetheless."

"Do you mind if we talked up on deck? The weather is pleasant this evening; I would prefer staying in the open air."

"Not at all, Malou," Solange replied, following her and the three kids to the upper deck.

Once everybody was seated, Damian said, "As you know by now, you are going to follow your father in his journey toward your future. However, we need to prepare you for your trip..."

"See, I was right, wasn't I?" Gaby exclaimed, shooting an accusing glance to Damianos. "You said we didn't have to prepare anything..."

"The devil in me made me say that," Damianos replied, laughing heartily.

"You're a typical cat, aren't you?" Stefano put in, "Always wanting the door open when it's closed, don't you?"

"Absolutely," Solange agreed. "When Damianos was just a kitten, he would have me leave the door open in the middle of winter and meowed to high heaven if I dared close it." She laughed.

"That's what I thought," Daniel agreed. "And you're still a terrible feline!"

"Alright, children," Malou interposed, "enough teasing for now; let's hear what Damian has to say, okay?"

Everyone returned their attention to the angel.

"Thank you, Malou, but a little bantering here and there is good for the soul." He paused. "Anyway, as I was saying, you all need some form of preparation for the journey you're about to undertake." He looked up at Damianos. "As your "terrible feline" mentioned earlier, Daniel, you have seen war but your siblings had no such experiences. So, Malou, Stefano and you, Gaby will need to acquire similar knowledge..."

"Do you mean we will have to enlist in the army?" Stefano questioned.

Damian shook his head. "No, Stefano, none of you will have to experience such things, nevertheless, you will have to experience life the way your dad saw it."

"What do you mean by that?" Gaby inquired.

"For one thing, you will have to forget all about using modern means of communication; all about computers, internet, cell phones and like devices."

"We can't use them around here anyway," Stefano put in. "So, that's not much of a new experience."

"We agree," Solange said, "however, being unable to use such devices and forgetting they ever existed are two entirely different things."

"What do you mean by "forgetting they ever existed"?" Malou asked.

"Just that," Damian said. "We are here to make sure you forget the future you had, Malou."

"You mean, wipe our memories clean?" Gaby uttered, agape now. "What about what we learned in school and that, will we forget all that too?"

"No, Gaby, all essential knowledge that you have acquired up to 2013 will remain in the back of your minds, to be retrieved when you go home."

"It'll be like temporary memory loss then?" Daniel said.

"Yes, Daniel. During your travels you will have no need for your previous memories, given the fact that you will forge new ones."

"But what about our house, our friends and all the things we left behind?" Malou asked, visibly concerned.

"Do not worry, my dear," Solange answered. "Again as Damianos explained earlier, to you Stefano I believe, the end result will be the same – or similar – but the route you take and your future as a whole will be quite different."

"And when is that likely to happen, I mean our loss of memory and all that?" Gaby asked.

"By the time you wake up tomorrow morning, you will have forgotten most of the future as you remember it today. You will have only recollections of events or occurrences that are necessary for your progress."

"What about our phones," Daniel asked, "When will we be able to use them again?"

"When ever you bought your current device will be the time for you to find them at your disposal," Solange answered.

"You mean we've got to spend twenty five years without a cell phone?" Gaby exclaimed as if she suddenly realized what was required of them.

"Yes, Gaby," Damian answered. "However, I need to remind you once again, as I believe Damianos explained earlier, you're not on the clock here. You're living in God's time, and what may seem as a long time to you right now, will only be seconds in Heaven. Besides which, your mind will not recall the existence of your cell phones, so you won't have any need for such devices."

"Bummer," Daniel said, "And how do you expect us to entertain ourselves without a computer, for example?"

"Oh, but computers did exist around that time, Daniel," Solange said. "But the internet wasn't accessible to the public until much later. And if it's games you're referring to, they were only available on floppy disks for the people who had personal computers."

"Ha-ha," Damian chuckled, "You, son, will need to return to the books and to playing games with your family..."

"You mean like Monopoly and such?" Stefano asked.

"Yes, and such as so many others," Damian replied.

"Besides," Solange put in, "You won't have time for much entertainment, I believe." She shot a glance at Damian. "Right?"

Damian nodded. "So, when ever you're ready to retire for the night, we will be ready to do what God has asked us to do."

CHAPTER THIRTY-TWO

A little more eager to turn the pages of his book and curiosity invading his mind, Dan looked up at Chippewa. "May I get on with it?"

"Of course, Dan. And that's another thing you'll have to consider throughout your travels toward your future – your timing."

"But I thought you mentioned something about traveling in God's time, so isn't He the one who would decide on my timing?"

"No, Dan," Chippewa answered. "Your timing is part of your decision process. If you chose to put the book down right now and have a sleep, for example – that would be your choice and the timing you would have chosen to tackle this particular task."

"It's like I'd have three days to get a shipment to Atlanta," Gustavo interposed, "but if I wanted to stop on the way for a while, it's my choice and my timing, right?"

Chippewa nodded. "Something like that, yes."

"So, if you want to turn the page right now or tomorrow," Gustavo added, "it won't make any difference, as long as you don't stop your progress altogether."

"Okay then, let's see what the next tool is," Dan said, turning to the third page of his book. He read the paragraph aloud.

Patience is a virtue with which we are all endowed. However, circumstances drive us to foster impatience rather than its worthwhile opposite. If frustration is allowed to set in, your opportunities will become obstacles and your goal will be farther than you ever expected. When you reach the level of patience required to tolerate and accept your situation, you will be on the road to accomplishing your goal.

247

"That's the thing Damianos kept mentioning to me. He always told me that I was short on patience and long on frustration."

This time Chippewa exploded in laughter. "And too right he was, Dan. Patience is very difficult to acquire and master. As the paragraph says, impatience allows for opportunities to become obstacles. Instead of your goal being in reach, every time you show a lack of patience, it moves farther away from you."

"But doesn't patience also foster frustration?" Gustavo asked, relaxing to the back of the sofa.

"Say you were patiently waiting for the mail to be delivered," Chippewa began, "you only will become frustrated if the mailman doesn't come by your house on time, such as he does every day. So, patience at that point, becomes impatience, which soon turns into frustration."

"But the mailman may have been delayed in delivering the mail; so why should we become impatient?" Dan asked.

"Very good, Dan," Chippewa said. "An event that is totally out of your control, such as the mailman being delayed, should not foster impatience, but it does. In fact, more often than not you're ready "to kill the messenger" on the spot as soon as he rings the doorbell, aren't you?"

Dan had to agree. "Yeah, when a delivery is not made on time, I would throttle the guy before..." Dan stopped and stared straight ahead.

"Have you seen something of your future, Dan?" Gustavo asked, getting used to Dan's flash backs – or forward flashes – by now.

"Yeah, something to do with pizza... A guy was delivering some boxes and he was late. I almost bit his head off." Dan switched his gaze to Chippewa again. "Is that what I'd have to watch for? I mean I shouldn't get all riled up when something out of my control happens?"

"Precisely, Dan. You will not go as far as throttling the delivery man, because your instincts are not those of a violent man, but you will be frustrated and showing your impatience nonetheless."

When the little family woke up, after a restless night encumbered of all sorts of imaginings and conjectures as to what life could be without electronic devices, they were surprised to find themselves in their bunks, in the cruiser cabins – nothing had changed.

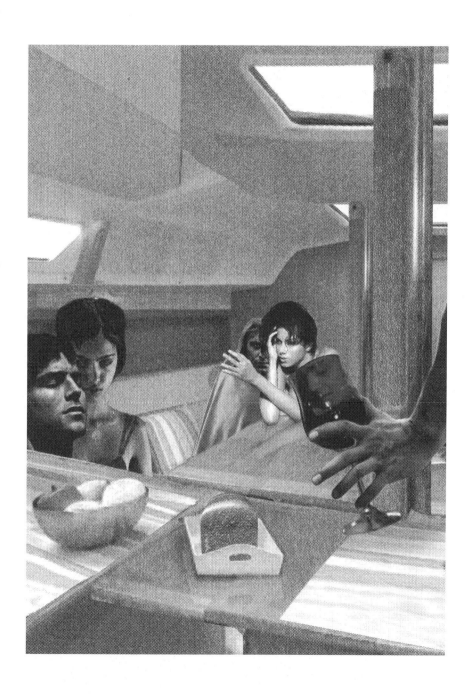

"What's going on here?" Daniel was the first to ask as he got out of bed. He looked around him and everything was the same. He went to the kitchen and sat down beside Damianos. "Have you been waiting here all night?" he asked him, wiping the sleep off his eyes.

"Not really, Daniel. I just curled up and went to sleep like you did."

"But I thought everything was going to be different somehow...?"

"Life without electronic devices at your disposal is not different..."

"What's not different?" Gaby asked, as she came to join her brother and Damianos at the table.

"Your life, my dear. As your brother remarked rightly just now, nothing of your life has changed overnight, except that your personal gadgets have disappeared."

"Good morning everyone," Malou said, stepping into the kitchen. She tied the belt of her robe and sat down beside Gaby. "How did you sleep?" she asked her daughter.

"Don't ask, Mom. I was tossing all night wondering what it would be like if I were unable to call my friends..."

"Same here," Stefano said, coming out of the cabin to join the family. "I really don't know what's going on, but I can't remember when I'm due to start university or which one I'm going to choose."

Damianos guffawed unexpectedly. "I see that you've forgotten your future, haven't you, son?"

"Is that what Damian meant last night when he said that we would have forgotten most of the future as we remembered it yesterday?"

"Yes, Malou. You remember most important events or turning points in your lives, but not those inconsequential items that could cloud your thoughts during the journey ahead."

"Does that mean my choice of university is inconsequential?" Stefano looked baffled, not to say displeased.

"No, Stefano, yet the choice you will have made by the time you return home will be perhaps different."

"How different could it be? I don't remember making the decision, but it must have been the right one. So why should *my future* be different just because my dad's future is going to be different?"

"Do you remember our conversation about the outcome being the same, although the path you take being different?" Stefano nodded. "Well, you can rest assured that nothing will have changed as far as your future is concerned, son. It all depends on your father's decisions and the future you'll be facing when he begins his journey."

"That's sounds like a trip into the unknown," Daniel piped-up. "That's neat!"

"There's nothing neat about it, Daniel, I remember..." Stefano began to say.

"Remember what, Stefano?" Malou looked up at her eldest who was still standing, his behind leaning against the kitchen counter.

"I have no idea, Mom. I can't remember anything much."

"What about you, Gaby, do you remember something of your future?" Damianos asked.

She shook her head. "I've been sitting here, wondering what I was doing before I came here with everyone. I mean I remember Dad being lost in time and all that, but nothing of what I was doing before we left."

"What about you, Malou?" Damianos pressed on.

"Nothing much, but I do remember sitting in the garden of our house..." She paused. "And something about being in the hospital with Dan. He had a skiing accident..."

"As I mentioned," Damianos interrupted, "that's what I meant by recalling major events of your lives." He looked at the children's faces. "That event is locked in your mother's mind so that she will not forget the impact it had on your family."

"Does that mean Dad will have another skiing accident?" Gaby asked, visibly troubled at the mere mention of her father being hurt somehow.

"No, it doesn't, Gaby," Damianos answered. "Yet the impact the accident had on his mind or even behavior afterward will remain with him in his future."

"What if he decides to go skiing again, should we stop him then?"

Damianos shook his head. "Not at all, Gaby. In fact, you'll only be able to express your opinion on the matter. But ultimately, your father will choose which path to take."

"And what about you, Daniel," Malou asked, "Do you remember anything?"

"Only that I was playing war games and that I went to Iran with Gustavo – Dad's friend – and saw that war was no game at all."

"Very good," Damianos said, visibly pleased with everyone's response. "And now, how about we take this cruiser out to sea and do some fishing for a change?"

"What about breakfast...?" Malou asked, already on her feet.

"We'll *eat on the run*," Damianos replied, laughing.

"Alright, Dan," Chippewa said, getting up from the chair. "Why don't we have a walk outside to stretch our legs...?"

"What about the book?" Dan was quick to ask. "Do I take it with me?"

"By all means, son. You'll have to read the next paragraph, won't you?"

Obviously hesitant to leave the house, Dan didn't move from the sofa.

Gustavo stood up. "So, what is it gonna be, Dan? Are you ready for a stroll or do you want to stay here and read your book all by your lonesome?"

"Okay, okay, I'm coming," Dan replied, closing the book and getting up. "Where are we going?" he asked Chippewa.

"To discover the world, Dan!"

"But I haven't read all twelve paragraphs yet." Dan was panicking.

Chippewa turned from the door in front of which he was standing. "It's just a turn of phrase, Dan. No need to panic. Besides, even in a square inch of grass, there is a whole world for one to discover. You will never have to go far to see what the world could offer you."

"Okay I guess..." Dan didn't sound very adventurous at the moment.

"What's the matter?" Gustavo queried. "Have you lost your punk or something?"

Dan shook his head as he put the book under his arm. "It's just that I don't know what I'm supposed to do. I'm kinda lost, if you know what I mean."

"Alright, let's get out of here first," Chippewa said decisively, opening the front door to a bright, sunny day, "and then we can continue this conversation." He extended an arm, inviting Dan and Gustavo to get out of the old mansion.

Dan turned around as soon as he was a few steps away from the front stoop. He looked up. "It looks so old," he remarked. "Almost as if it has been here for ever."

"Perhaps it has, Dan, perhaps it has," Chippewa replied, looking up to the roof as well.

"Is this like a half-way house or something?" Gustavo asked Chippewa.

He laughed heartily. "Yeah, you could say that. It's a safe haven for many and a house of learning for many others."

"Many others like me," Dan put in, returning his gaze to Chippewa.

"Yes, son. But for you it is a point of departure. From here you are called to go on a long road toward your ultimate goal. And during your journey, you'll need another tool…"

"You mean the one described in the next paragraph, right?"

"Precisely. But before we go into that, why don't we go to the back garden where there are benches – we could have a seat down there."

"That's not a very long walk," Gustavo said, grinning. "I thought you were going to take us on a trek through the forest"—he nodded in the direction of the woods abutting the lawn at the foot of the hill—"where we would pick up berries or something."

"Are you hungry?" Chippewa asked, returning the grin.

"Well, a sandwich wouldn't go unnoticed right now, I'd say."

"Okay, Gustavo, let's go to the backyard and see what we could cook up for you."

Gustavo turned a querying glance to Dan. "Don't look at me, I have no idea what's in store," Dan replied, following Chippewa to the back of the house.

When they rounded the corner, a whiff of aroma reached their nostrils.

"Oh wow; how did you manage that?" Gustavo exclaimed when he saw a bunch of hamburgers and hotdogs sizzling happily on the barbecue.

"That's one of my tricks," he replied, going to the table beside the grill. "And before you ask, this is no magic, although it may look like it."

"What is it then," Dan asked, going around Chippewa to have a closer look at the buns lined up on top of the upper shelf.

"That's the power of imagination, Dan. When you imagine yourself somewhere, doing something, hard enough, your mind turns your wish, or dream into reality."

"You mean like "my wish is your command"?" Gustavo asked.

Chippewa shook his head. "Not at all, Gustavo. It has to do with your power to make your dream come true. We all have the power to transform dreams into reality, with a little perseverance and determination."

"Okay…, when can we eat then," Dan asked impatiently now.

"Ah-ah," Chippewa said, "here it is again – that impatience of yours – isn't it, Dan?" He lifted a kindly glance to his pupil.

"Yeah, that's because all this made me hungry."

"Okay, okay, why don't you two help yourselves to hamburgers or hotdogs? Then we'll go and sit on the benches behind us."

Gustavo and Dan turned their heads all at once. And yes, there they were — benches alongside a table covered with all the trimmings that could accompany the best of cook-outs.

CHAPTER THIRTY-THREE

They were about ten miles at sea when Damianos turned the engine off and called the family to the aft of the cruiser. He had transformed the back of it into a platform where he had placed four chairs and rods — one for each of his passengers.

Quite surprised to see the new fishing deck and chairs, Gaby was the first to ask, "Are we suppose to catch our lunch?" She giggled.

Damianos remained impassible and waited for her siblings and mother's reaction.

Malou looked up at the shepherd and smiled. "This is an all-in-one lesson, isn't it?"

"Quite right you are, Malou. You see, it takes patience, determination, acceptance and some other skills to fish. I thought you needed to acquire these skills, or honed them"—he switched his gaze to Daniel and Stefano—"same as your dad is doing right now."

"What do we do if or when we catch something?" Daniel asked, taking a seat beside his mother.

"Not if, Daniel. But when you will catch a fish, depending on its size, I will show you how to clean it and ultimately, your mom will show you how to cook it."

"And I would have to do that, too, I suppose," Gaby said, visibly unhappy at the prospect of it all.

"Why not, sis?" Stefano said. "I guess we all need to get out of our cocoon sometime."

"That's yucky stuff, if you ask me," Gaby remarked, sitting down on the other side of her mother. "Do you know how to do all this?"

Malou nodded. "Where I grew up, I learned the simple pleasure of catching a fish and cooking it with my dad." She smiled at the memory. "You'll see; you'll learn to enjoy it as much as I did."

When they finished eating and they had drunk a couple of beers, Dan and Gustavo felt a little more relaxed, as if they were on holidays. For his part, Chippewa, noticing that Dan was now more receptive, felt it was time for him to return to reading his book.

"Alright," he said, "now that you've eaten and drank to your heart's content, I believe it's time to see what is written next, don't you think?" he looked at Dan.

"Right you are, Chippewa. I've still got nine tools to acquire before we can leave for that future of mine." He chuckled, as he brought the book to the top of the table and opened it in front of him. He had left it on the bench beside him while they had their lunch. He read the next passage aloud:

There is much to learn on the road of accomplishing one's dream. Together with patience, tolerance and acceptance, you will need determination to reach your goal. Giving up or quitting should not be part of your life now. Only with determination to reach your goal will you be able to have the patience, tolerance and acceptance to attain your desired aim.

"What's the difference between determination and stubbornness," Gustavo asked after a moment. "I know myself, when I want something bad enough, I can get very stubborn about it, and they say that's no good." He fixed his gaze on Chippewa.

The latter grinned. "I will not pretend to know why God has chosen you to accompany Dan in his quest, but I will have to say that you always ask the right questions." He shook his head, obviously pleased. "But to answer your question, Gustavo, stubbornness is determination's naughty cousin. You, Dan, will need a lot of determination to reach your goal as the book says. However, stubbornness may lead you astray – you'll have to watch yourself in that regard."

"Could you give me an example?" Dan asked, putting his forearms on either side of the open book.

"Ah yes. You were determined to take the navy pilot training, weren't you?"

"Yes, so?"

"Well, that determination, although, well aimed in the first instance, transformed itself into stubbornness the minute you refused to acknowledge the consequences that could befall you if you ever became a navy pilot."

"Don't remind me," Dan said, bowing his head. "I wanted to fly one of those aircrafts so bad, I didn't see what could happen if I was called to shoot down an enemy jet..."

"Exactly my point, Dan. Your desire to fly overcame any reasonable appreciation of what could befall you in such instances as those of warfare. Besides which, when your son was dead-set in enlisting in the army, you told him everything you should have told yourself when it came to take the navy training. By the time your son was old enough to enlist, you had learned what could happen to him, and what could have happened to you."

"Yes, I agree with what you're saying, Chippewa, but how do I stay determined without becoming stubborn about my endeavors?"

"If I may, Chippewa?" Gustavo interposed.

"Yes, by all means, go ahead."

Gustavo turned his head to Dan. "When you asked me to promise you to get a job in return for offering me a place to stay, I was determined to fulfill that promise, but I opposed some reticence when it came to driving semis. I didn't know anything about these big rigs. And if I had been stubborn about my promise, I could have gone down the street and found a job, any job, like tending bar, or sweeping the gutters, without thinking ahead of the consequence. So, as I understand it, determination will lead you to do the right thing, while stubbornness will lead you to do almost anything as long as you get what you want." He returned his gaze to Chippewa. "Right?"

"Yes, you're absolutely right, Gustavo. The end doesn't justify the means, Dan. You will need to take time to analyze your options as they present themselves to you, and then *determine* the best course of action."

Dan looked down at the paragraph again. "What about quitting? I don't think I ever given up on anything..."

"Ha-ha-ha," Chippewa laughed. "Again, you're right on point, Dan. You never wanted to quit, and that's another aspect of stubbornness. You see, if your determination is well directed, you will not need to quit or give up, because you would have made the right choice initially. However, if you chose the wrong path, quitting will become your only option if you want to redress the situation."

"How would I know if I chose the wrong path – or the right one for that matter?"

"It's like cooking," Gustavo answered. "When you want to make some pancakes, you set out to prepare the batter, put the butter in the skillet and scoop a little of the batter, let it sizzle, turn it over, and voila – you've got pancakes. However, before you started you had all the ingredients needed, and the tools required to accomplish your goal." He paused. "But let's say you didn't have eggs and you still wanted to have pancakes for breakfast. You would either stubbornly cook something inedible or you would quit until you got some eggs, wouldn't you?"

Dan nodded. "Although having pancakes for breakfast was the right choice, I needed to consider all angles before I started, is that it?"

"Yes," Chippewa said. "You will know you have chosen the right path if you have all the tools and ingredients to accomplish the task." He paused and smiled. "If you don't have eggs, having pancakes for breakfast is most probably the wrong choice to make."

A half-an-hour after they had started throwing their lines in the water repeatedly – without much success – impatience set in. Gaby was the first to get up from her seat. "I've enough of fishing to last me a lifetime," she declared. "This is crazy." She looked down at her mother. "I'm going downstairs and prepare something to eat, do you want to come?"

Malou shook her head in reply. "No, Gaby, I don't want to go anywhere. Besides, knowing Damianos, there's probably nothing in the fridge left to eat."

Damianos, who had been sitting on the engine hatch at their backs, chortled.

"Oh don't you start, you crazy cat," Gaby said, stomping off to the front of the cruiser.

"Hey-hey, hey, Gaby, come back here," Daniel hollered at the same moment. "I think something is biting," as he felt a strong tug on his line.

Gaby swung on her heels and rushed to come to stand behind her brother's chair. "You have to have all the luck, don't you?"

"No luck, Gaby," Malou said, "just patience. Why don't you sit down and watch?"

Daniel was having a hard time; the fish was really pulling on the line now.

"Here, let me help," Stefano said, replacing his own rod in its holder and getting up to help his brother.

Malou watched her sons fight to get the fish close to the platform with a broad smile on her lips. "Here," she said, getting up and grabbing the landing net, "As soon as it surfaces, I'll get it in," and getting down on all fours.

Damianos watched. He had known that Gaby was going to be reticent to anything that was out of the ordinary for her. He stepped down from the hatch and whispered in her ear, "Why don't you go and help your mother? I think she'll appreciate it."

Turning her head up to him, Gaby nodded and got up. She knelt down beside her mom just when the fish was in sight. "Oh no!" Malou shouted. "It's a catfish. It's going to be far too big for the landing net…"

"Hold on," Damianos said, snapping his fingers. As soon as he did, the catfish released its own catch, which landed easily into the net.

With a big sigh of relief, Daniel and Stefano reeled in the line while Malou took the hook off the fish's mouth.

And that's when Stefano exploded in roaring laughter. "We did it, Daniel," he shouted, high-fiving his brother. "Not only did we catch our lunch but we had to fight a catfish for it! Splendid!"

"Now what do we do?" Gaby asked, looking down at the wiggling fish in the landing net.

"Now, you have to kill it," Damianos replied. "You'll have to hammer its head as quickly as you can so it doesn't suffer."

"I can't kill anything," Gaby screamed, running away again.

"Here," Damianos said, handing the hammer to Stefano. "Why don't you do the honors?"

Seeing that her son was hesitating, Malou grabbed the hammer from Stefano's hand and with a well-directed blow ended the fish's life.

"How could you do that, Mom?" Gaby shouted, as she returned to the "scene of the crime".

"When you buy fish or chicken at the market, Gaby, have you ever considered that someone had to kill the creature before you could eat it?"

"But didn't God say, "Thou shalt not kill"?" Gaby argued.

"Yes, Gaby, He did say that, but He has always created food for us, and killing to eat is no sin. Killing for pleasure is. That's the difference."

"I don't think I could eat any of it though," Gaby went on arguing. "I'll rather eat vegetables for the rest of my life…"

"Alright, Gaby," Damianos cut in, "I think it would be a good idea for you to come down from where ever you are right now and try understanding what your mother was teaching you."

"This is all too gross for me, Damianos…"

"Maybe it is, but you're losing focus…"

"What do you mean? All I can see is that you killed some poor fish for us to eat."

"That's exactly the point," Malou rejoined. "Sometimes, you may be face with difficulties, whereby fishing will be the only means for you to fill your tummy and avoid starvation."

Seeing that Gaby was going down the path of stubbornness, Stefano suggested to Daniel, "Why don't we try catching another one while Mom cleans this one up?"

"Yeah, two is better than one, isn't it?" Daniel agreed, returning to putting another bait on the hook.

As the two brothers threw their lines into the water again, Malou took the landing net and grabbed Gaby by the arm on their way down to the kitchen.

Damianos regained his seat on top of the hatch and smiled to himself. He knew Malou would be able to show Gaby what the lesson meant to achieve.

CHAPTER THIRTY-FOUR

"**D**o you know anything about indulgence?" Chippewa asked as he saw that Dan was about to turn to the next page of his book.

"Ha-ha-ha," Gustavo laughed. "Dan probably doesn't, but I do," he said, slapping Dan's back. They were still sitting in the lounge room. "See, Chippewa, I've indulged into everything that would make me feel good, or help me forget where I had been and what I had seen. But Dan here, he doesn't know what temptation really means. He's had it hard when he had to fend for himself, but I don't know that he ever broke down and succumb to any temptation or indulge into anything that would have hurt him."

"Is that right, Dan?" Chippewa asked.

Dan smiled and switched his gaze from Gustavo to Chippewa. "I wouldn't say that. I was always thinking of ways to get back to the life I had known. I worked hard for everything I got, but I was tempted many times to chuck all that for spending money on things that I didn't really need."

"And did you succumb to these temptations?"

"No, I didn't," Dan replied. "You see, Chippewa, I've always had a little voice inside me telling me if I was doing the right thing. I'd say I would indulge in partying with Fabio when we were in college, yes, but apart from that, I had fun restoring cars — one at a time — because I couldn't afford to buy all the cars I saw, and they paid for themselves, and for part of my college tuition."

Chippewa nodded. "Well then, I think you'll find that the next page of your book contains both paragraphs — one dealing with indulgence and the other with temptation. I don't think you need anymore than you know already to fight temptation or succumb to indulgence."

"But I'll be interested to see what it says," Gustavo piped up.

And with these words, Dan turned to the next page of his book.

Thus far you have been given tolerance, acceptance, patience, determination. In your future there will be time for you to face temptation and the indulgence necessary to avoid your falling at the grips of evil. Indulgence will steer you away from the wrong temptation, however, indulging in the desirable or appealing things in life could be detrimental to your well-being and could be very costly indeed. If tolerance, acceptance, patience, determination, compassion, indulgence and resisting temptation will help you in forging your way into the future, perhaps endurance will crown your efforts with equal rewards. But remember, enduring the worst of life's torments require perseverance and untamable will. Your dream will be etched in your mind and none will be erased once you have attained your goal.

"That's interesting," Dan said, raising his gaze to Chippewa. "It says that my dream will be etched in my mind and none will be erased when I have attained my goal. Does that mean I could start another goal or working on another dream with these same tools?"

"Let me ask you this, Dan," Chippewa said, "Does life end with the accomplishment of one dream?"

"No, of course not. But this is to build my future, and once I have reached my goal, I could work on something entirely different, right?"

"Yes, you could," Chippewa replied, nodding. "However, think of your future as the foundation of your house. It wouldn't be a good idea to demolish the foundation if you wanted to build another house, would it?"

"What if I get bored with what I've chosen to do? I hate things that are only a repeat of the previous day's venture. What then?"

"Let's examine your question one step at a time, okay?" Dan nodded to Chippewa's suggestion. "Although attaining one's goal is laudable, the journey to your destination should provide you with experiences that will enable you to go further than your first target." He paused. "Perhaps an example will help. If you decided to drive to Miami with your Porsche, yet you knew that it would need some adjustments to the engine before you could start on your journey. The goal is to drive to Miami, but making the adjustments is a hurdle that you have to cross before making a start, right?"

"Sure," Dan replied. "And once I would have bought the new carburetor, I could be on my way, couldn't I?"

"Yes, Dan, you could, and indeed you would be on your way, as you planned. Yet, when you arrive in Miami, you remember how enjoyable the trip was. So, you decide to go somewhere else, perhaps exploring places in Florida you've never visited."

"But what about time?" Gustavo interjected. "Would Dan have time to go any place else once he arrived in Miami?"

"For the sake of this example, let's say that Dan is on holidays and has time to venture a little farther out, shall we?"

"Okay," Gustavo said. He turned to look at Dan. "Where would you go then?"

"Well, if the car was in perfect working order by then, I'd probably drive along the coast to Virginia."

"Very well," Chippewa said, grinning. "The reason for which you chose to go to Virginia, at this point, is not important. What's important for you to remember, however, is that your Porsche has to be in perfect working order for you to venture farther. And it will be the same once you're on the road to forge your future. You will have to ensure that each building block is fully secured before putting more layers on top of those you've just constructed."

"Yes, I understand all that, Chippewa," Dan said, showing his impatience. "But what I wanted to know is if I could do something else with my life once I've done what I wanted in the first place."

"Ah yes, if you don't like the house you've just built, you can always redecorate or remodel it as you wish…"

"What if I wanted to build an entirely different house, somewhere else, could I do that too?"

"Within the confines of the future you will have chosen to trace for yourself — up to 2013 — after that you will be free to do what ever else you wish to do."

"You mean my first destination will remain the same?"

"Yes, Dan. You are destined to return to your house with your family, but what you do with your life in the meantime should be different. Remember, God has given you the opportunity to alter your future, but where you land will remain the same."

"You won't be able to have another wife or other children," Gustavo suggested, "is that what you mean?" He looked at Chippewa.

"Not that I would ever want to," Dan said, chuckling. "The woman I saw at the race track and those kids — they were all beautiful. Who in their right mind would want to have another family when I've got one like that?"

Chippewa and Gustavo had to laugh at Dan's enthusiasm.

That afternoon, aboard the cruiser, after catching another three fish, the family was sitting down having a delicious dinner, which Malou had cooked, with Damianos providing all of the ingredients she needed with a snap of his fingers. Gaby, however, was not enjoying her meal.

"I can't get it out of my mind...," she blurted, putting her fork down.

"What's that?" Malou asked her.

"You killing that fish, that's what, Mom."

"Well, if you don't want to eat your meal, that's fine," Malou said. "You can leave the fish aside and I'm sure Damianos will delight in eating it tonight." She turned her gaze to their cat. "Wouldn't you?"

"Absolutely," he replied, grinning. "As long as I know that it was caught not for the sport of it, but to fill one's tummy, then yes, I will enjoy it."

"Why can't we just eat vegetables and cereal?" Gaby continued arguing. "We wouldn't have to kill anything then."

"Because God has created omnivorous human beings, Gaby," Damianos explained. "He has made you so that you could eat everything, including meat, poultry and fish along with vegetables and cereals. You, as every human being on Earth, have been created equal, and that means that all humans are designed the same way."

"But there are many vegetarian people who are very healthy..."

"Yes, Gaby, there are, yet to maintain their health, they have to replace all of the ingredients they miss by not eating meat or fish with something else. Otherwise they would die."

"Damianos is right, Gaby," Malou went on. "There's nothing wrong with people eating only vegetables, but God did not design you that way."

"Besides," Stefano piped up, after swallowing a mouthful, "there is the natural restoration of flora and fauna that occurs every day."

"What does that mean?" Gaby asked, returning to eating a bite of her fish.

"It means that if all the animals never killed anything to feed themselves, they would all die. The Earth needs to be re-generated, Gaby. That's God's plan."

"Okay, okay," Gaby said, "but killing that fish still grossed me out!"
After silence had broken among the three men, Chippewa said, "Why don't we analyze another of the statements made in those paragraphs?"

"Which one?" Dan asked, returning his gaze to the book opened in his lap.

"The last sentence dealt with endurance. And I believe you will need quite a bit of it to attain your goal, Dan."

"But aren't there more than one form of endurance," Gustavo asked Chippewa.

The latter nodded. "Yes, absolutely. When you're running a marathon, you need physical endurance to reach the finish line. The average human body is not built the same as the one of a gazelle. Humans need far more endurance to run the same distance as a gazelle would effortlessly. On the other hand, endurance is also present when faced with personal problems or hurdles that life puts in front of you from time to time."

"And I will be facing problems and having to surmount obstacles, I suppose," Dan said.

"Yes." Chippewa nodded. "But I believe you will have to develop both types of endurance in your case."

"But I'm not intending to run a marathon anytime soon," Dan argued, a broad smile crossing his lips.

"Perhaps, Gustavo could expand on that subject," Chippewa said, looking at the man.

"Well if you mean I'd need endurance to drive one of these semis for eight long hours on an endless highway in the middle of the night, I'd say you're right, Chippewa. It demands constant concentration, staying focused and above all resist the temptation of falling asleep."

"Very good," Chippewa said, bobbing his head up and down. "And the same will be true when you'll be at the control of an aircraft flying 30,000 feet above ground with 200 or 300 passengers aboard, Dan. You will need to develop the endurance required to accomplish such a task."

"Yes, but doesn't the captain have a co-pilot or even getting the plane on auto-pilot when he's tired?"

"In the year you're presently living, Dan, the technology exists, but it is not as secure or practical as it will probably be in years to come. However, depending on technology to save the day is not always the best course of action.

If you were ever called to pilot a long-distance carrier, you will have developed the endurance required to stay alert for ten to twelve hours on end."

"That's like driving a car in the Paris–Dakar race," Dan said. "Every day, these guys have to cross as many miles as they could under horrible conditions…"

"Perfect example, Dan," Chippewa interposed, chuckling. "These drivers have endurance to pilot their vehicles for long hours and endurance to go through any obstacle in their path."

CHAPTER THIRTY-FIVE

If there was ever a time when impatience began to invade Dan's mind, it was that night. He had closed the book, had left it on the coffee table and had retired with Gustavo to two of the upstairs bedrooms. Chippewa had told them that he would be back in the morning with breakfast waiting for them when they would get up.

Lying on top of the covers, Dan couldn't get to sleep. He was wondering why he couldn't just turn the pages of his book and read the whole thing at once. Of course, there would be many questions to be answered with each recommendations or tools that he was given through these paragraphs, but he couldn't wait to reach the end of the chapter. He wanted to get going. He felt sure he could find a way to build a future with what he had learned already. The thought of being sitting in the cockpit of an aircraft was as tempting as ever. Yet, he knew that if he decided to leave the house before he finished reading the book, he might have to face the worst of problems.

Nevertheless, and since he couldn't contain his curiosity, Dan decided to slip down to the living room and see if he could sneak a peek at the next few paragraphs so that he would have an idea of what the subjects were.

He had noticed that there was a candle on top of the mantle above the fireplace and some long matches beside it. He went down the stairs stealthily, not wanting to wake Gustavo, and soon reached the living room. The moonlight streaming through the front windows as well as the red embers in the hearth helped him locate the candle and matches.

As soon as he had lit the candle, he carried it to the coffee table and placed it beside the book. Sitting on the sofa, he was about to open it when a breath of air extinguished the flame of the candle. Dan swore under his breath, and went to relight the candle by the fireplace. As he was about to place the match on the embers, a spray of water put out the fire. He looked around him to see who could have thrown a pitcher of water onto the burning embers. But only darkness and silence met his searching eyes and ears. Shrugging, he returned to sit on the sofa and with the moon rays at his back illuminating the book, Dan opened it and turned to the sixth and seventh pages – they were all blank.

"I can see that stubbornness, impatience, and succumbing to temptation have not yet abandoned your mind, have they, Dan?"

Startled, Dan lifted his gaze, only to see the shepherd towering over him across the coffee table. With his arms crossed over his chest, Damianos asked, "What have you got to say for yourself?"

"I'm not a child anymore, Damianos, so please don't treat me like one!" Dan was angry.

"If you didn't behave like a child, I wouldn't treat you like one."

"Okay, but what are you doing here? I thought you were watching over my wife and children, so what do you want with me?"

Damianos chuckled. "What I want is not important, Dan, but what you want out of life is. If you want to continue being stubborn, impatient and giving in to any temptation that may present itself in the future, you're no where near leaving this house. You're actually regressing. And if you go far enough down that path, you'll find yourself sitting at a desk at Seagate for years to come. Is that what you want?"

"Of course I don't want that. But I find it a little tedious to have to read all this stuff"—he pointed to his book—"when I know most of it already. It's like watching a rerun of the same movie."

"Okay, I can understand that, yet tedium is not a bad thing when you're trying to build something as complex as a future for yourself and your family."

"You know, every time someone mentions my family to me, it's like you're punching me back into consciousness."

"And it feels good, doesn't it?"

"Yes, it does," Dan replied, nodding.

"Well then, every time you're tempted to do something as idiotic as taking God's time as your own to manage, I suggest you think of your family."

Dan looked down to his lap. "Why is it idiotic? Chippewa said that I was free with my timing. He said I could read it anytime I wanted."

"Yes, but that doesn't mean you could just read all you want in his absence."

"Then, how long will it take for me to finish reading all these paragraphs, do you think?"

Damianos guffawed to Dan's surprise.

The shepherd uncrossed his arms and went to sit beside Dan. "Your son, Daniel, has asked me a similar question some time ago, and do you know what I told him?" Dan shook his head. "I asked him how long is a piece of string."

"So you have no answer for me. Is that it?" Dan snapped, his anger returning.

"No, Dan. I have only one answer for you: Be patient and listen to Chippewa. Remember, he is the only one who will be able to transform your dream into reality. He is the *Dream Maker*, Dan. And you should feel privileged to be his pupil for a while."

"Oh, don't get me wrong, I'm grateful to have been given another chance, Damianos, but can you understand that I want to get to the end of this road sooner than later?"

"The joy is not in reaching your destination, Dan, but in experiencing the journey while you try reaching your goal."

"What do you mean by "try reaching my goal"? Is there any doubt?"

"There is always a certain amount of doubt in everything you endeavor to achieve, Dan. If there wasn't, what would be the fun in journeying toward achievement? Doubt or lack of confidence in one self will lead you into hesitation, but it's in that very thing that you'll exercise your freewill."

Dan had been listening attentively. "So, there's nothing wrong in doubting or hesitating about anything, as long as I make the right choice in the end."

"Yes, Dan. Always think twice before you decide to jump across a ravine. If you know you can cross the distance without falling to your death, then do it. Yet, if you hesitate at the last moment, or if you doubt you could leap that far, you will be doomed to fall."

"Meaning that once I have considered all aspects of the problem, it's no longer time to doubt or hesitate, right?"

"Yes, and now that you've been given another lesson that's not in your book; I think it's time for me to rejoin your family and for you to get some rest."

When Dan slipped under the covers later that night, he thought of how Damianos always managed to make sense of everything in life, and he had no problem falling asleep.

When Damianos returned to the cruiser, he was surprised to find Stefano sitting at the kitchen table, reading.

"Couldn't sleep?" he asked him.

"No, couldn't close my eyes. I kept thinking of my dad." Stefano put the book down and lifted his gaze to the old shepherd. "Have you seen him lately?"

"Yes, son. I've just returned from the house. Like you, he couldn't sleep."

"What was he doing?"

"He was trying to jump ahead of the schedule."

"What do you mean by that?"

Damianos sat down across from Stefano. "Your dad wants to get on the road of his future and can't contain his impatience. He wants to finish reading his book before he is given all the tools he will need to reach his goal."

Stefano grinned. "Yeah, that sounds like Dad alright. He likes things to happen and he's always getting bored when things are running smoothly."

"Your father has an inquisitive mind, Stefano, and when he's attained what he wants in life, or reaches a point where he's achieved what he wanted, he needs to get onto something else. However, in this instance, he's like a construction worker who would climb to the top of the ladder without the hammer he needs to fasten the shingles on the roof of his house."

"And he's got to get back down to get the hammer to finish the job," Stefano added, nodding. "What did you tell him then?"

"I've just given him an opportunity to think about a couple of things."

"Such as what?"

"Such as thinking about the tools he's carrying before he steps onto the first rung of the ladder." Damianos shook his head and smiled. "But this time he wanted to grab all of the tools in the toolbox without knowing what they were for."

Stefano laughed, picturing his dad at the bottom of the ladder and loading his tool-belt with everything in sight. "I can see him doing just that, you're right. He likes to be prepared, he always says."

"Yes, and that's fine to a certain extent, son. But you also need to sort out the tools you need and those you won't need before you climb all the way to the top of that ladder, don't you?"

"Yeah, if you don't need a saw or a power drill just to plant some nails in the shingles, why would you take them with you?"

"Exactly, and that's what your father was trying to do tonight. He wanted to read every paragraph of his book before he understood what each tool was designed to do."

"Everything in God's time, right?" Stefano concluded, returning to the page of the book he was reading.

"What are you reading?" Damianos asked, his curiosity peeked.

"*No Place Like Home,* by Mary Higgins Clark." Stefano closed the book and showed the cover to Damianos.

"Ah-ah, yes. I thought you might like to read this story," Damianos said.

"Did you leave it here for me?"

"Not specifically for you, no, Stefano. Yet, it's good that you've found it. How do you like it so far?"

"It's intriguing — the husband buying the house where his wife grew up and apparently murdered her mother. It's quite something."

"How she felt when she entered the house is perhaps what I wanted you or your siblings to understand. What ever happened in that house came back to the woman's mind as if she was reliving the terrible events that occurred twenty five years ago..."

"And why did you want us to read this?" Stefano inquired.

"During the journey ahead, you will see, feel and relive events of your past in the same way as this woman did. She too had the chance to alter her future, and she too reached her goal. However, returning to her house wasn't in her plans." Damianos paused. "You see, you have forgotten most of the things you have experienced before you left, but, as I said before, those important events that have occurred or the teachings that you have acquired along the way are still there, in the recesses of your memory. And once you will be exposed to similar circumstances, those memories will surface and will be as vivid as if they just happened minutes previously."

"So, like in this story, we'll be more or less expecting the unexpected, right?"

"It depends on you opening your mind to the possibilities, Stefano. But most importantly, you will be prepared and you will know which tools to grab before climbing the ladder."

Stefano chuckled, looked up at Damianos and then returned to his reading.

When Gustavo reached the bottom step, he looked into the kitchen. Chippewa was there, busy preparing a feast.

"Ah-ah, you're up, good morning, my friend. Have you slept well?" he asked Gustavo.

"Top of the morning to you too, Chippewa. And I've slept like a log. It must be the air around this place," Gustavo replied, going to the cupboard above the counter and grabbing a mug out of it. "Where's Dan? Hasn't he shown up yet?"

"No. He must still be asleep. He's had a busy night I think." Chippewa put a couple of pancakes on a plate and poured some more batter in the skillet.

Gustavo had stopped pouring himself a cup of coffee and was now staring at the Dream Maker, coffee pot in hand. "What happened?"

"Nothing much, except that Damianos had to intervene before Dan would have found himself kicked out to the pavement."

"Why, what did he do?" Gustavo was obviously puzzled. He finished pouring the coffee in his cup and turned toward the kitchen table, and sat down.

Chippewa, meanwhile, continued attending to his cooking. When he was finally satisfied that everything was ready, he brought the pancakes and maple syrup to the table. He sat down too. "I think Dan needs to work on his patience. Last night, he came down here intending to read the rest of the paragraphs in his book."

"Good Lord, why?" Gustavo exclaimed.

"Because this little schooling does not seem to progress as fast as he wants."

"And did he succeed?"

Chippewa shook his head. "No, otherwise you and I wouldn't be here to talk about it. But it was a close call." He paused, pouring some orange juice in Gustavo's glass.

"And you said Damianos had to intervene...?"

"Oh yes. As soon as he learned that Dan was trying to open the book, he prevented him from doing so. But the point is, if Damianos hadn't been vigilant enough, Lucifer would have had his chance to grab Dan and send him back to Delray Beach to sit at a desk at Seagate Technology."

"And what happens now?" Gustavo asked, as he began eating his pancakes.

"The plan has not changed, yet I would suggest that we keep an eye on Dan's reactions to what the book is teaching him. He's opened a door last night, which should have remained closed. He's allowed the devil to tease his weaknesses and he's unfortunately responded to the tease. So, we need to watch him closely, Gustavo," Chippewa said, visibly concerned.

CHAPTER THIRTY-SIX

A few minutes later, Dan came down to join Chippewa and Gustavo at the breakfast table. He smiled as he sat down.

"Good morning," he said, his attitude somewhat subdued.

"Good morning, Dan," Chippewa and Gustavo replied in unison.

"Did you have a good night?" Chippewa asked.

"Not that great, no," Dan answered, taking a pancake and putting it on his plate. "I couldn't sleep and I came down to read some more of my book..."

"Why did you do that for?" Gustavo interposed, after swallowing a mouthful.

"Because"—Dan turned his face to Chippewa—"you said my timing was my own when it came to read my book." He poured some maple syrup on the pancake.

"I did say that, Dan. But what you had forgotten is that I suggested you chose the timing beforehand..."

"And why's that?"

"Simply because I am here to make your dream come true. If you run ahead of me and encounter problems, I wouldn't be able to help you or remind you of what you have learned. Besides, you and your family are deemed to take this trip together *in my company*, and that of Gustavo. This is not a solo flight, Dan!" Chippewa was visibly displeased. He got up and brought the coffee pot to the table. "But for now, have breakfast. We'll talk about this later."

A half-an-hour later Chippewa had regained his seat by the fireplace while Dan and Gustavo had plopped down on the sofa.

Dan stared at his book on the coffee table but didn't dare touch it. He raised his gaze to Chippewa. "Could we forget what happened last night and get on with it?"

"Why?" Chippewa asked. "Is it because you truly want to get to the end of the chapter sooner than later, or is it because you're afraid of what I have to say about the risks you've taken?"

"What risks are you talking about?" Dan's tone was far from amicable.

"By opening the book and, I'm sure, finding blank pages facing you, you've responded to evil's tease."

"I don't see any evil in wanting to progress a little faster than we've been doing," Dan argued.

"Hold on a little minute, Dan," Gustavo interposed. "Chippewa here is trying to help you accomplish what you couldn't do on your own..."

Dan stood up and started pacing the length of the lounge room. "I'm sorry, Gustavo, but I've been doing things on my own since I was a teenager. And all these tools; I've used them all, successfully, I might add."

"Yes, perhaps you have..."

"There's no "perhaps" about it, Chippewa. I have earned my keep without any help. So, what's the big deal about reading these paragraphs?" Dan stopped and pointed at the book. "They're just re-hashing old stuff." He paused long enough to regain his seat beside Gustavo. "I need to learn what I don't know rather than retrace my steps."

"Okay, Dan, you've made your point. Now, would you like to open your book to the next page, or would you rather I leave you alone to return to Key West. The choice is yours. The book has no value if you don't think of it as a valuable piece of advice from the All Mighty."

"Okay, okay, I'll read the next paragraph and the next and the next, as long as I see that I'm learning something I didn't know already."

"Belligerence and aggressiveness have no place in your behavior when it comes to building a future for you and your family, Dan," Chippewa said almost inaudibly. "You have been given an extraordinary opportunity, and you seem to forget that it can be taken from you as easily as it has been given."

Arms crossed over his chest, Dan still seemed unwilling to abide by Chippewa's counseling words. "Yes, sure, I've been given a great opportunity, and I thank the Lord for it, but re-hashing what I've known about my behavior for years, to me, amounts to a waste of time."

"Well, let's see if the next paragraph is new to you, shall we?" Chippewa suggested.

"Okay," Dan replied, extending both hands to take his book. As he put it on his lap, he noticed the latch was closed once again. "What the...," he practically yelled, "why is it closed again?"

"Perhaps it is because the respect that is due to its author has abandoned you, Dan."

"Who says I've lost respect for the Lord...?" Dan looked from Chippewa to Gustavo.

The latter shook his head. "You know, Dan, I don't know what's bitten you during the night, but you are really going crazy if you think that God is going to let you go one step further before you correct that attitude of yours."

"Thanks for the sermon, Gustavo, that's all I needed right now!" Dan shouted, slamming the book back on the coffee table.

"Alright, that's it," Chippewa said, getting up. "I think I'll tell Damianos that I can't go any further with you, so that he could let you return to your family and resume your life in 2013."

Suddenly Dan's face paled. "Okay, okay," he blurted, jumping to his feet, "I'm sorry, Chippewa," and grabbing his arm. "I don't know what's got into me, but I couldn't get rid of my anger just now."

"That's what anger does, Dan. It grows in you and invades the farthest recesses of your mind until you go insane."

"Please, can I re-open the book now?" Dan pleaded, not letting go of Chippewa's arm.

He looked down to Dan's grip. "Okay, let go..., please?"

"Oh, I'm sorry. I didn't mean..." Dan looked abashed.

"Right, perhaps now we could sit down and open the book again." Chippewa took the little key out of his shirt pocket and showed it to Dan. "You'll need this."

Dan smiled and took the key from the Dream Maker. He nodded. "Thanks, and again, I'm sorry."

As soon as he returned to the sofa, Dan sat down and grabbed the book hurriedly under Gustavo's approving gaze.

He opened it and turned to the next page. When he started reading the first line, Dan was surprised. "This is what we've just talked about. That's amazing!"

"Why don't you read it aloud for us, Dan?" Chippewa said, a broad grin appearing on his lips.

Every man experiences anger and belligerence at one point in his life. These character traits demand control and sufficient love to be tamed. Anger is often born of offensive and opposite behavior on the part of an enemy. Amiability and understanding are the weapons you will need to use against rising anger, irritation or adversity. You have already acquired tools that will combat the nefarious effects of anger. Amiability is another tool that you will need to use in your future. However, never forget that Amiability of character is by no means debasing or demeaning. You should stand tall, and proud of your accomplishments.

Daniel was up first the next morning. He looked around him. Everyone was still asleep. He crept into the bathroom quietly, took a shower and slipped into his swimming trunks. Since the cruiser was moored at the edge of the pier, he thought a swim would do him a world of good. He was truly tired of being cooped up in that boat day after day. Like his father, Daniel wanted this waiting for their journey into their future to end. He knew he couldn't leave the company of his family right now in case Damianos would come up and say that his dad was ready to make a start.

When he was ready, Daniel made his way to the forward deck and dove into the ocean. The water was warm enough not to shock his system and made for a pleasant swim. As soon as he poked his head above the surface, he smiled. It felt great, almost liberating. He began swimming toward the mouth of the marina and stopped for a moment before continuing toward the next beach. Mid-way to his destination, a cramp tackled his calf. He swore, but remained calm, lay on his back for a while until he felt his muscles relax a little. *I should have done some warm-up exercises before diving in,* he thought, as he looked around him. Suddenly he heard the roar of an engine. A hors-board was coming straight for him. He didn't take time to think and dove below the surface as far down as he could before the boat passed over him at full throttle. A few seconds later, he swam upward until his head emerged above the water, just in time to see the water-skier barreling down in his direction. He wasn't fast enough though. The water-skier clipped his shoulder and took a tumble into the waves.

Daniel lost his bearings for a moment, but soon realized that he was bleeding. As he turned around, he saw the man try to take his water skis off his feet without much success. Somehow the force of the impact had jammed the mechanism. Daniel didn't hesitate. He swam to his aid and brought the man's head above the water at the same time as the boat came back to the scene and the engine was switched off.

"What the heck happened?" the fellow on the boat asked, looking at both young men in the water. "It's okay, Dad, I'm okay – thanks to this guy."

"The name is Daniel, Daniel Politano." He put a hand on his shoulder.

"But you're bleeding…?" the father said, coming to the side of the boat. "Come on up here." He grabbed Daniel's able arm and hoisted him aboard. "Okay, Mike, let's get the ropes back in," he added, helping his son over the edge of the hors-board. "I'm Oswaldo Gomez." He paused. "What happened?" he repeated, looking at Daniel's shoulder.

"Please to meet you, sir." Again, he shot a glance at his injury. *It hurts like hell,* he thought. "I had a cramp, and I didn't notice you until you were practically over me…" Daniel looked down. He was feeling faint. "And…, and when I came up, I didn't see Mike until it was too late, sorry."

"Don't you think twice about it, Daniel. Let's get you back to where ever you came from. But first, let's get you patched up, okay?"

Mike had taken the water skis off his feet by then. "Here, Dad," he said, handing the man a first-aid box.

Once he had bandaged Daniel's arm, the man asked, "Where's your boat, or did you come from the beach?"

"We're moored at the end of the pier, at the edge of the marina, sir."

"Right. Let's get you back then." He regained his seat at the wheel and started the engine.

When Malou got up, she immediately noticed Daniel's absence. She grabbed her robe from the foot of the bed, put it on and trotted to the forward cabin, expecting her son to be sitting at the kitchen table. Seeing no one around, she climbed the stairs to the upper deck and again saw no one. Panicking a little, she retraced her steps and went to wake Stefano.

"Oh, hi, Mom. What are you doing up so early?" he asked after his mother had shaken him awake.

"Where's Daniel?"

"What. . .?" Stefano said, jutting his chin to the next bunk. "I don't know." He slipped out of the bed and stood up. "Have you looked up on deck?"

Malou was visibly anxious. "Why do you think I'm asking you? Of course I've been upstairs. He's nowhere to be found." She gathered the collar of her robe with trembling hands.

Stefano turned toward the forward cabin and upon reaching the kitchen; he swung on his heels to face his mother. "Where is Damianos?"

"I haven't seen him either." Malou clasped her hand around her son's wrist. "What's going on here, Stefano?"

"I haven't a clue, Mom. But let's get up on deck. Maybe Daniel went to the marina shop. . ."

"But nothing's open at this hour," Malou argued, following Stefano up the steps.

"Where are you guys going?" they heard Gaby ask from behind them. "Where's Daniel?"

"That's what we're trying to find out, sis," Stefano replied as soon as Gaby joined them.

"Do you think he could have gone for a swim?" Gaby suggested. Clad only of jeans shorts and a faded t-shirt, she looked over the railing into the water.

"If he did, he'll be back soon," Stefano said. "But what bothers me most is Damianos's absence."

"Yeah, you're right. That cat is usually waiting for us to get up." Gaby turned toward the stairs again. "Anyway, I'm hungry. I'll get breakfast going."

When Oswaldo Gomez slowed the hors-board down toward the pier, where Daniel had told him the cruiser was moored, there was no boat or yacht in sight.

"Are you sure this is where your brother has moored the cruiser, son?"

Daniel's head bobbed up and down. "Absolutely, sir. That's where it was an hour ago anyway." He stood up from the bench and looked around. Their cruiser was definitely gone.

"What's your cruiser's name?" Mr. Gomez asked.

"I think it's *Destiny*," Daniel replied, sitting down again. "I don't understand."

"Okay, I'll get back to our spot and then we'll go to the marina's office to verify *Destiny's* location," Mr. Gomez said, already pushing the throttle in reverse and then turning the hors-board around.

CHAPTER THIRTY-SEVEN

Dan didn't know what to say. He knew that he had done wrong by trying to jump-start the journey into his future but couldn't understand why he had flown off the handle so readily. It was totally out of character for him. Yes, he was a passionate man, but he usually managed to direct his passion to accomplishing whatever task he tackled at the time.

"Again, I am very sorry, Chippewa," he finally said, closing the book. "What happened to me?"

"I believe you have opened a door that should have remained closed, Dan..."

"That's what you said this morning," Gustavo interrupted. "But how does Dan close it now?"

"I don't think anyone could close it, unfortunately," Chippewa replied, obviously disappointed. "The best way to avoid evil's interference is by heeding God's counsel. And in the instance of anger, as it says in your paragraph, amiability is the best weapon to use against anger."

"Like turning the other cheek, right?" Gustavo put in.

"Good of you to remember, Gustavo, but not quite, no. You see anger flares up when someone or something has offended you, but the most disarming weapon you could use then is letting the offense course down your back as you turn away from the enemy."

"Shrug away, you mean?" Dan asked.

"Yes, Dan. The purpose of offensive behavior is generally to rile you up. To get you angry. Therefore, if there is no anger ignited when you've accused the shock from the offense, the enemy and his purpose will be defeated." Chippewa got up from his seat and went to the book shelf to the one side of the fireplace. Being a rather small man, he couldn't reach to the top row to take any of the books located on the upper shelf. However, he passed his hand over the spines of the books that were in his reach. "You see, Dan, all of these books pertain to someone's past or problems. Each of them, were you ever able to open any, would highlight qualities and moral values or character traits that the person concerned would need to work on. Yet, there is one common aspect to each of these books and to each of these moral values." He turned to look at the two men sitting on the sofa. "Could you tell me which of the character traits is common to all?"

Gustavo and Dan exchanged a querying glance, smiled and shook their heads.

"No idea, Chippewa," Dan said. "What is it?"

"Why don't you re-open your book and see for yourself?"

Dan brought the book back to his lap. When he opened it, he was quite surprised to see that he had reached the last page of the chapter.

"I thought there were twelve tools. What happened to the ones we've not checked yet?"

"I believe you're referring to perseverance which is synonymous to persistence and force of character. Then there is trust. And lastly you have forgiveness of others for their trespass, which comes in the wake of amiability. Is that what you meant?"

Dan's gaze was one of puzzlement. "I guess so." He sounded hesitant.

"Ha-ha-ha," Chippewa laughed, sitting down again. "Yes, of course, you wouldn't know for sure. Yet, I can tell you that these three, together with the ones we discussed already are contained in the one you're about to recognize."

Dan and Gustavo bent their heads to the paragraph.

"Fortitude! You mean that's the one that encompasses them all?"

"Absolutely, Dan. But please read on."

And Dan did – aloud.

Fortitude and force of character is the crowning and underlying trait to all the tools you have received to this day. Fortitude will help you to be more tolerant toward others, to accept the hand you have been dealt, to endure the severity of enmity, to show humility in face of extravagance, to display determination in face of hindrance, to cast your eyes away from temptation, to persevere in your chosen task, to have the patience to pursue your endeavors and to impart trust to deserving parties, and ultimately to forgive yourself for your misguided pursuits.

Therefore, fortitude will assist you in overcoming all problems that may be ahead of you in your future. Remember, you are made of a cloth that will not accept defeat as an inevitable outcome.

When Dan stopped and lifted his gaze to Chippewa, the jolly old man looked as pleased as a Cheshire cat. He was grinning from ear to ear.

"Very good, very good indeed!" he exclaimed, getting up again and dancing a jig in front of Dan and Gustavo. They smiled, then laughed, then stood up and began dancing with the Dream Maker.

When they stopped, they looked at each other and exploded in roaring laughter.

"You've done it, Dan!" Chippewa finally said, plopping back into the old English chair. "You've gone through your schooling with just one hitch. And that, to me, is fantastic."

Sitting down beside Gustavo, Dan said, "But what does that mean? Am I going to see my family now?"

In the space of a breath, Chippewa's face returned to being severe. "NO, Dan! Do not jump ahead of yourself again, please. Remember, all in God's time. As to what will happen next, we shall wait to hear from Damianos. He shall be advised shortly of you closing your book. When he will come, it will be time for us to depart."

"This is getting exciting," Gustavo remarked. "I can hardly wait to get out of here and start on this journey with you, my friend." He threw a glance at Dan.

The latter was smiling. "Yeah. I wonder what's in store beyond that door." Dan nodded in the direction of the hallway.

If Dan, Gustavo and Chippewa were ready to start on the journey that would take them through the tracing of Dan's future, Damianos was facing one of the gravest problems he had encountered in his nine lives. "Where did Daniel go?" was the question he asked himself repeatedly.

"What happened?" Malou yelled at the top of her voice when she saw their cat come down the cruiser's steps. "Where could he have gone?"

Gaby and Stefano were standing at their mother's back.

Damianos looked at them intently before he said, "Please sit down..."

"I have no intention of sitting down, Damianos," Malou flared, her concern not abating one iota. "I want to know where my son is. Just tell me!"

"The short answer is that I don't know."

"How's that possible?" Gaby shrieked. "And where were you? Did you go and get some fish from the garbage at the back of the restaurant, eh?"

Damianos sat down at the kitchen table and looked up at the three worried faces staring down at him. "Please, I've got to explain something to you." He extended an inviting arm for Malou and the two children to sit around him.

Once they did, Damianos went on, "You see, in this boat or where ever we go together, we are navigating in the cloud of your imagination. Time has no meaning, and space is only one you envisioned at the time of the events that occurred around you."

"But that doesn't tell us where Daniel could have gone," Malou interposed, wringing her hands on top of the table.

"No, it doesn't, Malou, but it explains why we cannot find him." He paused. "When Daniel went to Iran with your dad's friend, God allowed him to be separated from you three for awhile. In this instance however, Daniel must have gone on his own to a time and place of which I had no knowledge."

"But that means he's lost like Dad was...?" Gaby began crying.

"Not quite, Gaby," Stefano piped-up.

"I don't see the difference. Do you, Mom?" She stared at her mother.

"I think I see what Damianos meant, Gaby," Malou replied, passing a reassuring arm around her daughter's shoulders.

"Sis, listen to me," Stefano went on. "It's like he's gone out of our bubble for a bit, but if he returns he'll find us"—he turned his head to Damianos—"Right?"

"You're partly right, Stefano. But I think we need to find him as soon as possible." He shook his head. "You see, the reason I was not here when it happened was because I was advised that you're dad is ready..."

"He is?" Malou erupted, not knowing if she should laugh for joy or cry for her son's disappearance.

"What do you propose we do now?" Stefano asked. "Should we try retracing his steps or something?"

"Yes, Stefano. I think you'll find that he's probably gone for a swim, and instead of staying close to the boat, he's ventured out to sea..."

"Oh my God," Malou shouted, putting a hand to her mouth. "The book...!" She turned to Gaby. "Don't you remember? I told you about my dream when we started on this trip." Gaby looked baffled. "Yes, yes. I had this strange dream about the ocean swell coming up and drawing down around me. And then the book said something about *not to stray toward the swells of your memories, for they will be wasted errands.* Don't you remember?"

A worried smile drew on Damianos's lips. "Yes, dear lady. The sentence has significance, but it's not going to solve the problem. However, we now know that Daniel has gone on a wasted errand and we need to find him." Getting up from his seat, Damianos added, "Let's get up on deck," and climbed the stairs leading to the wheel house.

"What for?" Gaby argued, "It's not like Daniel is going to re-appear all of a sudden."

"Don't be such a pessimist, Gaby," her brother scolded, taking her by the hand and dragging her out of the kitchen behind their mother.

"I don't want to move the boat from its mooring," Damianos said, once the little family had joined him. "Losing ourselves in another time and place would only make this problem worse."

"What do you plan to do then?" Malou asked, switching her gaze from the floorboards to their shepherd's face.

"I will call on Solange and Damian and hear what they suggest. They're probably aware of what's happened to Daniel and maybe they've located him already."

"Let's hope so," Stefano put in. "But since Daniel is gone alone, they might not have kept an eye on him specifically."

"Now, who's the pessimist?" Gaby said, looking up at her brother.

A few minutes later, Solange appeared first in the wheel house. Seeing the troubled and expectant faces looking at her, she smiled reassuringly. "Do not be so troubled. All of you need to trust in God. And for now, let Damianos go on his own to search for Daniel. You, Malou, and you, children, definitely cannot leave the cruiser. You need to stay in this time and place so that Damianos can always locate you."

"That's all fine and dandy," Gaby interposed, "but now that we were about to join our dad, we've lost our brother. What's next?"

"Don't worry, Gaby," they heard Damian's voice behind them as he was coming up the steps. "We will find Daniel. But this is another test perhaps..."

"A test for what?" Malou demanded. "Haven't we gone through enough already?"

"I understand your rebellion, my dear," Damian answered, "But trust in God, as Solange said, is all you need now."

"I can't bear this anymore..." Malou's voice trailed off as she went to nestle in Stefano's arms.

"Fortitude, Malou, is what you all need now. Feeling sorry for yourself is not going to help you."

"Yes, this is all good, but how are you going to find my brother — that's what I'd like to know!" Stefano sounded obviously irritated.

"And what about the seven days — we only had seven days to find Dan and return to our future," Malou demanded, regaining some of her fighting spirit.

Damian's eyes traveled to each of the three worried faces pleading for an answer. "I believe I should remind you that even though you have been told you had seven days to return to Pahokee, time is now God's time and reality has stopped, to give way to The Dream Maker's work."

Knowing that he had probably gone too far from the cruiser and after Oswaldo Gomez and his son Mike had left him on the pier to wait for the yacht to return, Daniel was wondering what he should do.

Mr. Gomez had verified that in fact there was a cruiser moored at the end of pier 31, but according to the marina manager's record, *Destiny* was due to leave that morning. *Have they left without me?* Daniel wondered for the umpteen times. But once again, he shook his head. "They couldn't have done," he told himself. However, it was now late in the morning, and the cruiser had gone.

EPILOGUE

Faced with yet another loss, Malou, Gaby and Stefano will need to gather their strength and their resilience in order to find Daniel.

Meanwhile, Dan, Gustavo and Chippewa are to start on their journey, even though a cloud of anxiety would assuredly damper their enthusiasm once they learn of Daniel's disappearance.

Will they find Daniel before they all have to leave 1988?

The next book, *Dream Maker 3* should provide us with an answer.

ABOUT THE AUTHOR

At the end of World War II, Arnaldo Ricciulli's parents decided to leave the torments and sequels of war behind and move to Venezuela. Arnaldo was very young when his parents left South America for the warmth and tranquility of Florida where he grew up in Boca Raton. After graduating from high school, he attended college. Obtaining a Bachelor's Degree in Electrical Engineering, Arnaldo, thirsting for adventure, thought of joining the US Navy where he was readily accepted as an officer. Yet, destiny had other plans for the young man. Instead, Arnaldo went to work for Seagate Technology, SyDos and IBM. But Corporate America wasn't for him – Arnaldo wanted to be his own man, and manage his own business. It was then that he opened a restaurateur chain, which, eight years later, counted no less than seven restaurants and a gas station. Following the sale of his business, he founded the Millenium Limo in December 2001, in the wake of nine-eleven. Somewhat to his surprise, the business took off and rapidly became the top exotic limo service, not only in the State of Florida, but across the country.

The father of three children, Arnaldo remained true to his adventurous spirit until one day a skiing accident locked him down. Beaten in his purpose, but undefeated, he decided to put "his dream" on paper and The Dream Maker Trilogy was born.

www.thedreammaker.co www.thedreammaker2.com